When the lady and the stranger came to the courtyard, as the servants watched, and the grooms at the stable door stood watching, the stranger stopped where he stood and loosened the lacings of his tunic, and two squirrels leaped out onto the ground, one gray and one fox-red. And they turned into a bright chestnut horse and one of dapple gray, each with curving neck and coddled mane and each bridled and saddled and ready to ride; the sidesaddle, for the lady, being on the gray. And her horse went gloriously arrayed in trappings of spring-green and violet. Lightly she mounted it, and took the reins in one hand while she carried her flowers in the other, and with the stranger at her side on the red horse she rode out the fortress gates and away, the way no one but woodcutters went, toward the forest named Wirral.

NANCY SPRINGER

CHANCE & Other Gestures of The Hand of Fate

BAEN BOOKS

CHANCE—AND OTHER GESTURES OF
THE HAND OF FATE

ACKNOWLEDGMENTS: The following originally appeared
and are copyright as follows: "The Boy Who Plaited Manes,"
The Magazine of Fantasy & Science Fiction, © 1986 by Mercury
Press Inc.; "The Wolf Girl Speaks," *Star*Line*, © 1982 by
Nancy Springer; "Bright-Eyed Black Pony," *Moonsinger's
Friends*, © 1985 by Nancy Springer; "Come In," *Night Voyages
Poetry Review*, © 1982 by James R. Page; "The Prince Out
of the Past," *Magic in Ithkar*, © 1985 by Nancy Springer;
"Amends," *The Magazine of Fantasy & Science Fiction*, ©
1983 by Mercury Press Inc.; "The Dog-King of Vaire,"
Fantasy Book, © 1982 by Nancy Springer.

A Baen Books Original

Baen Publishing Enterprises
260 Fifth Avenue
New York, N.Y. 10001

First printing, September 1987

ISBN: 0-671-65337-7

Cover art by Gary Ruddell

Printed in the United States of America

Distributed by
SIMON & SCHUSTER
1230 Avenue of the Americas
New York, N.Y. 10020

CONTENTS

CHANCE

Chance walked softly through Wirral, silent in doeskin boots, more stealthy than seemed possible in a man of his broad-shouldered brawn and middling age. His duty as Lord's Warden was to see what happened in the vast forest named Wirral, whether poaching or spying or, sometimes, murder, a corpse left in the boskage. Sometimes he glimpsed things stranger yet: the small faces that were gone in an eyeblink, vanishing into the hollow of an oak. Denizens. Them he did not report, for Roddarc son of Riol, Lord of Wirralmark, gave no credence to the hidden folk who were even holier than the Wirral and never spoken of by name. Chance did not like to believe in them either, for the tales related of them were fearsome. Squirrels, he told himself. Squirrels rustling the branches of the oak.

The beast with two backs was commonplace within the fringes of the forest, especially in the springtime. It, also, he did not report, nor did it much trouble him. If squires and servant girls needed a private place to enjoy their sport, he would not begrudge it to them, though another with his secret might have. But he was long-suffering, Chance. He would turn his face away and leave the place as silently as he had come.

Only, this time, he could not help seeing that it was she whose name he never heard without a leap of his heart.

Halimeda. He remembered the day she was born. Her lady mother, dying after the birthing, had chosen the name. Halimeda, "dreaming of the sea." Chance had never seen the sea, but even at the age of ten he had known what it was to dream. A lovely name, and the girl had grown to suit it, tall as befit a lord's daughter, her eyes gray-green, her mien quiet, her look often focused somewhere beyond a stormy horizon.

Halimeda on a bed of violets and spring-green moss. She did not moan and squeal like the servant girls, so he had come quite close without knowing. And she was naked, and so lovely, slender as befit a lady of the blood, fallow-fawn skin and dark, dark hair. So young, so bold. She lay silent and rapt, her eyes lidded, the dark lashes trembling. Head next to hers—that handsome young buck of a commoner, Blake. "Love," he whispered to her, and her lips moved against his neck.

Chance moved away for a few silent paces, then recklessly abandoned silence. He ran, crashing through bracken like a stag. When he finished running, he leaned against a birch and retched.

Halimeda would never be his; he had always known that. For more reasons than could be counted. But his feelings were not amenable to such reasons.

That evening Lord Roddarc came to see him in his

small lodge that stood outside the forest walls and beyond the tilled ground, under the shadow of Wirral.

Chance heard the rapping, hurried over and flung open the door at once, for he knew that signal well. His lord strode in, but no retainers stood at guard.

"You should not come here alone," Chance scolded. "Have me summoned if you wish to speak with me."

"Bah!" The lord crossed the room in three paces, sat down on a bench by the hearthfire. A tall man, finer of feature than his warden, not as rugged of build but perhaps just as strong. His hair and short beard shone red-gold in the firelight. His high black boots shone even brighter with hours of some servant's polishing.

"Rod, would you think with your mind instead of your hind end! Out alone in the dusk, fit game for assassins—"

If the lord's retainers had been present, Chance would not have bespoken him so bluntly, nor would he have called him by name. But as they were alone, he let go of ceremony. He and Roddarc had been reared nearly as brothers. As young warriors they had fought the blue-painted barbarians side by side in the front line. Roddarc had been with Chance when he had taken his worst wound—it could as featly have happened to the lord himself. Roddarc had shielded his comrade while they fought out the rest of the battle, and when Chance had weakened and fallen at last the young lord had borne him away to the tents and cared for him. Ten years and more it had been since that time, but Chance was not likely to forget. And later, when Roddarc came into his holding, he made Chance his warden—Chance, the commoner with the sorrow-child's name, orphan and bastard, unclaimed by any family. Roddarc had made him a man of authority in Wirralmark, and Chance would not forget that either.

Therefore he scolded his lord and friend from the heart.

"All the mutterings of the malcontents, the rumors, and you must come a-visiting when anyone could aim a bolt at you from a shadow!"

The lord of Wirralmark sat grinning broadly, as if he wished for nothing more than to be railed at by his friend. Indeed, Chance could hardly have better rewarded him for coming alone.

"At twilight! Alone, to the edge of Wirral! Of all the jackass—

"I'll go where I like," the lord interrupted, still smiling, "and alone if I like."

"That's what you said to my Lord Riol when you were seven years old, and he thrashed me until I bled."

For Chance, of an age with Roddarc, had been reared at his side as the whipping boy, the one who took punishment so that the noble buttocks need not be scarred. It was an honor, an opportunity for a child of low degree.

Roddarc's smile darkened into a scowl. "The old bully is gone, praise be," he retorted, "and I am not a child any longer."

"You act like one!"

But Chance's ardor merely made Roddarc smile anew. Amused, he was. Chance raised clenched fists in despair and gave it up, slumping onto the other bench. He fed thornwood to the fire. The two men watched the leaping flames companionably.

"Nothing out of the ordinary in Wirral," Roddarc remarked after a while, for Chance would have told him if there were.

"I have seen nothing, no."

Halimeda's dalliance—should he reveal that? He felt a hot flush at the thought, and realized he would

4

not. She was Roddarc's younger sister, ten years younger, and the lord treated her much as a father might. He would be upset, angry with her, perhaps even furious enough to punish her in some way, though he was not a punishing lord. Chance did not care to gift her with wrath. Nor could Halimeda's affairs have any connection with his lord's difficulties. Or so he deemed.

"Wirral is vast," he added, "and I am but one man. What might be moving in the deeps of Wirral I cannot say."

"I know it." Roddarc studied the flames, their hearts shadowed with blue and green, and when he spoke there was unhappiness in his voice that he would not have revealed to anyone else but Chance. "If only I knew who was behind this unrest. . . . Old friend, I have not been a bad lord, have I?"

"Hardly! You are among the best; you know that." Roddarc was for the most part just, and in many ways not unkind.

"Then why . . ."

"Because men are fools, that is why!" Chance spoke with vehemence. "They would prefer a lord who rules by the sword and torture, it would seem. For when a gentle lord rules, they can think of nothing but overthrowing him."

"Well." The lord looked up, his jaw firmed. "If they should succeed, Chance—"

"Say no such thing! They will not."

"It is devoutly to be hoped you are correct. But if they should succeed, I want a promise from you."

"Rod, you know you have it."

"Not so reckless, my friend. It is hard." The lord was faintly smiling, his look wry. "It is this: that you should protect my sister. For if I am killed, this

5

demesne by right goes to Halimeda, should she ever be able to claim it."

Chance took a deep breath and nodded. Roddarc was right; the task was hard. For likely he would see Halimeda wed to some lord powerful enough to champion her, and he could never make any claim on her except that of a loyal servant, for all of his heart's clamoring.

Chance prowled through the Wirrel the next day in a panic barely concealed. He had never known Roddarc to speak of his own mortality. And when he had walked his friend back to the fortress, parted from him at the gate, Roddarc had reached out for a moment and clasped his hand, the grip of a comrade facing battle.

Plain battle was a matter ill enough, but this hidden one yet worse. He and Roddarc knew not even the names of their enemies. Who were the conspirators? Where might they be mustering? Six men had been missing from the fortress guard that morning, deserters. . . . If there were rebels gathering in Wirral, they ought to be somewhere in the skirts of it near the Mark. But Chance had stalked all those ways, every moment expecting attack, and found nothing.

A movement—he froze, crouching, bow raised and arrow nocked. But it was nothing. A flicker of brown, a shadowy face peering for a moment from the hollow of a lightning-torn oak, then gone before he could draw breath.

Chance straightened and aimed his arrow at the ground. A daring thought had taken hold of him, and he seized the moment.

"Little one there in the tree," he said softly, "come out, please, and speak with me."

There was a scrabbling sound as of a squirrel inside the trunk, and then the face appeared again, eyes bright. Quite by accident Chance had hit upon a lure well-nigh irresistible to the Denizens of the forest—the lure of words at coupled sport, of rhyme.

Chance stood still, not utterly afraid but very wary. In a moment the small man of a nameless race stepped boldly out of his refuge and stood on a branch at the level of Chance's eyes, entirely revealed.

Chance knew that he had been reckless beyond belief.

The creature was far less human than he had thought. Twig-thin limbs and a torso very narrow, covered with skin like the bark of a young cherry tree, by the looks of him as hard and tough as an ash switch. No clothing. Chance had to force his eyes away from brown genitals that lumped grotesquely large in proportion to the skinny body, scarcely a foot tall. He had heard that the nameless woodfolk were lustful; now he believed it. No wonder Wirral grew so thick. . . . The small man's hands and feet also seemed overlarge, and his nose. Even so, Chance perceived his face as eerily beautiful. A narrow face, fine of jutting bone, subtle of mouth, taut of russet skin, with eyes so large and bright they seemed almost luminous.

"Chance Love-Child," said the oak-dweller in a strong, dark voice, "what do you want?"

Chance could not speak. The Denizen laughed, a sound like the song of a wren, and strutted on the branch where he stood, his massy cock thrust forward.

"Nearly ten years you have trod this way," he cried, "and never showed lack of sense till today. What ails you, Chance?"

From trees all around came the sound of bubbling laughter. Chance felt his small hairs prickle.

7

"Is it the maiden who is maiden no more?" the Denizen mocked. "The lady Halimeda who is maiden no more? She lay with Blake in the violet glade, no more a maid, and when Chance saw—"

Anger such as he had not felt in years rushed over him, jarred him out of his frozen fear. He raised his bow. But that scion of Otherness faced him, bright-eyed, fearless and laughing, and he could not take aim. He lowered his bolt again. A saddened ease stole over him, the calm of utter defeat, and he found that he could speak.

"It is for my lord Roddarc's sake that I make bold," he said.

Birdlike chirps of delight rose all around; a subtle rhyme! The brown woodsman strutted again.

"Why?" he demanded. "He has said, the lady is yours, should he die."

Chance nearly lost his voice again. If they had heard Roddarc's bidding, then even in his lodge one of them had been listening. "You go everywhere," he whispered. "You see everything."

"It is our nature so to go, so to see. What do you want to know?"

"Where the rebels muster," Chance said with a dry mouth. "Who is their leader. When they will strike."

The Denizen stopped his posturing and stood still in what might have been genuine perplexity.

"Surely you know," Chance urged.

"I know full well. But why would I tell?"

Chance stood with his mouth agape. "Why not?" he burst out at last, and the small woodsman warbled with laughter.

"Why not?" The little man turned to the listening forest. "What say ye? Should I tell?"

There arose a piping clamor. A few strong voices

8

shrilled above the others. "Tell! Tell!" cried one. "We love to meddle!" one sang out gaily. "And we meddle full well!" called another.

But before the visible Denizen could speak, another appeared, from where Chance did not see, and stood on the branch beside the first. He was gray, like beech, and mossily bearded, and as massy of cock as his russet comrade, for all that he seemed older.

"Chance," he said in a taut voice, "ten years you have averted your eyes. Now you grow unwise. Think again."

"There will be a price to pay," said the brown one, singsong, "a price to pay, some day, some way."

Their gaze met his as if from out of depths of another time, another order of being, and he knew that he was facing a power he could in no way control, relentless as fate, capricious as the turning of fortune's wheel. Perhaps as cruel as old Lord Riol, and not likely to go away, like Riol, and die. The Denizens would live forever in the forest, and what they might do to him. . . .

Still, he had to know. For Roddarc's sake.

"Tell me," he whispered. "I will pay when I must." *Whipping boy that I am,* he thought.

The forest fell to silence. The brown Denizen sat down on the bough; the gray one remained standing and spoke formally, with no attempt at rhyme.

"The rebels are gathering at Gallowstree Lea. Blake is their leader. Their numbers are small, fifty and a few, but they are clever. They will not need to penetrate the fortress. Roddarc will come to them, for they have with them a hostage."

"Who?" Chance demanded, though already he knew.

"Lady Halimeda."

*   *   *

All the miles to the fortress he ran. The day was more than half spent, but, powers be willing, there might yet be time—if the forest folk had told truth. He had heard tales, and he knew they might be making a jackass of him, burbling their uncanny laughter. Or betraying him, luring him off on a fool's errand, perhaps setting him to lure Roddarc off on a fool's errand while Blake took the fortress. The thought burned in him.

But instinct told him that there was truth in them this one first time. Truth to make him always hope thereafter.

Roddarc was at the gate, at horseback, with a troop of mounted followers, just setting out when Chance ran up to him, stumbling and streaming sweat and grasping at the steed's mane for support.

"Halimeda is missing," Roddarc told him tersely.

Chance nodded. Gasping for breath, he could not yet speak.

"What is it, man! You have news of her?"

"Gallowstree Lea," Chance panted, finding voice. "Blake, their leader. Fifty men. They will be expecting you."

Halimeda had gone on horseback and left a plain trail. Roddarc rode grimly along it, with Chance on a warhorse beside him but not armed for war. When they neared the lea, they dismounted and left their steeds and men, stalking ahead to scout the enemy's preparations. It was not fitting that the Lord of Wirralmark should do this; Chance should have done it for him. But Roddarc had insisted that they go together.

"I trust no one but you these days," he murmured as they made their way softly forward.

The lea was a meadow in the midst of Wirral, a

place where lightning had seeded fire a few seasons before, now lush with grass and shrubs. Off to one side stood a surviving tree, an elm where outlaws had once hung a renegade. Cocky of Blake, to choose this place; did he not fear the same fate?

Roddarc did not tread as silently as Chance would have liked. But it did not matter. Blake was indeed overweening. He and his followers stood chatting in boyish excitement, and his sentries heard nothing but that babble. Of course, they were not expecting spies, but a troop of men on horseback, blundering along a plain trail.

Halimeda stood tied to the gallows tree.

"How did they lure her here?" Roddarc wondered, whispering, very softly, directly into Chance's ear.

Chance knew well enough how it had been done. A message of love from Blake, an elopement planned, perhaps. Hoping Roddarc need not know, he did not answer. But suppose Halimeda stood bound merely for appearance's sake, actually there of her own will, to watch her brother be killed . . . could infatuation have made her so false? Chance felt sick.

"Go around," Roddarc whispered, "and when you are behind her, signal me with a bolt in the air. Then I will sound the horn, and do you free her and take her to safety."

If Roddarc's troop charged at the blast of the horn, all would be well. But if they tarried, Roddarc would face fifty men alone. Chance shook his head in protest.

"Do as I tell you!" Roddarc commanded, the words soft between clenched teeth.

The bolt, Chance decided, would be in Blake's back rather than into the air. He made his way with all stealth around the lea to the place where Halimeda stood captive.

And when he had stalked to a place where he

11

could see her hands, his heart warmed with relief. She was tied, truly and firmly tied; her wrists ran red with blood from her attempts to free herself. She stood with her head bowed, her dark hair hanging so that he could only glimpse her face.

He could not shoot Blake. Halimeda and the tree stood in the way. By no maneuvering could he manage it.

At last he gritted his teeth, sent a bolt into the air, and heard the mighty blast of the horn. Halimeda's head came up as if jerked by a hangman's rope.

Then Chance reached her side, cutting her bonds.

And on the far fringe of the lea, Roddarc was striding forward, sword at the ready, roaring for Blake to meet him in combat.

If the rebels had any honor at all, he would not yet be killed. . . . Chance reached for Halimeda's arm, to lead her to safety. But the look on her lovely face, the blaze of hatred, stunned him, and in his astonishment he let her snatch the long knife from his grasp. Dumbfounded, he stood with the hand that had reached for her arm still reaching, in air.

She turned and ran straight toward Blake, the knife raised.

There was small honor in the renegades. They were closing in on Roddarc on all sides; he held them off with mighty arcs of his sword. Running to his aid and her own revenge, Halimeda hurled herself at Blake with a harpy's shriek, clawing at her erstwhile lover's neck, stabbing at his back. The knife hit the shoulder blade, doing little more than startling him. He flung her off, sent her staggering with a blow.

Chance got hold of her around her waist before she fell. Enemies were everywhere; he flailed about him with his bow, using it like a club. Halimeda raised the knife again, but not, he saw, against him; she was frightened now, and with reason. "Roddarc," she pleaded.

Her brother was hard beset, taking blows and wounds.

Then the troop thundered in, clearing away the rebels from around him like so much smoke, and Roddarc seized Blake and held him at the point of the sword.

Three days later the execution took place. By hanging, at the courtyard gallows within the fortress walls. It was as well, Roddarc said, that Halimeda had not killed Blake. Treacherous schemer that he was, he deserved strangulation, not the clean death of the blade.

Everyone in Wirralmark was there to witness, for by longtime law all were required to be. Halimeda stood near the wooden stairway leading up to the high keep door, and Chance shifted his place, seemingly at random, until he stood near her, hard put not to look at her too long or too openly. She stood very still, very lovely, in a slim dress of oak-green velvet, the raw rope cuts on her wrists hidden by long sleeves that tapered nearly to her fingers. Threads of real gold bound her dark hair into braids and tendrils that rippled down her back. The bruise on her fair, pale face was already fading.

Not so, Chance thought, *the bruise on her heart.*

Hands bound, Blake walked out of the dungeon tower between two guards—or barely walked; they more carried him than not. The coward. There was not a mark on him except Halimeda's knife scratch; Chance knew that. Roddarc practiced no torture in his prison, not even on traitors.

The lord came out of the keep and stood by his sister.

"Our father would have ripped out his tongue," she said to him, her voice not quite steady, "and his eyes."

And taken away his cock as well, had he known.

"Do you wish it done to him?" Roddarc asked, gazing at her levelly.

"I—" her voice failed her, and she was silent.

Perhaps she does wish they had gouged out his eyes that gaze at her so piteously. But no need to take his tongue. He is too craven to speak.

The noose was slipped over Blake's head, hitched to the plowhorse which would draw it tight. Halimeda looked straight at her former lover and proudly lifted her chin.

Roddarc raised his hand and gave the signal.

The horse walked forward, and Blake was lifted into the air. His handsome face turned to a horror. His feet convulsively kicked, and there was a stench as he befouled himself. The watching crowd burst from silence into a vengeful roar.

Roddarc was staring stonily at his dying enemy. But Chance watched Halimeda more than he did Blake, and he saw the pallor of her face increase, a fit of trembling take hold of her. Moving only a few inches, he slipped his strong bowman's hand under her elbow just as she started to sway.

Startled, she looked up at him, but did not take it amiss that he aided her. Chance was her dear and lifelong friend, like an uncle, her brother's all-but-brother. . . . He did not meet her eyes. If he had answered her glance with all the compassion in his own, she would have wept, and it would not be well for folk to see her weeping. Worse yet, she might have perceived the love. . . .

14

Blake had ceased to writhe. Halimeda took a deep breath. Her brother turned away from the dead renegade, offered his arm to his sister, and Chance eased away from her without, he hoped, anyone's noticing. The lady walked up the long flight of stairs to the great hall at Roddarc's side, her head held high, and Chance went back to Wirral.

He had an inkling what tumult was in Halimeda. He thought of her as he walked in the shadow of the forest. And on toward dusk he made his way to the place where Wirral groped nearest the fortress, where he had a clear view of the postern gate, and there he waited.

And there, when day had nearly turned to dark, she slipped out and came running as if hounds of hell were after her.

He met her as she plunged into the forest, tears already shining on her face, and he blocked her way. "Lady—"

"Oh, Chance, let me be!" she wailed, trying to make her way around him. He knew what she was thinking. She had spent a long day withstanding the gaze of all the world, denied even the wretched release of tears. And now this big, bumbling fool of a warden was keeping her from entering her only refuge, the wild place where she had thought no one would see her weep.

"Lady, no, you cannot! There is danger. Listen to me, Halimeda!" He took her by the shoulders, met her eyes; she could not see much in him now, not in the dying light. "There is no need to hide your grief from me. I know you loved Blake."

She stood still, gazing up at him. "You—you *know*?" Her voice rose on the final word; she sounded glad.

"I know much of what happens in Wirral," he said,

then winced and tried to soften it. "Couples walking—clasped hands—"

She did not care what he had seen. She was weeping freely, and for all that caution cried out to the contrary he gathered her into his arms so that her head rested against his shoulder. Words joined her torrent of tears.

"The—more—fool I—"

"You couldn't know he was a liar," Chance said.

"Handsome—liar. He—made a laughingstock—of me."

"No one is laughing."

"They—will be." She raised her head, tears clinging to her face. "Chance, you don't—know all."

His heart froze.

"He—I—I am with child."

A spasm afflicted his arms so that he pulled her yet closer to him, rocked her against his chest. "Could you be mistaken?" he begged when he could speak.

"No. I am—sure."

She grew still with a despair too deep for weeping, turned away from him and spoke numbly.

"He sent for me, and I went riding out to meet him like a—like a—"

"Brave and loving lass that you are," Chance told her.

"Happy," she said with a bitter wonder. "I was so happy, all the way, I had such news for him. When I reached the lea, I ran to him, he kissed me. And I told him I was bearing his baby—I could scarcely speak for happiness. Then he was laughing at me, and there were men all around."

Anger was boiling up in Chance. "I did not see him laugh when you came at him with the knife," he said.

She turned her face to him with a grim smile. "I

16

wish I had struck more true! I wish I had done it
sooner. But I could not believe what I was seeing,
hearing. They were leering, and telling me that I
was going to help them kill my brother and take his
lands."

"The scum," Chance raged. "The piss-proud dregs!
And they needs must tie you to that foul tree, like a
felon—"

"Not then, not yet! It was worse. Blake—Blake
seemed to think that I would stay with him willingly,
that I was so much besotted—"

Choking on the words, she wept again.

"So much his toy, that you would betray your own
brother," Chance said huskily. "Well, the more fool
Blake, for thinking so." *And I, for thinking it even
for a moment.* He put his arms around her, and she
wept wearily against his shoulder.

"Roddarc was—so magnificent—"

Chance nodded. Roddarc had indeed been splendid. His feat capture of Blake and his outlawing of
the remaining rebels had made him shine in the eyes
of his troops and his people. Trouble was behind
him, for the time.

"How am I—ever to—tell him."

His despair matching hers, Chance had no answer
for her.

The Denizens danced in the mushroom ring.

A place of great antiquity, this, where the revels
had been held time out of mind. All the woodsfolk
came, swarming in their hundreds, as thickly as tad-
poles in a rainpool. Not all were like the first ones
Chance had met, with their sapling bodies and twiggy
limbs, their smoothbark skin and the gall-like swell-
ings between their legs. Many were like them, and
there were females like them, too, with tough brown

protuberant breasts that reminded him of oak apples. But some of the females were miniatures of the most lovely of human maidens, so slender, so dainty, that they seemed nearly transparent. Looking at them, Chance thought achingly of Halimeda.

He sat off to one side in the starlight and firefly glimmer of dusk, watching the swirling and strutting of the dance with a quiet half-smile, listening to the wild skirling of reed pipes and squirrelgut strings. If the small folk had taken a fancy to invite him to their vernal revels, it was hardly his place to refuse, but he would not be drawn into that ring of yellow mushrooms. Knowing the Wirral Denizens better day by day, nevertheless he knew only that they were changeable, as likely to mock him as greet him. Or as likely to harm him as help, he deemed. If Blake had bespoken them fair, perhaps he would be alive and Roddarc dead. Perhaps they would have aided him instead of Chance. None of this would Roddarc have believed had Chance told him, so Chance told him nothing of it, though he disliked having even so small a secret from his lifelong friend.

Halimeda's secret was the heavier one. . . . She was pale and silent whenever he saw her, and there were whispers among the people; what ailed her? But her secret would not keep much longer. It was blossoming in her, as spring blossomed into summer.

When the dancers in the starlit ring began to pair off into couples and slip away amongst the ferns, Chance rose and took his leave. He smiled wryly, walking back to his lodge. No lover awaited him there, but the Wirral would grow lush this year.

Roddarc sat waiting in the lodge when Chance came in.

"Are you a werewolf," he asked tartly, "that you have taken to roving under the moon?"

"Have I bitten you?" Chance retorted. He lighted a lantern and looked at Roddarc, then sat down with him by the cold hearth.

"What is it?" he asked.

"What is what?" Roddarc snapped.

It was the chilling anger in him that Chance meant, anger such as he had never seen in his friend. But he did not say so. "What you came to tell me," he said instead.

"Halimeda." Roddarc hurled the name out as if it were a curse. "She is with child."

Chance stared. Perhaps Roddarc took the stare for shock. It was shock indeed, but at the lord's rage, not at the tidings.

"I looked at her today," Roddarc went on with a terrible fury, terrible because so cold and controlled, "and I saw the swelling of her belly. It is just beginning, but I knew. So I made her tell me the truth of it, and name a name, and I did not take tears for an answer."

So there had been shouting, ugliness. And Halimeda was disgraced. Chance felt ill at the thought.

"You must have guessed some of it before now," he said stupidly.

"Of course I guessed. What sort of fool does she take me for? She goes about all ribbons and smiles before Gallowstree Lea, and then she turns into a wraith afterwards; how am I not to guess? I knew she was lured there. And who would her lover be but that calf-faced, honey-tongued Blake."

"Whom she tried to kill for your sake."

"She tried to kill him because he had betrayed her," Roddarc said coldly, "using her as bait to bring

19

me to him. If he had confided in her, belike she would as readily have killed me."

"Rod! You cannot believe that!" Chance spoke with a force that gave Roddarc a moment's pause.

"What am I to believe?"

"All good. She is ardent, innocent, betrayed. She has suffered. She came to your aid, and stood by you bravely while you exacted a lord's vengeance on a traitor."

"If she is so brave," said the lord in cutting tones, "then why did she not brave my ears and my presence with some words of truth?"

"She was afraid of hurting you. I'll warrant she thought to spare you pain as long as she could."

"Spare me pain?" Roddarc laughed harshly. "As if it were no pain to wonder! I guessed from the first, and my heart went out to her, and I wanted nothing more than that she should confide in me. More than once I asked her in all gentleness what was wrong, and she would make no reply, only look at me and weep. After a while I grew annoyed with weeping."

Chance said nothing. He knew Roddarc, or so he thought. Heartfelt gentleness was painful for the lord to sustain; annoyance, far easier. But perhaps, after he had vented his spleen, gentleness would return.

"If only she had spoken with me," Roddarc railed, "trusted me, I could have forgiven her. Even though her foolishness means the disgrace of us both. But she was afraid to tell me. Afraid! I, who do not practice torture even on felons and traitors, what was I likely to do to her? I, who do not use the lash even on my horses and dogs?"

"Lady Halimeda is no coward," Chance protested, but Roddarc seemed not to hear him.

"Child and youth, when I had done wrong I had to stand before my father and endure his wrath—"

"Which was visited on my body!"

So that the lord need feel no constraint. It was wonder, Chance thought, that he had not been killed entirely. A hard edge of anger nudged somewhere inside him, edge which had never been there before, or not for more years than he could number on the fingers of both hands. And without clearly knowing why, he began to remember things he had not thought of since he had been a man.

Starting with the day Roddarc had scanted his courtesy before his lordly father's seat of honor.

Not so great an offense, merely a stripling's newfound arrogance. The two lads, Rod and Chance, had just turned thirteen. But it was not in Riol to humor anyone's arrogance but his own. Not even that of a stripling, not even his noble son. His face flushed bloody red with rage, and he darted out a long hand and snatched Chance by the arm as he made his own proper obeisance, jerking him forward and landing a blow on his head that sent him sprawling, all within the moment.

"Again!" he thundered at Roddarc.

Roddarc was very thin at that age. His limbs looked as if they might be broken by two fingers of his warrior father's heavy hand. But there was a look on his fine-boned face as of something that refused to be broken. He made a sweeping parody of a courtly bow.

"Strip!" Riol roared at Chance, tapping at the tops of his high leathern boots with the whip that was always in his hand.

Strip, before all those present in the great hall. But it was not so uncommon an occurrence, and Chance stolidly did as he was told. To do otherwise was unthinkable. Powers of hell only knew what his punishment would have been if he, himself, had ever scanted a bow. But looking back, with a flare of fury and anguish he wondered if little Halimeda had been there to see his humiliation. Belike not. Belike she was yet too young to eat in the great hall, or a nurse had taken her away so that she would not be frightened. Though he seemed to remember a child's crying. . . .

Riol had lifted the whip, a sort of rod covered with knotted leather, meant for the disciplining of hounds. With it he had commenced to scourge Chance's legs and buttocks.

This, also, was an occurrence all too common. Riol was easily angered, no matter how Roddarc tried to please him. Eyes narrowed with pain, Chance stole a glance at his foster brother's face, expecting the more inward, bittersweet pain that sustained him through these times. Roddarc would be starting to weep. In a moment, he would begin to plead with his father for Chance's sake. It would take much pleading to satisfy Riol, much begging before the flogging would be ended. But for days thereafter Roddarc would do whatever his father wished. . . .

The young lord's face was hard and dry.

"Bow," Riol commanded his son.

Roddarc stood without moving, jaw set, chin raised at a stubborn angle.

"Bow!" Riol roared, and he beat Chance with such fury that blood burst from the boy's mouth and nose; he would have fallen if it were not that the lord's hard hand held him up. His eyes, blinded by pain and tears, could no longer seek Roddarc's.

"Lash all you like," he heard the young lord coldly say. "Chance is a commoner and a bastard. He deserves whipping."

"Aaaa!" Chance panted suddenly aloud in a new experience of pain. He could not have said which hurt him more, Riol's rage with the whip or Roddarc's betrayal. Though of course Rod could not mean it—

"Is that so?" the lord queried in a soft voice, far too soft for comfort. "Chance deserves punishment?"

"Certainly. He is a commoner, and we of the blood do with commoners what we like. Do we not?"

"Truly? You flog him, then." Riol stilled his whip long enough to offer it to Rod. Not an offer, but a command. . . . Knuckling his eyes so that he could see, Chance looked at his friend. With an angry, arrogant smile, Rod was shaking his head.

"But I choose not to. And what will you do to me, my father? Turn the lash on me?"

With a wordless roar of fury Riol struck Chance across the face. Only the boy's raised hands saved his eyes from the rod.

"Go ahead. Kill him," said Roddarc. "And who will you beat then?"

Riol spun the whipping boy around and struck him with the rod featly across his cock, bending him double with agony. His head swaying above the floor, Chance felt that his world had spun upside down. Rod, condemning him?

"Cut it off," Roddarc said. "I don't care."

Riol straightened Chance with a blow of his heavy fist, then struck again with the rod.

"You are a filthy tyrant," said Roddarc with something of heat, more of disgust, and nothing, nothing at all, of heart.

Even in his agony Chance felt the lord's shock, the sudden silence, the rod hovering, stilled. "What did you say?" Riol inquired through clenched teeth.

"You heard me," said Roddarc with a weird calm. "A filthy, bloody tyrant. All goodly folk hate you."

Riol flung Chance to the floor and started to laugh, yell after yell of comfortless laughter. "Very truth, very truth!" he shouted amidst his laughter. "And someday you will be another."

It was over. No thanks to Roddarc, and not because the lord was merciful, either. Merely because he was amused. Lying half drowning in his own blood, slipping away into a swoon, Chance heard the yells of laughter, the lord's tipsy shouts. "Tyrant, is it? And someday you will be one, just like me."

Servants carried him away after the lord's back was turned, tended to him hastily and heaved him into his bed. He knew nothing until he awoke groaning in the dark of night.

"Stop your whimpering." Roddarc's voice sounded irritably across the chamber they shared. "Let me sleep."

"You swine," Chance breathed. "Every part of me is on fire. Do you not care—"

"Hold your tongue," Roddarc commanded more coldly, "or I will thrash you myself."

From mere pride Chance kept silence. He would not have Roddarc hear him weeping.

Later he understood, in a dim way, how Roddarc had needed to free himself from the trap formed by his own noble birth and the happenstance of his loving Chance. But at the time, the pain of the flogging had seemed as nothing compared to his heartache.

He lay in his bed for days, past the time when he could have been up and about, for all parts of him were healing cleanly. No one troubled him. Let the lad sulk; there were events afoot. Lord Riol was going off to war.

The war from which he never returned, all good powers be praised. And after he was gone, Chance and Roddarc had drifted gradually back into their former, brotherly ways. No lasting harm had come to

Chance from the flogging except a quietly continuing pain of spirit. For there had been no apology from Roddarc, nothing said between them of trust betrayed. No need for words, Chance had told himself. Forgive and forget. Better truth was that he was too needful to risk a quarrel with Roddarc. The young lord's regard was all he had. The young tyrant . . .

"I still bear the scars," he said angrily. The old, buried dagger-blade of anger, all but forgotten, edging up in him, after all the years; why? Roddarc's ice-pale face before his eyes.

"You think it is the easier lot," the lord said, "to stand by and let a—a brother be beaten? You will scoff, Chance, but it may have been almost—harder for me."

Long habit is not easily broken. Chance did not quarrel.

"Yes," he said, "there are punishments worse than blows." How well he knew it. "And my lady knows it as well as you and I. If she fears, it is not for her body."

"She knows full well I will never lay a finger on her to hurt her," Roddarc said stiffly. "I did not touch her even today to wrest the story from her." He stood up, his face stony. "But by all the powers, it will be many a long day before she sees my smile."

Chance stood up as well, trying to pierce that locked gaze with his own. "You're no gentle lord, then," he said. "Blows would be kinder."

But Roddarc only gave him a black look and strode out.

He will be over it in a few days, Chance thought, or hoped, for he had no basis for thinking so. And at the back of his mind he seemed to hear still the yelling of dead Riol's laughter.

* * *

As summer warmed into high summer he learned what Halimeda had somehow feared but he, Chance, had never admitted: that Roddarc was capable of an icy and relentless wrath day in, day out, sustaining it and feeding it as he had never been able to nurture tenderness. And even though his demands were the same as they had ever been and his rulings in the court of law not unjust, all his people felt his mood and began to mutter under it.

Every few days Chance went to see Halimeda.

At first he found it hard to find excuses. Business had never brought him much within the fortress. Later, he simply went, not caring for sly looks or whispered comments, taking blackberries, a delicate flower found beneath the Wirral shade, a drinking noggin carved and polished out of oaken whorl.

Halimeda needed none of these things, for she was a lady and had all she needed of baubles and good food, clothing and the gardens for roaming. But as her belly swelled with child, Chance sensed she needed his visits for nurture food could not give her. Though, truly, she was strong, all through the summer and early autumn, strong in body and steady in spirit, "bearing up well," as the gossips would have it. With awesome strength, for one so slender, so young, so defenseless, Chance thought.

"Does my brother come to see you still?" she asked him when summer was hot and golden before autumn.

"From time to time, yes." *Fleeing his own wrath*, Chance thought.

"Maybe there is still hope, then, if there is that much heart in him. I—sometimes I think he will never be a brother to me again."

"He provides for you," Chance said awkwardly, meaning, *love underlies the silence*. But Halimeda only pulled a face.

"Yes, he checks on me as he might on a well-bred birth in whelp, cursing me with his concern. He speaks to the servants, not to me." She shrugged, dismissing the matter as out of her control.

"He speaks of you from time to time," Chance added after a moment.

"None too kindly, I am sure," said Halimeda with bitter amusement, and Chance could only keep silence.

He sometimes took issue with Roddarc for Halimeda's sake, but not too strongly, hoping to do more good if Roddarc continued to think of him as a friend. Moreover, he was afraid to speak ardently of Halimeda. Afraid of what Roddarc might see in his eyes.

By harvest time, the lady had grown as round as the fruits of the vines, a very emblem of the full lofts. Those golden days were darkened for Chance. A fear was growing in him as the babe grew in the lady, and one evening when the smell of frost hung in the air he spoke plainly to Roddarc.

"It is time for you to give over this wrath," he said.

"Give over?" The lord glanced up, his look chill even in the warm light of the hearthfire.

"Yes. I know well enough that you love your sister, Rod. You cannot keep on this flinty shell forever. Suppose she dies in the birthing of the child?"

Chance felt his voice falter, speaking of that fear. But Roddarc's hard stare did not change. Chance plunged on.

"She is very young, very slender, it is not unlikely. How will you feel if she dies and you have not made your peace with her?"

"As I feel now," Roddarc stated. "That it would be her own foolish fault, for dallying."

"You cannot mean that!" Chance whispered, shocked

and vehement. No use, any longer, trying to hide his vehemence.

"I do mean it," the lord said, all too evenly. "No one made her conceive a child. It is not as if she were wed."

"Roddarc of Wirralmark," Chance shouted at him, "for whatever goes wrong, the blame will be on your head if you send her to childbed grieving!"

"Is it not fitting," the lord said with icy calm, "that a sorrow child should be born amid tears?"

"Does it mean nothing to you that she is your beloved sister?" Chance was on his feet now, raging. "Lord Roddarc, you are blind, locked like a felon in a dungeon of your own digging, as bad as your father Riol at his very worst, for all that you give yourself airs of kindness!"

That stung. "Speak not to me of Riol," Roddarc snapped, and the lash of the words brought him to his feet in his turn.

"I will speak what you need to hear! My lady Halimeda was wise not to confide in you. She knew that you can be as cruel as any tyrant who ever wielded—"

"Speak no more to me of that wench!" Roddarc thundered. "What, are you besotted with her?"

"You pledged me once to protect her!" Chance shouted back just as fiercely. "With my life I was to shield her! What, am I to desert her now for the sake of your ill humor? Is she worth less than she was before?"

"She is worth nothing!"

"She is worthy of all love," Chance whispered. But the lord did not hear him, ranting on.

"What man of rank would have her? There is no noble in the land who will take such a sullied bride, be her dower far richer than I can afford. Once I had thought there would be perhaps a prince for her, but now—"

"I would take her in an instant," Chance said softly, and this time Roddarc heard him.

For the space of three breaths there was utter silence. Eyes met in a complicated communication; memory was part of it, memory of a time ten years and more before, of a battlefield. Pain for Roddarc in that memory, and pain angered him.

Lord Roddarc spoke.

"How very fitting, how suitable for her. You: a commoner, a bastard, and a castrate."

Chance stood as if frozen, unable even to breathe. When he drew breath and moved, it was to stride across his small home and fling open the door.

"Get out," he said.

"I will go when I please."

"It is not fitting that a lord should come so familiarly to the home of a commoner. Out!"

Roddarc shrugged and ambled out with apparent indifference.

The next time he went to see Halimeda, Chance found that he was no longer to be admitted to her presence. Nor did Roddarc come any more to his warden's lodge.

Autumn waned toward winter. Chill winds and rains tore the leaves from the trees until only a few remained, hanging in dark tatters, like rags.

The Denizens seemed not to mind the cold any more than the bare trees of Wirral did. They wore no more clothing than they had in the heat of summer, nothing more than their barklike skins.

Making his rounds of the forest one day, Chance went back to the same lightning-hollowed oak where he had first spoken with a small brown man. There he paused, feeling diffident, for he had been mocked and snubbed by the small folk often enough. He stood gathering courage until he heard a birdlike giggle within the blackened hollow.

"Little one there in the tree," he whispered, "come out, please, and speak with me."

A face popped into view. But as the body followed it, Chance saw that it was a female he had summoned this time. Her jutting breasts and pudenda were no less daunting than the cock of her male counterpart had been. More so, to Chance.

She saw as much, and grinned at him. Her narrow, bony face yet had a broad and sensual mouth. Chance forced himself to look not at that mouth, nor at the handspan height of the rest of her, but at her eyes, both merry and haunted, as he spoke.

"Have you any tidings—I mean—know you anything of the Lady Halimeda?"

The Denizen grinned more broadly but answered him directly enough. "We have seen her walking in Gallowstree Lea."

"Lately?"

"Yestereen."

"Alone?" Chance exclaimed. With her time so near, Halimeda ought to have been sequestered in her chambers. It was not right or usual that she should have been wandering so far into Wirral.

"Lone, alone, all alone, under the bloated moon."

Chance frowned uneasily. "No tidings more?"

"We stay in Wirral, we. Nothing more."

Chance slept restlessly that night, half waking. The wind was high and whined even through the stone walls of his lodge. Moonlight shone in through his single window, and tossing trees seen against that white luminous mushroom made him moan, dreaming first of flailing rods, then of the revels of the

Denizens. Clouds torn into dark tatters by the wind passed across the face of the bloated moon, casting shadows that crawled eerily on his floor. A skein of wild geese flew somewhere in the dark, their cries like the yelping of the hounds of hell.

Other cries, singsong cries, on the wind with the piping of the geese.

"Lady, Lady Halimeda,
Lone, alone, under the moon,
Lady, Lady Halimeda,
Lone, alone, under the moon,
Left the fortress, left her home,
Lady Dreaming-Of-The-Sea,
Bound for Gallowstree Lea—"

Chance sat bolt upright. The voices were real.

"Bound for Gallowstree Lea!"

Chance sprang up, pulling on trousers and boots in a panic, not pausing for further clothing. At a dead run he sped through the windy, shadowy Wirral.

Gallowstree Lea was swept with stormwind, cloud gloom and shifting moonglades. In the trickster light Chance could not at first comprehend the dark, billowing shape by the lone tree that groaned aloud in the night. Then he saw. It was Halimeda, round with child, all robed in black, with the black cloth whipping about her, Halimeda standing on a waist-high boulder under the boughs of the gallows tree—

For a heart-sickening moment Chance thought that already the loop clung around her neck, that she had only to jump and she would be swinging, strangling. Then he saw that she was still tying the rope. She was having difficulty in securing it. The storm had delayed her.

He was heartsick still, that she stood there so desperate.

Possessed by her own desperation, she did not see

31

him until he stood panting before her. Then she screamed with fury.

"Chance, no! Let me be! I—"

He lifted her down and led her away, an arm around her shoulders. She went with him unresisting, though she was still crying aloud.

"I cannot stand it any longer! He hates me! He glares at me with a curse in his eyes."

Her shoulders sagged, and she started to weep.

Blinded by her own tears she walked, and Chance led her to his lodge, as it was the closest dwelling. He sat her by his hearth, put fragrant apple wood on the fire, drew water and set it to boil for hot herb tea to soothe her. She looked up at him. Her face was white, drawn down by grief, ravaged by tears, her hair hanging down her forehead in strings.

"There is nothing for me any more," she told him with deathly calm, "for my babe, nothing. No hope."

"Hali, please." He had not called her by the pet name since she was a tiny girl, but that night it burst from him. "Do not say that!"

"How am I not to say what is but simple truth? What is there for me but to be a whore, and my baby a whore's brat? Unless I die—"

"Hail, no!" He knelt before her, his shoulders broad and bare in the firelight, reached up to touch her face, as if his touch could somehow heal her of tears. It did not.

"Far better that I should die. I am a blot, all goodly folk scorn me. My own brother hates me—"

"I love you," Chance whispered, his face upraised and his eyes meeting her eyes.

Her face grew very still, and she looked back at him as if she were seeing him for the first time.

"That was not spoken as my brother's warden," she said slowly after a moment, in a hushed voice.

"No." Chance swallowed, and shame tugged at his face, but still he met her eyes. "And it should not have been spoken, for it is unseemly, except that—it is truth, Lady, and something you needed to hear, tonight."

"You—love—me?"

The tremor in her voice smote him to the heart.

"How not?" he said. "Hali, you are of all maidens most beautiful, most brave, most—most dreaming. What man can see you and not love you? And you are wrong, Lady." His voice grew stronger and yet warmer. "There will be a worthy lover for you someday, after these dark days are behind you. A noble lover, I feel sure of it."

"You call yourself unworthy?" Halimeda's voice also grew stronger, and with her own hands she reached up and brushed away her tears.

"I, a commoner and a bastard?" He laughed briefly, harshly. "Yes, manifestly unworthy. I am a fool to speak."

"No fool. I know better." Halimeda was looking at him thoughtfully, desperation turning into a bold thought, and Chance saw. In a few moments, he knew, his heart would break—for still he must speak truth.

"Hali, I have—nothing to give you."

"No name, you mean, for the babe? No family? But already I am bereft of those. I came here with nothing, and you have offered me a commoner's love. It is that much more." She spoke not warmly, but in a settled, collected way. "Perhaps, in time, I could learn to return it."

Looking up at her, hope dawning in her gaze, he faced at last the agony that for years he had held at arm's length. He sobbed, bent as if by a blow, hiding his face behind his hands.

"Chance, what is it?" Halimeda drew him toward her, letting his head and shoulders lie in her lap, against the warm curve of her pregnant belly, as he choked on pain. "My life's friend, what is wrong?"

He stopped struggling and found the calm in the vortex of the pain, looked up at her.

"I have—nothing to give you, Hali."

Scarcely comprehending, unwilling to comprehend, yet she began to understand, and her face grew very still. She did not speak. He got up, found a shirt and put it on, made the tea, gave her some and himself some as well. Sitting near her by the hearth, he told her the tale.

"It happened the day of our victory in the long war. Roddarc and I fought side by side always, and he in the fore, as befits a lord's son. And he is a splendid warrior, I was proud and joyous to stand by him. And many a time had he taken a spear on his shield. But this one time of those many times, he erred somehow, and instead of deflecting the spear harmlessly he let it slip down and to the side, and it struck me featly in the groin."

He had never spoken of that day, not to anyone, and it was as though he felt again the blow; he shuddered and winced. But the lady's steady eyes were on him, and he went on.

"We fought on, both of us. We had to, or be killed. Luckily the battle was nearly over before I weakened. . . . Roddarc carried me to safety, and laid me down and tore open the clothing to bandage the wound. And when he saw what had been done to me, he wept. When I awoke, the next day, he was still weeping."

"How—how horrible," Halimeda whispered.

"He never told you?"

"No!"

"I think—he does not speak of it, any more than I do. I think—my lady, he has never said this to me, but it may be why he has never wed. So that he would not enjoy what I could not. He is—he is all bound up in honor and loyalty; he would think in that way. And he was a merry enough wencher before it happened. We both were."

Halimeda grimaced at him. "Did you make yourselves babes in the wenches?"

"We may have. I know Roddarc did." *And his punishment, as usual, was visited on me.* The thought, new to him, took his breath away, until he saw the look the lady was giving him. "No, it is not right," he told her.

"Or fair," she said hotly. "Men share the pleasure and escape the blame."

"It was a long time ago. We were young fools. And—Halimeda, do you think it may be part of Roddarc's spleen now, that you have enjoyed lovemaking. . . ."

She flushed and glanced down at her hands. Impulsively Chance reached over and touched her hair, straightening the straggling locks.

"I don't know when I began dreaming of you," he said softly. "Years ago. It happened stealthily. . . . And, you see, it did not matter to me that you were unattainable."

"I must think," she muttered, still staring at her hands.

"Take note, my lady, you are not so willing to hurl yourself away after all."

She looked up at him with a small, shamed smile, and he nodded.

"Truly, there will be someone better for you. Your case is not so desperate that you must settle for a bastard commoner with no manhead. Life's course is

35

full of strange quirks and turns. You are so lovely, there must yet be a worthy lover for you. I cannot believe otherwise."

"Chance," she said slowly, "I am all in confusion. You have made me see outside myself, and it is a comfort, but strange."

"Then go home, bear your child, wait. It will come clear. Only, Hali . . ." One last time he permitted himself that love-name, and he looked at her in plea. "Think no longer of Gallowstree Lea."

She gave him her hand for a moment. That was her pledge.

On a day when bone-chilling drizzle fell from a gray sky, Chance paused along a deer trail in Wirral to relieve himself against an oak—a thing he had done often enough before, forsooth. But this time he had no more than undone the lacing of his trousers and parted the fabric when a trilling laugh sounded, to be echoed from several directions.

"No nuts, and only half a stem!" a fey voice sang. "Chance, don't you miss them?"

Chance scowled and started to cover himself, then considered that it would be worse to be pursued elsewhere. He emptied his bladder, and as he did so the Denizen who had accosted him strutted into view. It was one of the tough-breasted females, to his chagrin, and he flushed deeply. The woodswoman laughed again.

"Chance, it is a wonder they call you man!"

He closed his trousers, fumbling with the laces in his haste, and burbling laughter sounded from all around. Then a small brown form shot through the air and landed like a squirrel beside the other. It was the Denizen Chance had first bespoken, the handsome russet-colored young prince of them all.

"Pay no mind, Chance," he said. "Fate is unkind."

"And you, I suppose, are kinder," Chance retorted sourly.

"Indeed so! Listen, and you shall know." The young Denizen paused for effect, and crouched down on his bough in a manner as of a conspirator. "In the midst of Wirral," he said in a lowered voice, "in the very fundament of it, stands a tree which bears nuts such as those you lack."

Chance snorted aloud. "You must take me for an ass," he said.

"You doubt it? When Wirral grows thick as grass?"

Chance scowled; they were rhyming with him, now. "What of it," he said curtly, "if there is such a tree?" For he did not know all that lay in the penetralia of Wirral; no one did. Stranger things than what the Denizen named might be there.

"What of it? Chance!" The Denizen prince seemed aghast. Still standing beside him, the female took up the tale.

"Just do as we say—"

Other voices joined in.

"Pluck the nuts from that bole,"

"And you will be whole,"

"And join the dance within the day!"

"Bah!" Chance exploded, but he did not turn away. If the small folk were bejaping him, they had judged nicely as to their bait. He could not turn away, not while there was even the fool's chance that they were speaking truth. In no mindly sense did he believe them, but he had heard tales of these folk, their many powers. He had to risk. . . .

"Danger?" he demanded.

The Denizen prince stood up, stiffly erect, cock jutting. "Some small peril," he admitted. "Do you

care for that?" Glint of his amber eyes gave the dare
to Chance.

"Bah!" Chance sputtered again. "Which way?"

Instead of replying, the copper-colored Denizen
turned to the surrounding forest. "What say ye?" he
cried. "Shall we guide him thither?"

Blast the cock-proud rascal, Chance fumed, *he'll
have me begging next for my chance to be gulled.*

The cry went up from all around.

"Away, say we!"

"To the cullion-nut tree!"

"Whither, thence! Hither, hence!" the Denizen
prince shouted crazily, and he vanished as handily as
a squirrel, within an eyeblink. A birdlike laugh
sounded somewhere, and then there was silence.
Chance lurched forward.

"Where are you?" he shouted, trying to keep the
fury out of his voice. Be cursed the lot of them, truly
they would have him begging! For what folly? A ball
tree!

"Here!" came a teasing voice from somewhere far
ahead.

"This way!" another cried gaily from a somewhat
different direction. "With a dildo hey! Away, we
say!"

Panting with anger even before he began, Chance
ran toward the voices.

"Full merrily away say we!"

And indeed they led him a merry chase through
the drizzling rain. Tearing through bracken and stumbling through stones, up scarp and down dingle, into
thorn thickets that pierced him even through his
leathern clothing, that would have liked to have taken
his eyes. The Denizens, he decided, must have some
plan for him after all, for they slowed their pace to
wait for him. But as soon as he stumbled out of his

difficulties they were off again as wildly as ever, and he must needs trail after, with no breath left even to curse.

"Chance Lord's man, he ran and ran . . ."

Already they were making a song of it. They would be amusing themselves with the tale, Chance deemed, for the winter's span, perhaps longer. No matter, for he had to know the end of the story. He ran through the waning day until the gray sky darkened into dusk. No matter, again. There was no loved one waiting by his cold hearth.

He splashed into fen. No matter, still; already he was wet to the skin. Though never before, even in Wirral, had he met with such a bog. Thick mud oozed up to his thighs, almost up to his crotch, slowing him to a snail's pace.

"How much farther?" he called into the dusk.

A babble of laughter sounded instead of an answer, and Chance stiffened: something large was bestirring the fen, rising luminous into the dusk.

The laughter of the denizens rippled and warbled from the forest all around. There must have been hundreds of them watching, as dense as a flock of starlings.

And Chance shouted with terror, falling back into the muck.

Looming over him, a sort of a snake of single eye, a dragon—but no, the thing was too stubby to be called a snake, too formless and squalid for a dragon. More like a huge worm or a maggot, fungus-colored, with the glistening soft skin of a catfish. Slimy fen water dripped down from it, and the single eye deepset in the center of its head peered toward him.

Chance floundered back from it, thrashing for balance and footing, and the Denizens shook the small tree limbs with their laughter. Gleeful voices shouted.

"Don't hurt it, Chance!"

"It only wants to dance!"

"Wirralworm, we call it!"

Above them all the voice of the young prince carried.

"Chance, there is no cullion tree. But see, we've found a phallus for ye!"

If I had a sword, he thought grimly, *if I had a nobleman's weapon. . . .* But what would be the use, indeed, of doing battle with the nodding monster? It had not moved from its place amidst the muck, and even as he crawled at last onto solid ground and stood, streaming bogwater and greenish slime, to face it, the thing went limp and collapsed beneath the surface. There was a faint glow as of something rotten, and it was gone.

"But it's always there," said a voice close by his ear, "hidden deep yet not asleep. Just like the manhood in you, Chance."

He turned, sluggish with disgust, to face the copper-brown prince of the Denizens, barely visible in the nightfall darkness.

"Very well," said Chance, "you've had your play. Now which way to my home?"

The handspan youth chuckled in delight at the happenstance rhyme. "The sun will show you the way, come day," he sang. "Sleep well!" Within the moment he and all the others were gone. Their laughing farewells echoed away into Wirral.

Chance did not wait for day. He blundered off, on the move to keep his chilled blood from pooling in his veins, and roamed all night though he could see nothing beneath cloud gloom that shut out the moon and stars. He did not mind the darkness; it matched his wakeful rage.

* * *

Halimeda's babe was born as the first snow fell thick and cold on turrets and trees. It was a girl. A hard labor, but the lady would be well enough after a ten of days, if she did not weaken with fever. This much Chance learned from the talk of the alehouse— he went often to the alehouse, those days, and made friends with those who muttered there in the evenings after a day of wearisome toil in the lord's service. He inquired of Halimeda also from Roddarc's steward, to whom he made his reports. The lord himself he had not seen since the night he had ordered Roddarc out of his lodge. Nor was Chance admitted to see Halimeda.

The talk had it, after several days, that she was on the mend and the infant thriving. But the tenth day came and passed, and there was no courtly gathering, no ceremony of welcome for the little one, no bestowal of a name.

Near Chance's cottage lay a broad, hollow log of apple, the most auspicious of woods. When that day had passed he worked the evening by lantern light and cut a section of it, took it in by his hearth. There in days that followed he cleaned and shaped it, polished it with wax, fitted ends to it, and rockers.

Snow after snow fell. The Wirral stood shrouded, white and cold.

"Any tidings?" Chance asked of a tree one day.

A small, cross face looked out at him. "We have said we will tell you, Chance Lord's Man."

He believed them in this, for he considered that they might be inclined toward kindness since the affair of the fen. For a time.

"But someday—" the Denizen grumbled.

"I will pay," Chance finished impatiently. The small woodsman scowled at him.

"Think not, fool, that you can pull from one of us a thorn. We take care of our own."

"Just tell me quickly when she comes."

As it chanced, he saw her himself and needed no telling. Barefoot in the deep snow she came, in the pale winter's daylight, slowly walking, gowned in black, carrying the baby in her arms. So as not to be seen from the fortress, he let her come well within the shelter of the trees before he met her.

"Chance!" she gasped, then burst out at once with her trouble. "He has said I must leave the little one here in the Wirral!"

"I know. So it would have been done to me if your kind lady mother had not taken me to the keep." Easily, as if he had done nothing in his life but handle children, he reached out and took the babe. "Now the little lady of Wirralmark comes to me."

"But Chance—oh, I am filled with hope, but how will you care for her? How will you feed her?"

"I will find a woman to nurse her. I will cherish her, my lady."

Halimeda's eyes filled, and she touched one of his weathered hands.

"How is Roddarc?" he asked her gruffly.

"Much the same." She sounded more weary than bitter, but then her eyes widened with fright. "He will learn that you have sheltered the babe, he will punish you for it!"

"He will learn," Chance agreed, "but I think he will not trouble me. There has to be shame in him, or he would have killed the child outright."

The infant in his arms stirred and began to wail.

"Go back quickly, Lady, before you freeze," Chance urged. "Only tell me, what is this pretty one's name?"

"I have called her Sorrow."

"She is worthy of better than that, Halimeda!"

The lady hesitated only for a moment. "Call her Iantha," she said softly, and she touched the babe's petalsoft cheek, kissed her on the forehead, glanced once at Chance and turned away, running.

Iantha. The name meant "Violet."

Chance carried her to his lodge, and the babe howled loud with hunger.

He satisfied her with a sugar-teat and the rocking of the cradle until after dark. Then he carried her to the village huts that huddled beneath the fortress wall. But he had misjudged, thinking his fellow commoners would be as brave as he. Not a woman of them would take the infant to nurse, or a man permit it, for fear of the lord's wrath.

By the end of the next day Chance knew that Iantha was starving. She could not hold down the milk of cows or goats, or even that of mares. Her wailing grew weaker, mewling and piteous.

Frantic, Chance bundled the baby warmly and began to stride through Wirral toward the distant demesne of a neighboring lord. He would be a renegade to Roddarc thenceforth. He had thought it would be a while yet before that happened; Iantha was upsetting his half-formed plans. But he could not let Halimeda's daughter die. . . .

"We will feed her, Chance Love-Child!" a voice piped from the beech tree at his elbow.

Chance stopped short, but he looked doubtfully at the twiggy female Denizen who had spoken. Greatbreasted she might be for her size, but the whole of her was no more than half the length of the infant, and maybe a quarter the mass.

"How?" he demanded, and the woodswoman gave him a dark smile. She was greenish gray as well as brown, with hair that hung in airy tendrils like liana, and Chance realized suddenly that her tough, narrow face was both grotesque and beautiful.

"Simply, as the sap rises in the tree. Take me up in your hand."

He did so, conscious of his own daring—he had never touched a Denizen, and he found this one dry, cool and pleasantly hard, almost like a lizard. He held her beside the baby's head, and she gave the breast. Her entire dug fit into the infant's mouth.

For a moment Iantha did not respond. Then she began to suck greedily, and she sucked at length.

"Is she being nourished?" Chance asked doubtfully.

"Does earth nourish yonder beech?" the small woman retorted. "Open her mouth; I must change breasts."

Chance pried apart the infant's lips with a fingertip, and Iantha bellowed angrily, a strong sound that was good to hear. Sucking on the second breast, she fell warmly asleep. Chance took the Denizen and set her back in the tree.

"Many thanks," he said, hoping thanks were warranted, for he felt a stirring of misgiving even as he spoke. The woodswoman did not speak to the thanks. She seemed exhausted.

"Take the babe back to your dwelling," she said, "and we will tend her." She turned, slipped away, and Chance did as she had said.

When Iantha woke and cried, some hours later, another great-breasted Denizen slipped down through a gap in the eaves, between rafters and thatch, climbed nimbly down the stones of the wall and gave the breast to the babe in the applewood cradle.

So it went for the space of many snows. A different woodswoman came each time; Chance never saw the same one twice, to his knowledge. Nor were his nursemaid visitors ever the lovely dancers he had seen, the ones shaped like the most lissome of human damsel, but always the bark-brown, twiggy-limbed females. The others would be too delicate, Chance decided, their breasts too small and fine. But he would not have minded seeing one of them again. They were in their way nearly as beautiful as Halimeda.

Of the lady, he heard nothing. She kept to the fortress. Presumably, she yet lived.

Sometimes he carried little Iantha with him as he made the rounds of Wirral or went to speak with certain folk he met within the forest for secrecy's sake. Sometimes he left her sleeping in his lodge, and the Denizens cared for her. Often he shirked his duties, but he always turned in a semblance of a report. In the evenings, and often during the day as well, he would hold baby Iantha in his arms and lull her and hum to her in his husky voice. No one from the fortress troubled him; if it was known that he harbored the babe, nothing was said of it.

By the time the snowmelt came, Iantha was drinking cow's milk and eating mush, and the Denizens no longer came to her.

Spring warmed. In Wirral glades the violets were blooming.

One day of soft rain, as Chance stirred porridge and rocked the little one in her cradle, his door opened and Roddarc strode in. By his side walked Halimeda, more lovely than the violets, robed in a dress of amethyst velvet, her hair looped up in braids plaited with thread of gold.

If Roddarc had come alone, Chance would have challenged him. But as it was, he simply stood and stared at Halimeda, porridge dripping from the spoon in his hand. The lady seemed well, her bearing grave but quiet, as if she had settled something within herself. She stood gazing at her daughter, and her smile shifted Chance's glance there also. Roddarc knelt on one knee by the cradle, putting his finger into the infant's tiny fist.

When his eyes came up to meet Chance's stare, his look was full of shame. "Ten thousand thanks," he said in a low voice.

Halimeda came with a rustle of velvet, as if she could not longer restrain herself, gathered baby Iantha up and cuddled her, conversing with her in the private way of mothers. Roddarc stood up, and Chance scowled at him, more than a little uncomfortable.

"Do you want me to go away?" Roddarc asked him.

Chance kept silence, undecided what to do. The lord's diffident manner both touched and annoyed him.

"I have hurt you," Roddarc said, speaking awkwardly, "and I have hurt Halimeda more. So much, both of you, that I doubt if I can ever make amends. But I want you to know—I am sorry."

Chance flung the spoon into the porridge pot. "Gaaah! Sit down," he growled, not wanting to hear any more. "What woke you out of it when all my shouting could not?"

"My own misery." Roddarc sat. "But it is a hard thing to face. . . . Chance, I am more like my father than I knew. My methods differ, but the venom is the same."

"It served him well," Chance said curtly. *Powers, can we make this limp worm into a man again?*

"In the long war, you mean? Then I am worse than Riol. He turned his poison against his enemies, but I vented all of mine on my sister and my only true friend."

46

"Gaaah!" Chance exploded again. "Be done!"

"There are things that need to be said. I know I still have your loyalty, Chance, but I know I cannot expect—"

I should say not. Though you do.

Roddarc swallowed. "I cannot expect your friendship. I cannot blame you if you hold it against me, what I have said, what I have done."

Chance looked over toward Halimeda, where she whispered to her baby, swirling about the room and rocking the little one to the imagined melody of a carole. "Does your lady sister hold it against you?"

"Halimeda is more noble than I can comprehend."

Chance wondered, but he could not disagree. With a grunt he sat down across from Roddarc at the hearth.

"If you can forgive me," the lord said to him, "it will be blessing far more than I deserve."

"Would you *stop* that!" Chance roared at him.

Halimeda looked over at them with a smile, came over and crouched by them, still holding tiny Iantha.

"She does not know me," the lady said wistfully.

Iantha gazed solemnly up at the three of them. Though she was but a fourmonth old, already her features were delicate, her pale fawn skin very fine and scarcely touched with pink, her eyes of a startling green. The wisps of hair on her head were reddish gold, very bright and true. When Halimeda caressed her cheek, she did not answer the caress, not even with her glance. She looked skyward with a mien at once innocent, knowing and very old.

"She is the same with me," Chance told Halimeda, meaning to comfort her. But the lady clutched her daughter in alarm.

"Changeling," she whispered, and Chance sat stunned at her boldness, that she should have spoken so nearly of the Denizens who were never named. Even Roddarc, startled, gestured her to be silent. But she stammered on, unheeding. "They—folk say babes left in the Wirral will be taken—"

"Lady, please!" Chance exclaimed, nearly knocking her over as he blundered to his feet. She caught at his hand, and he pulled her up.

"The babe is very young," Roddarc soothed, rising also. "She is not yet aware of us."

Sighing, yet smiling, Halimeda placed the baby back in her cradle, and without much more speech she and Roddarc went out. Chance did not need to wonder why they had not taken Iantha back to the fortress with them. He deemed he already knew.

Whisperings had grown louder. Rumor was turning into certainty.

Some few weeks later Chance went to Roddarc— for he was no stranger to the fortress any longer, but went there often, with Iantha or without her. He found Roddarc in his chambers and spoke to him in privacy. "Louts wink at each other again. It is said that you will be overthrown before the year is done."

The lord answered with a smile. "You had not heard ere this? The little one must be keeping you out of the alehouse."

"You *knew*?"

"There have been mutterings since before Iantha was born. When I was in my dungeon, I bruised many a nose, it seems."

And a few hearts, Chance thought. "Why did you not tell me?" he asked coldly.

"Could you keep watch better than you already do?" Then, seeing the stony look on his warden's face, the lord reached out to him. "Old friend, if I had told you, perhaps you would have thought I spoke you fair only for this, that you should aid me. And it would not have been true." He sat back, his manner quite settled and calm, almost happy. "Truth is, I do not care what happens."

"You—what?"

"You think I left little Iantha with you out of the hardness of my heart? When Halimeda longs every day to hold her? Chance, I entrusted the babe to your care because she will be safest with you. Pay no heed to the scheming of renegades. Tend the child, and let them do to me what they will."

"You cannot be serious!"

Roddarc laughed. "Oh, I will put up a fight, never fear! But I want you far from it, Chance."

Chance murmured in wonder, "You really do not care."

"Why should I care, with Riol's ghost leering over my shoulder and the smell of blood everywhere? Let some other lout take this cruel seat and rule by the sword. Why should I be lord when my folk scorn and spurn me, rule I foul or rule I fair?"

Chance could only stare at him. Taking the stare for shock or protest, the lord stood and grasped him by the shoulders, very seriously meeting his eyes. "Chance, please hear me, please trust me. I have seen the way to my redemption."

"It is true, folk scorn Roddarc," Halimeda said, eyes lowered. "And that is my fault."

Chance stirred broth and snorted. "As it is the cricket's fault that frost comes?"

"Things just happen, you mean?"

"Yes," he said, "they do."

His glance strayed to the baby sitting on her lap. Halimeda came often to see little Iantha, talking to her and trying to teach her pattycake and singing to her in a pure, sweet voice. The little one did not respond, not any more than she responded to Chance. Unsmiling, she looked past her mother with vivid green eyes, gazing off into the distance at the tree-tops of Wirral, as if she heard somewhere a yet sweeter music.

"But it was when I went about huge with child, and unkempt," Halimeda insisted, "that folk began to mutter again."

Chance snorted. "Say it is my fault, then, if old Riol rules anew in his son."

The lady looked at him in perplexity. "What have you done but show me kindness and care for my babe?"

"I could scarcely have let her starve!" His voice roughened, for it troubled him to remember how the babe had been fed. "And what have you done," he challenged the lady, "but give love?"

The word resonated in her. She met his eyes; silent echoes flew about the room. Slowly she set Iantha down, turned to look at him across the width of the stone lodge.

"There is love," she said in a low voice, "and sometimes there is lasting love."

"Lady, you know you have it."

She gazed at him and nodded, but pain flickered in her eyes. "I have been thinking," she said very softly, "that manly prowess is not the most important thing about a man."

Powers, she could not mean it! He would not let hope rise. "Lady," he told her, dry-mouthed, "do not let my devotion make a vestal of you. Love where you will."

She looked at him with an odd, saddened smile. "If only I could," she said, and she came over to him and laid a hand on his massive chest. "But, Chance,

I think it will not be a matter of loving for me, after all. I deem my brother will not long be lord of Wirralmark. I have had a dream of a dragon, and Roddarc lying bloody under its claws."

And which is the greatest tyrant, the dragon or Riol's son or love itself, I scarcely know.

"A woman taken as booty of war . . . there will be few enough choices for me, Chance."

"Then stand farther from me, Lady," he said huskily, "for this closeness brings but pain to both of us."

She nodded, kissed her daughter and went away.

Thereafter, when she came to see Iantha, there would be a doomed dignity about her, an acceptance, that made her seem older than her less-than-twenty years. She had grown, Halimeda. There was something in her as sturdy as oak, as tough as a Denizen's skin. Not for her, any longer, a noose at Gallowstree Lea.

Often Chance would leave Iantha with her and spend hours in Wirral, searching for the haunts of the rebels, or so he let her think. He lacked courage to tell her otherwise. . . . Summer had reached its height. The days were long, and Chance often stayed until after dark in the forest while Halimeda tended the child.

Iantha was growing rapidly, more so than seemed natural. She had long since outgrown the applewood cradle, and slept by Chance's cot in a great wicker pannier. Already she walked, and no longer needed diapering. Though tiny, she possessed nothing of baby plumpness; she was small and graceful, with the proportions of a slender four-year-old. She did not talk or even babble, and she never smiled, not even when her mother braided her red-gold hair and whispered into the flower petal of her ear. Iantha

seldom cried, but she played listlessly with the toys
that were provided for her, and often for hours on
end she simply sat and rocked herself or stared.

Roddarc came to see her in the evenings sometimes.

"She is so very beautiful," he said to Chance with
a touch of awe. "So delicate. Almost as if—what
Halimeda said—have you ever seen such folk, Chance,
in the forest?"

"Many times," he answered promptly, facing his
lord across a cup of ale. What made him divulge such
truth after all the years, he could not have said,
except that Roddarc truly no longer cared. And in an
odd way Chance felt closer to his foster brother than
ever before. Before too long, he would be meeting
him as an equal, to do him the final favor.

For the time, he told him how he had first made
speaking acquaintance with the Denizens. "But there
is no dependable aid to be had from them. They are
full of caprice, as happenstance as a puff of wind."

"A lucky chance, eh? Well, so were you, my friend,
that ever you were born."

He said it so easily that Chance did not need to
growl. The two of them sipped their ale, and in her
basket the love-child slumbered.

"Have you yet arranged a marriage for Halimeda?"
Chance asked after a while, just as easily.

"Powers know I have tried. I have sent missives as
far as the Marches. But no noble scion has yet proved
willing to take her."

"The more fools, they," said Chance with feeling,
and Roddarc looked at him intently.

"You told me once, you would take her in a
moment. . . ."

"Rod, all powers know I have loved her these
many years."

52

There. At long last it was said. Pain flooded into Roddarc's gaze.

"By my mother's bones, how I wish I had never been born," he whispered. "Better that ill-fated spear had taken me instead of your manhood. It was meant for me." Roddarc sprang up, hands to his head. "Chance, every step I take, it seems I am a curse on you."

"Had you not heard?" Chance spoke lightly. "Old Riol cursed us both, on his deathbed."

The tyrant had died on a distant battlefield, and no one had heard his last words. But Roddarc stared intently at Chance, as if for a moment he believed him. "By blood, I would not put it beyond him," he muttered, sitting down again, limply, leaning against the table.

"Bah! If it had gone otherwise, Rod, I would have been wed to a wench. Long since."

"Think you so? Chance, all has come to naught now, but how it would have comforted me if . . ."

"If?"

"Folly." Roddarc roused himself with an effort. "I am an ass, as you have often said. Does Halimeda know of this?"

"Yes. She was so in despair, last autumn, that I told her. It cheered her."

"More than cheered her, I think." Roddarc looked at Chance steadily. "And a dolt I may be. But I like to think that somehow—had a spear struck differently, Chance, I would have found a way to give you your heart's desire."

Chance woke with a start in the mid of night to see little Iantha out of her basket and pattering toward the door.

"No!" In a few steps he had overtaken her and

gathered her up. The tiny child did not cry, for she rarely cried, but he felt the stiff protest of her body as he carried her back to her bed. He knew she would not go back to sleep at once.

For his own part, he pretended to.

There had been a dream of voices, he remembered, before he awoke. Voices like those once heard in an autumn storm.

This time there was no wailing of wind. Instead, the small urgings, when they came, chanted and whispered amidst the insect chatter of a late summer's night.

"Come away, little one,
Come away, Violet!
Dance in the ring
And all mortals forget."

Once again, dreamily, intent, the child got out of her bed and started toward the door, and once again Chance sprang up and grasped her.

"No!" he shouted at the night. "You shall not have her!"

All that night until sunrise he sat holding the child, with his arms locked tightly around her. When the day had begun and folk were about, he went to the village and spoke with an old woman. Then, carrying Iantha and a length of vivid red cotton, he went to the fortress keep.

"My lady," he hailed Halimeda, and she left her morning meal to greet him and the child.

"I need a drop of your blood," he told her in a low voice.

She looked somber, but asked no questions—the less such uncanny matters were spoken of, the better. She took the dagger he offered and stabbed her fingertip with it. Chance blotted up the blood with the wadded end of the blood-red cotton cloth.

54

"Some of yours," Halimeda told him, "on the other end. You are like a father to her." For she knew the blood was for Iantha.

Chance looked at the lady a moment, then did as she had said. When his blood had moistened the cloth, he folded it into a sash and tied it around Iantha's waist, knotting it firmly in the back.

"There," he muttered to the child, "you're blood bound to this mortal world." The child stared up at him, great-eyed and soundless.

"Leave her here with me for today," Halimeda said, and he did so, but went to get her again before nightfall.

He made Iantha wear the sash at all times, even in her bed. And when, a turning of the moon later, the voices sounded again in the night, he did not get up, but lay watching.

"Come away, little one,
Come away, Violet!"

Iantha also lay still for a while. Then she struggled up, but her baby steps were slow. Staggering, she made toward the door. But before she reached it she slowed to a stop and, standing as if abandoned in the middle of the floor, she began a terrible weeping.

Chance hurried to her and put his arms around her, picked her up and rocked her against his broad chest, whispered to her, calling her by all the names of love. But all his comforting failed to soothe her.

"Let her go, Chance!" commanded a stern voice close at hand. The Denizen came in through the eaves, stepped out on the chimney ledge to confront him. Their young prince, he of the massy cock and the wide, fey smile, but he was not smiling on that night.

"You shall not have her!" Chance shouted wildly at him.

"But she is already ours! One of us! Let her go! You are hurting her."

It was true; his heart smote him, knowing it was true. "And you," he railed, "gentle one, have never done hurt."

"Not to my own kind!"

"Go away!" Chance roared. But the Denizen came closer, his look grave.

"Chance, the child belongs to us. She has suckled on our sap. Many of us gave up their lives for her sake, drained dry. Noble was their willing sacrifice, for we need not die."

The words only made Chance clutch the child more fiercely. "And why do you want her?" he challenged.

"For the wellbeing of our race! We do not die, but—listen to me! We become rootbound, voiceless, with age. We become immobile, like trees. If we did not quicken our blood from time to time—"

"So you want her for breeding." Harsh anger in the words. The Denizen creased his brow at the sound of them.

"She will not be unwilling, believe me! Chance, if it will comfort you, I will give you a promise to cherish her as my own. She will be my bride."

Iantha stretched out her arms toward the woodland prince and gave a gulping wail. Chance swore, suddenly blind with anger.

"You cockproud buck!" He snatched up a butchering knife from the table and hurled it. Startled, the Denizen dodged, and the knife clattered against the stone.

"Out!" Chance raged. A cooler fury answered his own in eyes the color of woodland shade.

"Many have been the favors you have asked from us. You were told that you would pay someday."

"Take your payment some other way!"

"We have already taken it. Iantha will come to us. Her hands will grow clever enough to tear off that rag you have tied around her—"

"Out!" Chance roared, and he drew his dagger. But luminous eyes met his, and he found he could not lift it. After a long moment, the Denizen prince turned and at his leisure took his leave.

Iantha did not cease to weep until morning. Chance held her close to his heart, and his heart wept with her.

When summer was waning toward autumn, the leaves not yet yellowing but the nights growing chill, the rebels formed their line of siege around the fortress. Their numbers were large, for nearly every man of the demesne stood among them, as well as outlaw rebels venturing from their refuges in the penetralia of Wirral. And few were the servants or warriors who remained at Roddarc's side.

After dark of that night, a starlit night of the dark of the moon, Halimeda slipped out through the postern gate and walked toward the rebel lines. Once again she went robed in black, but this time she wore it proudly, and the long flow of her dark hair was starred like the night with small gems. A larger brooch of silver and ivory pinned her mantle, shining like the missing moon.

At the points of polite spears, the rebel sentries took her to be seen by their leader.

Halimeda was very calm. Her child was safe with Chance. She had come to offer herself to the rebel leader for wedding, so that he would not be obliged to kill her on the morrow, and she expected him, whoever he was, to accept her offer. She could only hope that the man would not be utterly a lout. . . . A bleak prospect for one who had dreamed of love, but Halimeda faced it with wintery calm.

Her calm deserted her when she and the sentries reached the campfire where men drew lines in the dirt. The leader of the renegades was a broad-shouldered, blunt-featured man in jackboots and leathers. The heavy hobnailed boots of a war leader, but instead of a sword he wore a bow, and he held a child by his side. Dagger in his hand, stabbing the earth; he laid it down when he saw her.

"You!" she exclaimed.

Chance came and put Iantha into her arms.

"Lady," he said, "take the little one to the lodge and wait there. When all is over, you will be ruler here, if you wish. You will wed me or not, as you wish. I hope you will not hate me." His voice faltered for an instant, then grew firm and hard, the lines of his mouth very straight. "As for the lord your brother, I have a lifelong score to settle with him. The whipping boy has spurned the rod."

"You—he—I do not understand," Halimeda stammered. "After all, you hate him?"

Chance shook his head. "I hated him for a while," he said, "when he had you so in despair, when I remembered my own despair. But it is you who should hate him now, my lady."

Her eyes widened hugely, shadowed in the firelight, as she stared at him. Chance's voice sharpened.

"Lady, your brother is no fitting lord. He craves to be killed. Do you think I should let the neighboring lord oblige him, then hunt you like a deer through Wirral? Or some lout hack him down, carry his head on a spear and take you to wife? You are the Lady of the Mark, Halimeda! If Roddarc is too cowardly to care for his own honor, he should yet care for what is rightfully yours."

Misfortune had made Halimeda tame, but his tone moved her. Listening to him, she felt her chin rise, her shoulders straighten.

Chance said, "For the sake of my own hatred it would have been sufficient to look him in the face and kill him. But for your sake, my lady . . . these many months I have planned and labored and brought folk together, since before the little one was born. The outlaws of Wirral, I knew the ways to their lairs, though it was a subtle matter to speak to them without being killed. But after we had struck bargain all was easier, for they have no desire to skulk in the woods, and there are those in the village who want their comrades and brothers back. I made promises, and received the one I wanted in return: that you should not be harmed."

"I would rather you fought my brother for your own sake," Halimeda said.

Chance's straight mouth quirked into a smile; there was yet some pride left in her! "Indeed, it is also for my own sake," he said. "When I have made an end of him, I will deem myself a man again."

"Have you ever been less?"

His face grew still and haunted. "Can you doubt it? I have always been lessened by Roddarc, and still am. Halimeda—have you not felt it, too? How he speaks you fair, and yet old Riol peeps around the corners of his deeds?"

"I have come to an enemy encampment in the night," she said, her voice hard, "offering my body to save my life. Yes, I feel it, how once more my brother has had no thought for me. This indifference is what he calls forgiveness."

"There is food in the lodge," Chance told her, for though Roddarc had taken no thought for her, Chance had. "Enough for you and the child for some days. Go there, bar the door and wait."

There were not enough men within the fortress, Chance deemed, to hold the shell, the circular outer wall of the stronghold. Though all the next day they did so, for Chance preferred to spare his followers and take Wirralmark by degrees. Not for him, the piling of bodies in the ditch outside the wall. He and his outlaw archers picked off defenders one by one until nightfall stopped them. During the night four more of Roddarc's followers deserted to join the ranks of the challengers, and at daybreak Chance found the shell deserted. Roddarc's force had fallen back to the keep, the square tower where the lord made his home, and they had knocked away the wooden steps that gave entry. The only door, heavily barred, stood well above the level of a man's head.

Chance and his rebels spent that day battering at the thick stone of the corner buttresses, hoping to knock a hole, stretching ox-hides over the laborers to fend off the many deadly things hurled from the parapets above. Chance took his turn with the maul and wedge, but for the most part he watched from the shelter of the dungeon tower, waiting. Once his men had succeeded in loosening a stone, it was only a matter of time. In any event, Roddarc's overthrow was only a matter of time.

They made their entry, and widened and defended it during the night, and on the third day they stormed the keep. Roddarc met them at the top of the first spiral of stone steps.

"Chance," he breathed. "They told me, but I did not believe them."

"Who else? Would you wish an enemy to have the slaying of you?"

"Mischance, I will have to call you now."

Roddarc raised his sword, and Chance struck with his cudgel, the commoner's weapon of choice. All around them men fought hand to hand, with staffs and daggers, the renegades forcing the defenders back, opening the high, barred entry so that those outside could put up the scaling ladders to it; more rebels poured in by the moment. And Chance had not yet succeeded in touching Roddarc, nor had the lord harmed Chance, but with swift strokes of his sword he killed rebel after rebel as he and his few remaining men gave way. He was splendid, magnificent, as magnificent as he had been at Gallowstree Lea. Flung back at every charge, Chance could not come near him. Only sheer press of numbers forced Roddarc back.

One more stone stairway led to the upper chambers, the lord's last refuge. Roddarc leaped to a vantage on the stairs, planted his feet in the fighter's stance and waited there with bloodied sword at the ready, and for a moment no rebel came near him.

"Why!" the lord panted at Chance. "That is all I want to know; just tell me why!"

Chance's anger rose up in him like the one-eyed monster in its fen at the center of the Wirral.

"Tyrant!" he roared. "You yourself are the rod that has always scarred me the worst, son of Riol! You with your sniveling and your so-called friendship—be an honest tyrant, would you, or no tyrant at all!"

Rage flushed Roddarc's face to the hairline, twisted his mouth, blazed in his eyes, and those who watched stepped back as if they had seen a revenant; for a moment it seemed as if Riol stood there.

"Where are your balls, whipping boy?" the lord taunted, and Chance lunged.

Up that spiral stairway they fought, and this time

Chance took cuts, and the lord took blows. Roddarc fought on alone; the last of his followers had been captured or slain. He slashed Chance on the head and nearly toppled him, but others stood ready to steady their leader, to drive back the lord; Chance and the others drove him back to the head of the stairs, then quickly halfway to the wall. But at the center of his lordly chamber Roddarc let his sword fall with a clash to the floor, kicked it toward Chance.

"I'll not be taken in a corner, like a brawler," he said, standing lance straight. "Take that and use it, whipping boy." The sword spun on the stone floor, then came to rest with a clatter against Chance's feet. Chance stood as still as Roddarc, and a ring of rebels formed, watching.

"Take it, bastard, and my dying curse on you! I'll not be slain with a commoner's weapon."

Chance picked up the sword, hefting it, accustoming his woodsman's hand to the feel of this unfamiliar weapon. "And what is the curse?" he asked mildly.

Roddarc smiled, a hard, dark smile. "Riol have you," he said.

Chance killed him with a single blow of the sword.

Chance came to Halimeda in twilight, with a bloody wrapping on his head. The lady came out of the lodge and stood beneath an oak tree to meet him, the child in her arms, a question in her gaze. He met her eyes and nodded.

"Roddarc is dead," he said, "and he died well. The women are preparing his body for a lord's burial."

"I thought it more likely, the men would have put his head on a pike," she said.

"That, too."

Laughter like the shouting of birds fluttered out of the foliage of the oak. A rustling like that of squirrels, and small woodland folk by the dozen stood on the spreading limbs, broad smiles stretching the tough skin of their faces. Halimeda gasped and clutched at her child, but Chance merely rubbed his nose in annoyance.

"What do you want?" he demanded of the Denizens.

Despite himself his glance shifted to the child. Having not seen her for a few days, he saw Iantha anew. The beauty of her—but how pale and thin she had become, the little girl so quiet in her mother's arms.

The Denizens trilled with laughter and did not answer his demand. Instead, they chanted at him. "Well, indeed, Chance! And you've become like us, as hard as trees, as fickle as mothflight; was it happenstance? Or mischance, Chance?"

"What do you *want*?" he asked them fiercely.

"Why, to honor you, Chance." It was the russet-brown prince who spoke. "The lady and thee. Come to the dance. A revel for your bridal."

He gave a single snort of laughter. "A quaint revel you'll have from me!"

The prince of the Denizens beckoned. "Come."

There had been no time to talk with Halimeda concerning bridals. Nor was there now much choice. "It is best to do as they say," Chance told her in a low voice, and she nodded, only her widened eyes showing her fear. He took the child from her, shielding the small head against his shoulder.

Leaping and scampering atop the branches, the Denizens led them through the darkening forest. A new moon, rising, gave not quite enough light. Chance and the lady stumbled over logs, felt their way through thickets, fending off twigs that seemed to search for their eyes. Iantha slept in Chance's arms. By the time they reached the meadow and the mushroom ring, Chance and Halimeda felt weary enough to sleep as well. They sank to seats on the tussocky grass. Chance laid Iantha down, wrapped his mantle around her.

All that happened that night seemed like a dream. The music, humming and buzzing and piping amidst insect music and birdsong in the moonlit darkness. And the whirling and circling of hundreds of tiny dancers within the luminous ring, the mushrooms that glowed like small yellow moons amidst the grass. And wine served in acorn cups. And a heat in the blood. . . . Chance dreamed that he took Halimeda by the hand, led her within the moonglow circle, danced with her there, and she came with him willingly, and he danced with a nobleman's skill. Later, he dreamed that he was lying with her there, her warm, womanly body close to his. And the passion, the sensations he had thought long gone, long dead and turned to dirt and worm on a distant battlefield, his once more. Dreaming . . . but such a blessed, vivid dream. Hands moving, and Halimeda's mouth meeting his, and soft importunity of her breasts, and the welcoming, sweet, warm haven under her skirt. He entered it. Reverent, nearly weeping with joy, home coming, he entered it.

With sunrise he awoke, blinked, gazed. Her face lay close to his, her hair in disarray, and her tender smile matched his own. His mantle covered both of them. Around them grew a ring of yellow mushrooms.

"Chance," she whispered, "darling Chance, you rascal, will you never stop surprising me? There's nothing amiss with your manhood."

"But—Hali, I've not deceived you—" Hope growing in him like passion itself, but still he hardly dared to believe. . . .

"I know." She kissed him. "I felt it happen. The healing. Wirral magic."

Healed. He was whole, entire, a man again, as he had not been for many years. He hugged her wildly, shouted aloud in joy. From somewhere close at hand, someone laughed.

Chance started to jump up, but something jerked him back. Looped from his wrist to Halimeda's, and knotted around each, lay a bright red sash. He untied it and fastened his clothing in haste, all the while glaring around him, but even as he did so he knew that it had been no human laugh, no human trick played on him, no human joke. He had nothing worse than Denizens to face.

Denizens . . .

"Iantha's gone!" Halimeda exclaimed.

Chance got up, numbly winding the blood-red sash around his hand. Halimeda scrambled up as well.

"Come, hurry," she pleaded, "we must find her!"

"No," Chance murmured, "perhaps it is for the best." As she turned on him to protest, he pointed. "Look."

A birdlike laugh sounded. At the outer edge of the mushroom ring a delicate beauty faced them, a fawn-gold maiden less than a foot tall. Shining red-gold hair curled down below her waist, and her large eyes sparkled vivid green, full of leafshifting woodland light. She was smiling, the sunniest of wayward smiles. Before they could do more than gape, she waved at them merrily and scampered away.

"She's gone," Halimeda whispered, "to—"

Gently Chance hushed her. "Say no more."

"She—she looks happy."

"Is a butterfly happy, on the wing?"

They gathered up their things and walked away.

Halimeda wept softly until they came to the lodge. There she washed her face, brushed dirt from her clothing.

"We must go to the fortress to live," she said.

"Yes."

"We will—have our own child, Chance."

"I hope, more than one." He kissed her.

"Our children will—rule after us."

"We will have to be canny," Chance said, "to rule so long. We will have to be hard as the trees, merciless as winter."

Though few are the trees I will leave standing. I will make prisoners of those who disobey me, have them hew at the Wirral until it is leveled. There will be no refuge for outlaws or rebels near my realm. Or Denizens.

"A pair of tyrants, we will be, you mean," Halimeda said.

"Yes. Old Riol did not toughen my hide for naught."

He looked at her with a fey, changeling's smile tugging at the corners of his straight mouth, and in a moment she lifted her chin and gave him back the same wry, elfin grin. Her eyes lit with caprice, the willfulness that would save her heart from breaking, ever again. For she also had suffered.

From some hidden place in the eaves came a warbling laugh.

"Rule by the sword, Chance my lord," the unseen Denizen sang.

THE GOLDEN FACE
OF FATE

Having been conceived amid the mystic revels, within the dark mushroom ring in the midst of the wilderness called Wirral, in the center of the circling dance of those who are never called by name, and having been conceived by an act of most obscure magic, she did not make such a daughter as was customary for a lord. Even such a lord as Chauncey of Wirralmark.

Xanthea, her lady mother named her, meaning "golden," a gift, a treasure, but she was not. She grew to be dark of hair and eyes, and tall, far too tall even for a lord's daughter, gangling and grotesque. Her face grew narrow, almost hatchet-shaped, and large-featured. From the time she was old enough to care, she knew herself to be ugly. Her father Lord Chauncey and her lady mother Halimeda knew something more of her, of which they did not speak. She reminded them of something, or some beings, and they hated to look at her.

Humbly, during her growing years, she tried to

please them. But always they turned away their eyes from her face.

They were not cruel to her, though she knew, chillingly, that they could be cruel. Lord Chauncey in particular could be cruel and deadly to anyone who failed to render him proper obeisance, anyone who remembered a former name, that of a bastard commoner.

He made a proper lord, Chauncey. Half mad, as befitted a lord of Wirralmark. Arrogant, pompous, glorying in wealthy display, grinding down his people with his demands. His folk whimpered under his rule, and looked on him with wide eyes when he rode forth, and he ruled long.

They told tales of him on winter evenings. Some were the forbidden tales, whispered, of how he had been the old Lord's whipping boy and Wirral warden. Others were the plain tales, of how he hated the wilderness of Wirral. Even before Xanthea's birth he had set his serfs to cutting that forest back, back from the fortress, with great labor grubbing out the stumps and setting the wood in vast piles to rot, far more wood than could be used for fuel or building. For sixteen years Wirral had been pressed back, back, until it could not be seen even from the tallest tower of the Wirralmark fortress, and still Chance and his servants worried at it. He hated it. He wanted to destroy it utterly. Sometimes he himself rode out and took sword to it, as if in battle.

But Wirral was vast as the sea. It ebbed away before him, biding its time.

By the time she was grown, then, Xanthea had never seen Wirral, not even from afar. Her noble parents would not allow her outside the fortress walls, though her sisters suffered no such restraint. Because she was the eldest, they told her, a saying which made no sense, for her brother would be the heir. Perhaps, she sometimes thought with a pang, perhaps they cared for her in their aloof way. Or perhaps they were merely zealous to keep her pure for a noble wedding someday. But then, why might her sisters ride forth? Perhaps they were hiding her ugly face from the sight of folk who might scoff.

Sometimes, not knowing why, she dreamed of Wirral in vague, babyish ways: trees that danced and waved twiggy hands. She thought little of the dreams and did not mention them to her mother. Dreams were unaccountable and not worth her mother's concern. In no way could Xanthea know how Wirral whispered in her blood, how Wirral reached out to embrace her, reaching into her dreams, and how, on a certain evening of her sixteenth year, Wirral would lay upon her the hand of love.

It was the first year that she was old enough to take part in the festivities of Misrule.

Longtime custom made a stronger lord even than Chauncey. He disliked Misrule—though he had liked it well enough when he was plain Chance, and a commoner—but he did not dare to proscribe it. Tradition had it that, on the night of the early-winter equinox, servants would rule and mingle with the nobles as equals. Custom, which is often wise, also decreed that the mingling should take the form of a masque. Much of what transpired on the eve of Misrule needed to be hidden behind masks.

It could still be told which masquers were the nobles, of course. They were the ones who went gloriously arrayed. Months of tiring-woman's labor went into the making of their costumes and masks.

Xanthea had taken small interest in the preparations. She had dressed for occasions before, and no amount of finery could make her look pretty or even passable. Her mother's averted eyes told her as much. Moreover, her father had often made it plain that he regarded his part in Misrule merely as an irksome obligation. Trying, as always, to please him, Xanthea took care to think likewise.

Until the moment when she put on the mask.

It covered her entirely, even her hair. Golden, or gilt, its handsome face hid her own. Long lashes made of bronze pheasant feathers framed the eyes, and at the golden temples rose real falcon wings colored like new bronze, upswept as if for flight, and at the brow curved a carved wooden crest, like the crest of a helm, but fanciful. And from it a featherfall of rare peacock plumes, bronze and green and brilliant blue, trailed down Xanthea's back and shoulders. Emeralds jeweled her bosom, her wrists, her stomacher. Her gown of peacock blue, overgowned in bronze, flowed to the floor, and she stood tall inside it, and the golden face and feather headdress rode high, and she was not her ugly self any more; she was something else. Something strong and free and wild. Something chanting and barbaric, like a blue-painted warrior.

Striding into the great hall, she saw her plain, blunt-featured sisters, Anastasia and Chloe, younger than she but better loved, their faces so much like her father's, peeping at the masquers from behind tapestries. She watched their eyes widen when they saw her. She watched her small brother, Justin, his face too much like his mother's, too delicate and beautiful for a little boy, the future lord, watched his soft lower lip tremble. She loomed tall over him, and he backed away from her in fear and ran to meet the nurse who was coming to find him and take him away to his bedchamber. The woman would leave

him there unattended and join the masque herself.
Justin would lie frightened and alone in his bed.
Xanthea laughed aloud.

Beneath the golden mask and gold-girt dress her
blood ran hot. Masquers swirled all around her, many
of their mask-faces as grotesque as Xanthea knew her
face of flesh to be. Some, billed like birds, some
snouted like animals. Some, warted and bristled like
wild hogs. Xanthea saw butterfly masks with eyes
peering through the markings of their wings. There
were red-lipped harlequin-painted masks of wood
and elegant half-masks of fine fabric, beaded and
gemmed, held in place by slender wands lifted in
gloved hands. Many of them Xanthea knew from
years past, when she had peeped from behind the
hangings, like her sisters. Some of the masks were
generations old, for the commoners, unlike the nobility, cherished the weird or beautiful things and
hung them on their cottage walls as ornaments and
prized possessions.

The great doors opened, letting in a long reaching
arm of winter air, and Xanthea turned her head to
see who it was who came late to the masque.

She stared, and many others stared with her.

The man wore a mask she had never seen before,
a strange and striking mask in the shape of a wolf's
head, strongly carved and wildly furred, a beautiful
and feral thing. The body of the man who wore it
seemed as strong and beautiful and feral as the mask,
moving with a wild grace, and folk whispered each to
each, for no one could guess who it was. He wore a
tunic the deep blue color of the windflowers that
grow in woodland, and hose of woodland brown.

Music was starting. Someone took Xanthea's hand,
and she danced.

At the far end of the room she saw her father,

resplendent in cloth-of-gold under a smiling mask. She paid him no heed. She did not see her mother, nor did she look for Halimeda. She danced. Relieved from the awkwardness of being the lord's ugly daughter, her body danced with zest and grace. It did not matter to her that she stood taller than her partners. All was part of the masque. She was an Amazon. She wished her headdress stood a foot taller, bristling high like a crested bird-of-paradise. She wished she carried a golden bow and a quiver of silver arrows. Her eyes followed the wolf-masquer as he wound his way through the circling pattern of the carole. Something about him seemed to call to her. She felt her heart pounding. She loosened the lacings of her gown so that the white swell of her breasts showed beneath the emerald pendant.

Dances passed. Folk made shift to drink without showing their faces. Eyes gleamed whitely out of masks as if no more real than the masks themselves, as if made of clamshell. Some of the evening's customary ugliness began. Men ordered Lady Halimeda to bring them drinks and beat Lord Chauncey with bladders, trying to humiliate him. They knew better than to venture too far into vengefulness, however good their disguises. But the unknown man in the wolf mask went up to him and cuffed him on the side of the head as if cuffing a bastard.

Then the same bold rogue came to Xanthea and clasped both her hands in his, like a lover, drawing her close to him to dance.

Folk stared, for they knew the man would die within a few days, when the festival of Misrule was over and as soon as Lord Chauncey found out who he might be. And someone was sure to betray him, or many would die instead of just the one.

But Xanthea took no thought for her father, because the stranger was speaking to her. She could not tell whether under his mask his mouth moved. The words seemed to sound close to her head, as if he held his lips against her ear, though he did not. And his voice was low, with a faint burr in it, as if it might mask a wolf's growl.

"Greetings, Lady Xanthea," he said. "I am Wirral."

Beneath her golden mask she felt full of bold excitement, and she answered saucily, laughing. "But how can you be Wirral? Are you made of wood? Wirral is a mighty forest."

"The mightiest of forests, Lady," he told her. "You speak rightly. And I am Wirral."

Her sauciness left her, and though she did not feel afraid she did not know how to answer him. And she noticed for the first time that he stood taller even than she.

Speaking to her silence, he said, "You do not believe me? But all that I say is true. I will never tell you anything but truth." His voice seemed to come yet closer to her, though he himself had not moved closer, holding her at half the length of his arms and swinging her through the dance. "I will show you the ways of Wirral, so that you may know I speak truth. I will show you things you have never seen, and I will sing to you the songs you have never heard."

And he sang to her in his low, husky voice, and the words sounded right inside her mind.

"Come to the mushroom ring,
Xanthea, our oddling;
Come to the revel ring,
Xanthea, our own!
Wirral will take back its own, we sing.
Wirral will take back its own!"

And his voice was no longer the low voice of the stranger, but it was the birdlike voices of many, of the unseen many who are never called by name, but spoken of only as the Denizens. From the trees all around her they sang. For she was seeing Wirral, seeing it inside her mind, more plainly than her dreams could ever show it to her; she might as well have been standing in the midst of that vast wilderness. The glades where felons roamed. The briars, the bracken, the huge, old, watching oaks. The fens, with corpse-white stubs looming. The rank wild-meadow grass, and the ring of luminous mushrooms.

She stood dancing in that ring with—what, or who? But in that instant the vision faded. Back in her father's crowded great hall, dancing to the music of lutes and viols, with the wolf-masquer holding her closer than Lord Chauncey liked, she blinked, her lips parted beneath the golden mask.

"Go there with me," the one who held her said.

Something mad and shadowed moved in Xanthea. No longer was she a blue-painted warrior or an Amazon. She was something yet stronger and wilder, more animal, more drawn by the calls that can scarcely be voiced in words. Images of Wirral danced within her eyes; the twisted, ivy-strangled trees . . . she was something reckless, daring, not afraid of them, of anything. Yet she did not speak.

"Go there with me," said the stranger with the faint roughness in his voice, "for it is small love your lordly father will bear either of us in the morning."

It was true. Yet, Xanthea knew that Lord Chauncey would not kill her. And she knew no such thing of this other, of Wirral. Still, she did not feel afraid.

"Come," the other said, and he tugged gently at her hands.

Then Xanthea spoke, shyly, yet the words were bold and blunt. "What are you like, under the mask?" she asked. "Are you as ugly as I?"

Silence, for the span of several heartbeats. The stranger, whoever he was, stood still with her hands in his. Like him, she stopped dancing, and she did not hear the music still playing, did not see the masquers swirling around her.

"I am as ugly as you," the stranger said at last, the words catching on the burr in his voice.

She went with him, golden-masked and regally gowned as she was, out the door into the chill of a December night, and her mother cried out, and her father shouted a command she did not heed. The men-at-arms were drunk, or perhaps acted more drunk than they were, for this was the evening they need not obey their lord. Chauncey could not rouse them. Moments went by while he roared at them. Then he ran out after his daughter himself, readied a horse and rode after her himself. But though he rode long, he could not find a sign of her.

When morning came and Xanthea had not returned, Lord Chauncey mustered his groggy retinue and searched the countryside for miles around. And he sent his men-at-arms into the Wirral, though he himself did not go there. But nowhere could the lord or any of his servants find Xanthea, or even so much as a footprint in the snow. It was as if she had been carried off on a horse of air.

No sooner had Lord Chauncey settled down with his golden cup than Halimeda swept in to confront him. "You have not brought back our daughter," she stated, in the tone of one who had expected otherwise.

With a sour eye, too sober to suit him, Lord Chauncey looked up at his wife. He remembered a time when Halimeda had not been so strong, so apt at taking command. A time when she had needed him. A time when he would have run through storm or fire for her sake. He took a long pull at the hot mulled wine, a huntsman's due, in the cup.

"There is no sign of the girl," he said to Halimeda.

"You have been in Wirral?"

"I sent men. They found nothing."

"But you yourself did not go there."

"The wench is gone," Lord Chauncey grumbled by way of answer. "And good riddance, I say." He drank.

"For the sake of your lordly vengeance," his wife told him acidly, "I thought you would be eager at least to find the one who cuffed you on the head."

Lord Chauncey colored with displeasure at the reminder, but answered her evenly. "Of what use is it to search for one who leaves no footprints?"

"Do you not feel peril in the air? Do you not wish to know your enemy?"

Chance eyed her dourly, then turned back to his cup, saying nothing. There was too much that he was not saying. Halimeda had courage. She would speak to some of it.

"You think she has gone back to—them."

The lord looked up sharply. "Hush!" It was the worst of bad luck to mention the nameless ones, even so obliquely. But Halimeda was not so easily to be silenced.

"And you have given her up so easily? You are afraid."

"As would you be, had you the brains of a bat," Lord Chauncey shouted. "Which you resemble in other ways. Hush! Speak no more of it."

"I will speak what needs to be said!"

Halimeda remembered a time when this surly man had been her strong support and savior. She remembered a night when lifelong love had pleaded in his eyes, when he had laid his head in her lap and sobbed. Even then he had been willing to put her wellbeing before his own. It was he, Chance, who had spoken truth to her, helping her see clearly, freeing them both from the twisted trammels that bound them to her brother. The memories turned in her like a knife in a wound. Now he sat lumpen before her, a foppish lord drinking from a golden cup.

"You will ride out again in the morning," Halimeda said. Her tone, half command, half plea. "You yourself will enter Wirral." *You will be a man again.*

Her husband scarcely looked at her. "The girl is gone," said Lord Chauncey, lifting his cup to his lips. "I will waste no more days in searching for her."

Hot contempt rose in Halimeda, burned in her voice when she spoke. "You are no proper lord. You were more of a man when you were a castrate."

Even as she said the word Chance sprang to his feet with a roar that sent servants scuttling and cringing as far away as the kitchen, for it was not a word that he permitted to be spoken. Castrate! It was his most hurtful secret. Beside himself, he swung a fist at Halimeda. She held her head proud and still, and his heavy hand stopped a hairsbreadth from her temple.

"Be silent!" he thundered at her.

Halimeda looked steadily at him, into his eyes, facing and studying the thing that hurt her most. "Never fear," she told him bitterly. "I will not speak to you until you are Chance again, and my husband."

She was not permitted to say that name, not even in the privacy of their wedbed, in lovemaking. She might as well have called him bastard. Lord Chauncey wanted to kill her. His strong fingers twitched as if to throttle her where she stood. Kings had killed royal wives for less. But oddly, he did not speak or move.

"Until you are Chance and a man again," Halimeda said to him, and she turned her back and left him with his golden cup.

The next morning, Lady Halimeda put on her riding habit of ivy green furred with ermine, herself mounted horse and rode through the white winter day, seeking her daughter. And she rode out in like wise the next day, and the next, and many days to follow, uselessly searching as far as the fringes of Wirral, though she would not go within that vast wilderness. She did not find her daughter. Xanthea was gone.

The lady rode a gray gelding. Being of independent mind, she rode alone.

One day in deep winter she rode the long journey to Wirral, heedless of the cold and snow that lay deep on the cornfields. The lodge where Chance had courted her stood surrounded by cornfield. Gallowstree Lea was gone, turned to cornfield like the woodland that had surrounded it; Chance had seen to that. But Wirral yet lived, somewhere far ahead.

At the reaches of Wirralmark the forest stood waiting, the butts felled by autumn woodcutters lying silently beneath a shroud of snow, and the many, the countless many yet standing waiting as silently for something beyond the reach of men's dreaming and striving. On the gray gelding Halimeda picked her way through the felled boles and into the realm of the living ones. Oak, beech, chestnut loomed huge to either side of her and for miles ahead. Her horse pushed its way through snow chest-deep.

Only a little way. Halimeda glanced over her shoulder. She would not go out of sight of the light of the cleared fields. Should she venture too far into this forest, darkness would take her.

She looked for a likely tree, a huge old oak or elm, perhaps, full of hollows and squirrel holes. Something unspoken lay heavy between her and Chance—she still thought of him as Chance. Nor was it silence alone that dismayed her, for he had never been one to speak to her overmuch, even when he was a commoner and her secret lover. But she could sense the unspoken trouble as she sensed foreboding troubling her sleep, and she had come to beard it if she could.

She stopped her gray at a lightning-riven oak. One of many in Wirral, but the Denizens were many, also. Likely there would be some holed in the oak. Likely they were watching all around her, and had been peering and smirking since she had approached the forest.

Halimeda spoke. For the first time she willingly bespoke those who were never called by name. "Little ones there in the tree," she addressed them, "come out, please, and speak with me."

Then she waited. No Denizen gave her answer. No large-featured faces appeared, no narrow bodies with twiggy limbs and barklike skin. But within the treetrunk she could hear the trilling and warbling of their laughter.

"Little ones there in the tree," she said again, humbly, "pray come out and speak with me."

Not in that tree, but in a beech nearby, in a comfortable hollow, the prince of the small forest people lay dallying with his longtime love. She would not live immortally as he did, but while she lived her sap would run quick and merry. She was one of the human-born ones, a dainty, chestnut-haired beauty, and her name, though she no longer remembered it, had been Iantha. She smiled in amusement, hearing not far away the humble beseeching of her mother's voice, and she broke away from her lover's arms to peep.

"These foolish humans," she grumbled, bright-eyed. But then her look turned wistful as she gazed upon the beautiful mortal woman in her garb of ivy green.

"Very foolish," the prince of the Denizens lazily agreed with his lover. "But the fortress lady is not as foolish as her mate."

With butterfly quickness Iantha's mood turned from wistfulness to glee. She smiled, foretasting the joke. "How so?" she asked.

"Chance has let us gift him with his own doom."

"Please!" Halimeda's tone turned sharp, and she abandoned rhyme. "I want to ask you about my daughter!"

Laughter chirped yet louder. "Which one?" a voice cried from the oak.

Halimeda paled as white as the ermine that trimmed her sleeves, as white as the snow. Anastasia and Chloe were safe at the fortress, she told herself fiercely. The mocking questioner could not threaten them. The voice meant—no. She would not think of—that other. They could not make her think of— that other.

She paled, but she did not crumple. A Denizen had spoken to her. It was a start.

"Chance thinks he can keep us away," the prince remarked to his mate. "Cutting the trees. The more fool, he."

The voices in the oak had started a chant.

"Which one, which one, which one, we say?
Wirral will take back its own one day,
Wirral will take back its own!"

"And Wirral is worse than we," the prince added darkly.

"Tell me where Xanthea is," Halimeda begged the

forest. Though she deemed she knew. For the trouble between her and Chance was this: that both of them knew well enough where Xanthea was to be found. Xanthea, or her body. At the heart of Wirral. But neither of them would say it, or venture there.

The prince of the denizens squirrel-leaped past his mate and out of his hollow to stand on the winter-stripped branch of the beech.

"Where is Xanthea?" he mocked. "Where can she be?"

Halimeda's gray-green eyes turned to him. He vaunted and strutted on the bough where he stood, and he sang.

"With bone of deer and outlaw's skull
And fur of wolf and fox she lies,
With limb of oak and linden leaf
And all that in Wirral dies!
But Wirral lives."

Halimeda heard the taunting menace in his voice. She felt her throat fill with terror, and she turned her horse toward the fortress and fled, floundering, through the snow. Chanting voices followed her.

"Which daughter, which one, which one?
Wirral will take back its own, and soon!
Wirral will take back its own."

Xanthea stretched her long limbs and sighed with pleasure. The canopied bed, piled with silks and furs, was soft, and sizeable enough so that her tall body need never be cramped, even with that other tall body lying beside it. From one bedpost, hers, hung a golden mask with peacock feathers streaming down. From the other one hung the furred wolf mask.

Smiling at the masks, Xanthea remembered. . . .

Fleeing her father's great hall with the stranger.

The night had not felt cold, for her blood ran so hot and strong that it seemed to her she could warm the whole wintertime world. A horse waited close at hand, saddled, with a pillion. Wirral had known when he came what he wanted, the rascal. He picked her up by the waist—and there were few men who could have done that—picked her up lightly, for he was very strong, and set her sideward on her cushion on the horse's rump. The steed was moon-white, and comely, and splendidly caparisoned, and mannerly beyond belief: it bowed for Wirral's mounting so that he need not pass his foot near the lady. Then, when its riders were settled, it sprang away into the air.

With the strange excitement pounding in her blood, Xanthea was not frightened. With her arms around Wirral's waist and the golden mask keeping the cold rush of air from her face, with peacock plumes trailing behind her and her peacock-blue gown flowing down around her feet, she rode. She looked down often to see how strange her father's land lay far below, moonlit and starlit and rushing away beneath the horse's hooves. The steed flew and bore her, but she felt as if she herself were flying, she, Xanthea the warrior, the falcon wings straining on her helm, flying away from the place where she had been kept prisoner, where someday she would return. . . . The horse had no wings. Yet it flew, so smoothly that it seemed at one with the still air, the night, the moon.

Then the world of white came to an edge; Wirral forest lay below, and stretched dark as far as Xanthea could see. The horse flew on until the snow-covered fields lay far behind; all was darkness below, dark branches so massed, so striving that only jumbled bits of white showed between them like drunken stars fallen into a pit.

"The size of it!" Xanthea whispered. She spoke

only for herself; she had not thought the other could hear her.

"Wirral is vast," he replied, his voice hushed.

It seemed immense as the sea to Xanthea, and though the horse flew swiftly she could see no end of it. But after the passing of a time, without warning the horse swooped down toward the trees, and Xanthea almost screamed, clutching at the stranger in front of her. The next moment, branches rattled against her mask. Then with dizzying suddenness she was under the canopy of boughs instead of above it, and the horse came to a stop, standing on the snowy ground. The wolf-masked stranger swung his booted foot over the white steed's neck and slipped lithely to the ground. Then he reached up for Xanthea's waist and as lightly lifted her down.

Dawn was coming on. Pale light drifted down like fine snow from around the stars. Lady Xanthea and her escort stood side by side in the midst of wilderness. The horse walked away.

"Tell me what you see," the stranger said.

She stood staring about her at ferns and deadwood and towering trees, for she had never seen true forest before, or even woodlot, but only the tame walled garden of her father's fortress.

"I see . . ." She blinked, for she had seen the white horse turn to a white squirrel and leap up the trunk of a massive oak.

"Take off your mask," said the stranger, "and feel the air, and breathe deep of it, and see."

Dawn's light had turned from white to golden. Xanthea regarded her companion steadily. "You take off yours also," she said.

He did so, and he was the most beautiful man she had ever seen or envisioned in dream.

His eyes were wild, and burning with a soft fire,

and fixed on her. His hair was the color of a red fox in summer. His brows were like the wings of an eagle; his face, a warrior angel's. When he moved, he was the deer for grace and the oak for strength, and when he stood still, as he was, looking at her. . . . She saw nothing but that face, those eyes. Ardent eyes, brown as a deer's, and as soft, yet fierce as the yellow eyes of a wolf.

His wild beauty frightened her as nothing else could have; it made her feel small inside, and cold, with all the heat in her blood chilled. She took a step back. "You said you were ugly," she whispered.

"As ugly as you," the man agreed. With both hands he reached out and lifted the golden mask by gentle fingertips. Peacock plumes rustled soft as the whisper of death, coming away, and Xanthea stood bared, shrinking, like a pale mollusk bereft of its shell, biting her lip and not meeting his eyes. The chill sting of the winter air on her face made her shiver. She clenched her cold, blue-fingered hands.

"Look at me," said the stranger with no hesitation, no revulsion in his voice. "See."

Xanthea shook her head. "I have seen," she mumbled, and she averted her face.

"See," Wirral urged. "Look in my eyes. See yourself."

The low tremor in his voice—threat, or ardor? Xanthea could scarcely believe, ardor. Still, something in his voice made her remember courage. Made her take a deep breath of the heady forest air, made her straighten her slumping shoulders and turn her head toward him. She looked straight into his soft, vehement eyes.

And in them she saw herself as Wirral did.

She saw herself in small there at first, and stared, and then saw nothing but the stranger's feral eyes and herself, in them. With a rush like heat in the blood the image filled her sight. A tall maiden with a proud bearing and long, dark hair—she had never noticed the honey-colored lights in her hair—and wearing the hair like a crested helm: a striking, strong-boned face, unlike the face of any lesser maiden, a face with flashing eyes and a wide, feeling mouth. A questing face, tender yet hawk-keen. A strange face, better than a jeweled mask for gazing on. And the hot-blooded daring that had been Xanthea's at the masque was hers once again; Wirral had given it back to her, and she no longer felt the cold.

"You see?" Wirral gazed gravely at her and took her hand in one of his, carrying her golden mask in the other. "Come."

By the hand, held in courtly wise, he led her to the massive oak. A fissure showed in the trunk, puffy-lipped, large enough for a man to squeeze through, no more. He stood aside and let her step in ahead of him, into darkness, or so it seemed. Then he followed, and found Xanthea where she stood blinking.

Outside, their tree-shelter was a wild, warty, gouty old oak with sprouts bristling from its gnarls. Inside, it was a palace.

Halimeda was not one to weep easily. The misfortunes of her youth had hardened her. Seventeen years of holding power with Chance, and sometimes against him; several lyings in childbed, one infant boy born dead, three babies miscarried; it had all hardened her. Therefore she did not weep for Xanthea. She would not weep until the girl's body lay in front of her, ready for burial. One long-ago night at Gallowstree Lea she had been in such callow, whimpering despair she wanted to kill herself, but she had seldom wept since.

Therefore, she did not weep as she rode home from Wirral, where the Denizens had mocked her.

Moreover, she had not loved Xanthea overmuch. There had been something uncanny about Xanthea. . . . Halimeda searched for Xanthea, not so much because she wanted this particular daughter back as because she sensed power, being one who knows the ways of power; she sensed menace. And she loved the daughters remaining to her more. And she scorned her husband Chauncey, who would sit at his cups and see to his lordly clothing and do nothing, for fear of facing the thing that was happening.

Halimeda returned to Wirralmark at nightfall and gave commands. Then she called her daughters before her.

"Anastasia, Chloe. Until I tell you otherwise you are not to venture even so far as the village. You are to stay within the fortress walls."

Their plain, blunt faces congealed, like hardening dough, to show their displeasure, for Anastasia and Chloe had been petted since birth and did not lack for boldness. "Mother," Chloe objected, "it is not fair."

"You ride out every day," said Anastasia.

"No longer will I do so," Halimeda told them.

But that night she dreamed a strange, dark dream of trees. Oak and ash and elm and linden, birch and beech and fir, all mingled like a masqueing crowd, all danced, tossing their leafy heads, and she stood tiny in their midst, trying to evade the huge tramplings of their roots, and then she knew with terror that they were not unaware of her. For their branches swung out and seized at her, their boughs became hard, twiggy hands that clutched at her, and they were so strong, she could not escape them, she was flung like a toy from one to another, and somewhere near at hand she heard the growl of a wolf. . . .

She awoke in her cold bed—for Chance slept elsewhere except when he came to her to service her, as happened seldom enough, any longer—Halimeda awoke shaking and lay awake until morning.

Then she had her daughters summoned to her again. "You are not to venture out of the keep," she told them. "You are not to venture even into the fortress gardens, or any place where there are trees."

Anastasia and Chloe were aghast. "Mother!" they protested.

"Go to the rooftop," Halimeda snapped, "if you need air." Then she did what she had told them she would not. She called for the saddling of her gray, and she rode out again.

At dusk she returned, her face pinched and shadowed. That night no trees groped and clutched in her dreams. But in the darkness of sleep she sensed a nightmare far worse to her, an ineffable, flowerlight touch, a presence like a song long pressed out of mind springing up once again from the dark soil of dream: the gossamer fragrance of violets.

Halimeda awoke nearly screaming, for there were things she had taken care not to allow in her mind for sixteen years, and this soft touch held for her far more terror than the hard hands of Wirral trees. She did not sleep again, and rode out at the first light of dawn, and was gone until dark. The next day she rode out again, and the next day, and every day, that long winter. Nothing came of it except that her face grew ever more thin, and taut, and pale, until even her daughters, petulant though they remained at being confined indoors, felt concern for her.

"Mother," Anastasia urged, "stay home one day,

warm yourself by the fire, rest. You look like a wraith."

Halimeda stared straight at the girl with a gaze that seemed to look through her, as if sturdy Anastasia were herself a wraith.

Chloe added her plea. "Stay home tomorrow," she begged.

Halimeda spoke, and her voice sounded hollow as the voice of winter wind. "Iantha is gone," she said.

The two girls stared at her in perplexity. It was a name they had never heard. "You mean Xanthea," said Anastasia gently.

"Iantha is gone," repeated Halimeda woodenly, and she rose from her place by the fire and went to her chamber, where she would sleep a few hours until some dream awoke her. She rode out again on the morrow.

Lord Chauncey sat with his feet sprawling and his golden cup in hand, regarding the delicate-faced boy who stood cowering before him.

Lord Chauncey was a man of two passions, a man whose thoughts ran two deep courses, like the deeply worn ruts of a well-traveled road. One was that he should not be scorned. He dressed splendidly, lived lavishly, strove in all things to make folk forget that he had been born a commoner and a bastard; and therefore, he never could forget it himself. The more he turned his back on his past, the more it sniggered and giggled behind him, like Denizens taunting him from their hidden places in the forest trees.

The other was that he hated and feared Wirral. That forest knew his secrets. Wirral knew, and the small folk who lived in Wirral knew, and the outlaws denning in its penetralia, the nodding monster in its fens, they all knew the most hidden thing about

Chance. Likely the Denizens were still singing it in rhyme from the treetops. Chance the castrate, scarcely man, Chance the castrate, ran and ran through Wirralwood in search of balls, and found them there, and found them good. . . .

The Denizens had gifted him with manhead, and he hated them for it.

Halimeda knew Lord Chauncey's secret. And since the matter of Xanthea, Halimeda scorned him; he felt it. Sometimes even before the matter of Xanthea she had scorned him, and he never failed to sense it, though she said not a word. Halimeda was proud, and would not rail.

The boy standing before him bore Halimeda's face.

He loved her. Hidden, like his secrets, pushed out of sight, like his past, was his love for her; but it held him and entrapped him as did his memories. He lived trammeled, helpless in the grip of that love. It was the reason he had not killed her for her scorn. It was the reason he had not killed her long ago for the secrets she knew.

He suspected she had been riding to the edge of Wirral, but he would not ask her, though he had heard her footsteps as she came in. He had not spoken to her, or she to him, for these many weeks. The winter days were lengthening toward springtime. It must be late, that she had returned. The room seemed dark. No one had lit the lamps or offered him supper. Lord Chauncey did not care, so long as someone kept his cup filled.

The boy Justin stood shaking in the chill of the damp and darkened room. Justin. What a weighty name for such a waif. The face was Halimeda's, but the boy's thinness reminded him of Roddarc at that age. It was a reminder Lord Chauncey did not like.

"Bow," Lord Chauncey commanded.

Eight-year-old Justin bowed, promptly and low, though he had already done so upon entering the audience chamber to stand before his father. Perversely, Lord Chauncey was not pleased by the boy's compliancy. He would have liked to toughen Justin by beating him. Lord Chauncey remembered his childhood as a whipping boy sufficiently so that he kept no whipping boy in his own court. But he also remembered, proudly and bitterly, that the whipping boy had become the lord. And he knew a lord only held power as long as he was hard and cruel. He knew he should beat Justin.

Instead, he drank from his golden cup, as he had been doing for some hours. "Justin," he said.

The boy looked up at him with Halimeda's eyes.

"It is a shame on both of us that you, the heir, cower here in the keep when your sister is missing, Justin. Where is your valor?"

The gray-green eyes widened. The boy had never in his life done anything valiant. He had never done anything but what he was bid. And like his sisters, he had been bid to keep within walls.

"Someday you will be a man."

The scrawny child had thought it hardly possible, but his father said it was so. Justin listened intently.

"It is time you began to think like a man." Lord Chauncey lifted a hand unsteady with drinking. "It is time you began to act like a man." The hand wobbled through an imperious gesture. "Go. Ride to Wirral. Find your sister."

With great difficulty Justin moved his lips to wet them with his tongue. He swallowed and spoke. "May I have my supper first?" he whispered.

"No whit." Chauncey felt annoyed at the thought of anyone's having supper when he had not yet had his. He was the lord, was he not? His fierce glare sent the child a step back from him. "Go! At once."

Justin bowed, backed awkwardly away from his father's presence, then turned and ran.

Down the stone corridor toward the courtyard door he ran. Was there permitted enough delay to fetch his cloak? His father would be angry. He had not said "Yes, Father." He was supposed to say, "Yes, Father," when Lord Chauncey commanded him something, but his mouth was always so dry that he could scarcely manage the words, and he was always so terrified he forgot. Better not risk taking time to find the cloak. God only knew what Lord Chauncey would do to him if he dawdled. He felt no assurance, such as Xanthea had, that he would not be killed.

In tunic and breeches, with no other covering, Justin ran out into the snowy courtyard and across it to the stable.

"Saddle Ebony," he ordered the first groom he found. His voice sounded clear. He was not afraid of servants.

The man raised his eyebrows. "Young my lord, it is growing dark! You'll not be riding out now."

"My father commands it," said Justin.

This was not a saying lightly to be questioned. The man looked anxiously at the sky, at the snow lying thick on the ground, at Justin's bare head and cloakless shoulders, but he brought the pony Ebony. It was not truly a black pony, though Justin, who had named it, liked to think it black as a black knight's warhorse. But in fact it was sooty brown, round, short-legged and sour-tempered, and so small that its back rose not much above the groom's waist.

He saddled and bridled the beast, and the young lord mounted. The pony balked at leaving the stable, for it wanted its supper at least as much as Justin wanted his. But the boy was determined, and set his slender lips in a hard line, and kicked and urged Ebony for all he was worth, and rode out at the postern gate. Night had fallen, very clear, full of frosty stars, and very, very cold.

Lord Chauncey awoke in the morning with a thundering headache and a dim memory of having said something foolish to his son. In the morning also, the pony came back riderless to the stables, trotting into its stall and looking with bright eyes and searching muzzle for food. The groom who had saddled it stared at it a moment, then ran and hid in the hayloft, but it was no use. Lord Chauncey found him and killed him, and the man was counted fortunate that rage made the lord kill him quickly. Lord Chauncey killed the pony, also, hacking its head asunder from its body with his sword. Then he roared for his own steed and rode to find his son.

This time the trail ran clear. Justin had found his way straight across snowy fields to the shadow that was Wirral. The pony had taken him under the trees. Chance ventured in far enough to find the place where the boy had fallen. He saw the depression in the snow, exactly the shape of Justin, as if the boy had been playing at making snow-angels but had fallen asleep. There was no blood. There was no sullying of the chaste white surface of the snow with signs of struggle. All lay still. Chance noted the tracks of the pony where it had turned back toward the fortress. No other tracks led away.

Yet no body lay there.

Chance felt the small hairs at the back of his neck prickle. He felt the amused stare of many small eyes. Grief made him more than ever hate-possessed. With a madman's roar, he snatched out his sword and slashed again and again at the forest which surrounded him on all sides. But the wood of the trees did not yield to his weapon as softly as had the flesh of the groom and the pony. Its resistance maddened him. He whirled his horse as if beset on all sides; he trampled his son's image into mud. He charged Wirral.

But the horse, frightened by its rider's passion, took opportunity and ran, like the pony, back toward the fortress, back toward its stable and safety. Chance had not been reared a horseman; he could not control the runaway beast. Or perhaps its fear agreed with his own. And as he fled Wirral, the sound of high-pitched, trilling laughter followed him.

> "Wirral is harsh and Wirral is fair,
> Sweet as the fragrance in springtime air.
> Wirral is soft and Wirral is stark
> As shadows blooming in the dark."

The voices woke Xanthea from her sleep. She could hear them clearly, piping and trilling in the night, and though around her she saw only the richly-draped canopy of her soft bed, she knew that the Denizens were singing in the branches of the oak that formed her refuge.

She turned at once to the one who lay next to her, for she loved and trusted him, and joggled him awake. "Listen," she told him.

> "Come to the mushroom ring,
> Xanthea, our oddling!
> Come to the revel ring,
> Xanthea, our own."

Wirral sat up in bed, his fox-red hair shining in moonlight—for the moon shone down through high palace windows, or the crevices of the oak. "It must be the night of the quarter-year," he said. "Come, array yourself." He took her by the hand and led her out of the bed, but she stood naked in the chill room, questioning.

"What do they want of me?"

Xanthea had seen Denizens more than once, for dawn, dusk and daytime she and Wirral wandered, and he showed her many wonderful things she had never seen in the forest melting toward spring; the scaly stems and barbaric blossoms of callow-come-early, the coiled fronds of bracken lifting the leaf litter, the hiding places of newts under stones. And the tough, thin, bark-skinned Denizens would come out of their tree hollows and speak to her with such impertinent courtesy as they could. Pranksters that they were, it was hard for her to tell whether they wished her ill or harm. And as many times as she had looked on their narrow, large-eyed, wide-mouthed faces, both grotesque and beautiful, she had never seen her own face in theirs. For it is not in the nature of anyone of human kind to see self truly.

Wirral gave her a soft glance, not unkind, but did not answer her question, and slowly she put on a gown he had given her, a silken gown of oak-leaf green.

The night was damp and chill, though smelling of treebud and earth; most of the snow had melted. Soon violets would be blooming. Wirral stepped out first into the darkness, hearkening for danger, then gave his hand to Xanthea. The oak stood silent; the Denizens had gone on before. A gray squirrel scampered down and turned to a horse, saddled and caparisoned for their mounting. But this one did not fly. By the forest ways it took them quickly to the wild meadow where the revelers awaited them, and shrill cries of joy greeted them as they drew near.

"Welcome, Wirral!"

"Welcome, Wolf-face!"

"Welcome, Xanthea of golden grace!"

The moon was waxing near the full. And though the snow still lay in patches under the holly and laurel, the mushrooms stood in their ring on the meadow, each one as plump and white as the moon. Xanthea gazed at them, for they seemed to shine. And she stared at the crowd around them, the Denizens as many, it seemed to her, as there were trees in Wirral. Numbers beyond counting. The cock-proud males, and the twiggy females with their hard, protruding breasts, and those other females, the dainty ones, humans in small, but fairer than any woman who ever walked.

One of them scampered up to Xanthea: a handspan-tall beauty with hair of red-gold, wisping finer than any babe's, and eyes of vivid green. And with her, by the hand, she brought—a boy?

A tiny, delicate youth with—she scarcely knew him, because of his look, unaccustomed, so merry. Nevertheless—Justin's face. Xanthea gasped, swaying where she stood with the shock of seeing him there, naked and joyous, ready to join the dance. A hand caught her arm to steady her; Wirral stood by her side.

"My—my brother!" she blurted.

"I found him!" declared the green-eyed beauty, gazing up at towering Xanthea. Justin paid no heed to his sister—either of them. Blithely he wrinkled his nose at the one, he broke free of the other and scampered away into the swirl of revelers.

Xanthea begged of the night, "But—how?"

"Look into my eyes," said Wirral softly by her side, "and I will show you how it was."

So she looked into his eyes, and saw.

The boy, riding the soot-black pony, his lips blue, his face ice-pale. Riding into Wirral, through the deep snow beneath the trees, and the pony growing slower with every step, and Justin, numb with cold, not noticing. Swaying on his small mount's back. Until, scarcely caring, he slipped sideways off his saddle, slipping into the sleep that comes before death by freezing, falling softly into a bed of snow, whiter than any bed of pillows and linens. And the pony turned and galloped back to the warm stable where death awaited it.

Then the girl, the tiny damsel who had once been named Iantha, peeping from her tree-hollow like a wary forest creature at the small human lying in the snow.

It took her a long time to come down, for it is not in the nature of the Denizens to leave their trees, their havens, and walk on the ground, except in numbers at the revels, and then the risk is part of the thrill of those nights. But on this winter day Iantha was alone. Sense told her to stay hidden. But despite sense she came out, risked thin boughs for a closer look at the boy, and something in his still face and his lidded eyes caught at her heart, tugging at memories she no longer owned.

So by hesitant degrees she went down to him, walking on top of the snow, her feet leaving no more impression than the feet of butterflies. She stood by Justin's cold face, gazing at him, feeling the tug in her heart for which she had no words, and after a time her mate found her there.

"Come away!" he called from the trees overhead. "Folk from the fortress are likely to come for that one, any moment!"

Iantha did not move. "Is he dead?" she breathed.

"Maybe not quite. But soon he will be, whether they come for him or no. Love, come away!"

She said, "Can we not take him for our own,

as—as—" And she could not go on, for she had small comprehension of how she had been taken as a babe.

And the prince of the Denizens saw the ache in her heart, and slowly replied, "As we sometimes take those who are left in Wirral. Never a boy, before. But he is fair. Very well, my lovemate. Kiss him."

Was that all? It was so simple a thing to do. Iantha leaned forward and kissed Justin's cold cheek. And the boy opened his eyes, blinking, and got up, for he no longer felt cold. Nor did he any longer feel the fear of his father's command. He did not remember his father, or miss him, or miss his mother or sisters: he felt nothing but a fey joy. Just being alive was enough, though he did not know he had been near death. He stood a scant foot in height, a little taller than the slender, shining-eyed maiden who faced him, and he laughed and followed her as she skipped away, and she led him to the dwellings of the many other small folk in the trees.

All this Xanthea saw in the eyes of Wirral, for Wirral knew all that went on within the forest, even to the mouse's cry in the hawk's claws.

Xanthea took a deep breath and steadied herself, then looked away, seeing the revel once again, seeking out another sight of Justin in the crowd of those who waited to dance. "He is better off now," she said softly. "He was always afraid. Now he is bold and joyful. He need never cower before my father again."

"Are you also better off now?" Wirral asked her.

She looked up smiling into her lover's eyes. "Assuredly."

Wild, skirling, piping music began. Justin caught hands with a female Denizen, her skin, the color and texture of cherry-tree bark, in odd contrast with his that was pale and smooth. They slipped between the mushrooms of the ring, joined the whirl of dancers within.

"Is that what they want of us," Xanthea asked Wirral, "that we should dance?"

He looked at her with a hint of smile showing at the corners of his keen, feral eyes. "I think not," he said. "That for the sake of which they dance, we have been doing for some months now."

She gazed up at him. "What, then?"

"Listen," he said.

Birdlike voices were singing with the piping and thrumming of the instruments.

"Welcome Xanthea, Wirral's bride,
Welcome Xanthea, golden one!
One with Wirral, one with woodland,
One with cousins who have died."

"What do they mean," Xanthea whispered to her lover, "cousins who have died?"

"Trees," said Wirral starkly. "Cut down. Made into lumber, or burned, or lying rotting. All trees are beloved. Some were—more than trees."

"Welcome, Xanthea, Wirral's bride!
Golden fate, of Wirral born.
By Wirral loved, with Wirral one;
Avenge the cousins who have died."

"More than trees?" Xanthea murmured.

But Wirral told her no more, for the prince of the Denizens stood before her, and a graybark who might have been his father, and many others, standing formally ranked. The music fell silent, and the dancers stood still and looked on, and the graybark spoke to Xanthea gravely, with no attempt at pun or rhyme.

"Daughter of Chance, your true name is Fate. You were conceived here, in our mystic circle, by an act of our magic. Your face is like our faces."

98

Xanthea gasped, seeing it for the first time, but the elder Denizen spoke on.

"For a while Chance and his lady tried to keep you from us, but now we have taken you back. You are at one with Wirral, and we are the spirit of Wirral and the flesh of Wirralwood. When we gifted Chance with you, we gifted him with Fate."

The speaker fell silent, and the Denizens all stood bright-eyed and silent, awaiting some response from her.

At first Xanthea could not think what the graybark had meant by gifting Chance. Then she remembered some whispers she had heard about her father's provenance, his change of name. All such talk was forbidden, and the matter had never been made clear to her. This matter of which the elder Denizen spoke seemed even less clear.

"I do not entirely understand," she said to him, speaking as formally as he had to her.

"You will understand," he replied, "When the time comes."

"Time for what?" Xanthea queried. But the music had begun again, the dancers had whirled away into their lightfoot circling, and the prince and his elder and their retinue turned away in like wise. The prince flashed a wide, fey grin at Xanthea over his narrow shoulder, then frisked away as featly as a coney. Xanthea looked at Wirral, and Wirral looked back at her with his marvelous eyes, dark as oak-shadow, soft as dew, fierce as a falcon on the wing.

"They are done with us for now," he said.

Already the dancers were pairing off and slipping away to private places.

"Between them and us," Wirral remarked, "the forest will grow mighty this year, hack your father as he will."

He laid his arm lightly around Xanthea's shoulders, and the two of them walked away like the others.

Halimeda in a sense did not know that her little son was gone, the boy who bore her face. Lord Chauncey had not told her, for they were not speaking, and he saw no reason to share his shame with one who scorned him already. He took his sorrow to his golden cup, and stayed with it. The servants were afraid to tell the lady what had happened, and as she rode out every day early and returned late, for some days there was no need to do so. And bound up in youthful self as they were, even Anastasia and Chloe did not notice for several days that their brother was missing. When finally they found out, they spent their long, tiresome day in the fortress questioning the servants, hearing the tale over and over again. Then when their mother returned, pale-faced, at dark, they ran to her and shouted to her what had happened, jostling each other and fighting to be the first to tell, for it was the most exciting news that had ever been theirs to impart.

Halimeda listened to them, and her lovely, pale face never moved. Finally her daughters had no more to say, and little by little fell silent under her stare, and felt its remoteness, as if their mother was a stranger coming in out of another time to shelter the night with them, and felt the unseemliness of their welcome to her, and sensed for the first time their own ungainliness, their noses like lumps of dough, their puff-pastry cheeks, and stepped back awkwardly. Their mother stared on. They tiptoed to a doorway, and still Halimeda stared, standing in the cold stone corridor with the March damp on her boots and dripping down from the hems of her clothing.

Then Chloe and Anastasia perceived that their mother did not see them. Halimeda stared past and through them to something—other. And at last the pale face stirred, the gray lips moved, spoke. "Iantha," Halimeda whispered.

"No, mother!" Anastasia exclaimed. "It is Xanthea and Justin who are missing."

Her mother seemed not to hear her. But suddenly the pale, still face moved, contorted, its serenity gone like a mask that has been whisked away, and Halimeda screamed, a cry that made every servant in the fortress jump and then stand shaking, that made the horses in the stable tremble and caused the hounds in their pens to whine and howl. Again and again Halimeda screamed, and her daughters ran to their rooms, flung themselves on their beds and covered their heads with their pillows, trying to stopper their ears, and the servants came running to the lady in their dozens from all parts of the keep and courtyard, speaking soothingly to her and trying to calm her, to no avail. Halimeda screamed on, her outcries taking the form of a single word.

"Iantha!" she screamed. "Iantha!"

Lord Chauncey, brooding over his golden cup, was not much moved by the screaming. But the sound of that name brought him to his feet; his golden cup crashed down unheeded, spilling its wine. Enraged, Lord Chauncey ran to confront his wife, to whom he had not spoken for many weeks. Servants scattered before him, but Halimeda seemed scarcely to see him. Again and again she shrieked, "Iantha!"

"Silence!" her lord thundered at her.

Her face confronted him mottled red and bruise-blue, twisted out of its lovely shape, lips curled, the eyes narrowed to slits with screaming, but the slits turned on him. "Iantha!" she screamed, and the name tore at her throat like a sob.

"Be silent!" Lord Chauncey roared.

But she took a step forward and spat at him, for she knew only that she hated him, he had taken a babe away from her, and she ached, she wanted her babe back again. "Iantha!" she shrieked.

Worse than ever before Lord Chauncey wanted to kill her. His hands curled, his temples throbbed, his nose and cheekbones turned chalk-white with his rage, though his face was flushed with drink. But despite wine, despite rage, something stubborn and well-hidden inside him kept his hands at his side, the words of deadly command inside his throat.

"My lord," spoke a chamberlain, a man perhaps braver than other men, "the lady has gone mad."

And still Halimeda shrieked, "Iantha!"

"Take her to her chamber," Lord Chauncey ordered, "and keep her there." He turned away and went back to his own darkened room.

The servants took charge of Halimeda, and coaxed and urged her to her chamber, and there tried in every way to comfort and silence her. But she screamed on, and her screams rang throughout the fortress in spite of closed doors, and few folk in that place ate much at that evening's meal. Only late at night did the lady finally cease to cry out, when her voice had turned to a hoarse wail and she lay breathless and exhausted. But she ate nothing, and slept restlessly, and in the morning she began again to scream of Iantha. She did not ride out that day, or many days to follow, for her chamber door was locked, and she knew nothing of what went on around her, for she had gone quite mad.

* * *

Anastasia and Chloe, like all others in the fortress, could not escape their mother's constant screaming. Even on the roof, during the daytime, they could still hear her. Even with their ears muffled by pillows, at night, they could hear her yet.

Within the first day of the harrowing noise they had taken counsel with each other, and they went to their lordly father, where he sat in his dim audience chamber with his golden cup in his hand. And they got down humbly on their knees, but their homely faces shone with their sureness, for their father had never denied them anything they had begged for in this wise. He liked to please them in all things, because they were younger daughters and because they looked so much like him.

"Father," spoke Anastasia, the elder, "Chloe and I are repining from being always within doors." And Chloe attempted to look like one who repined. "Might we take a retinue," Anastasia spoke on, "and visit for a while at the home of Lord Robley and his lovely wife? For a fortnight, perhaps?"

Robley, the neighboring lord, his holding farther from Wirral than was Chauncey's, had taken a young wife. Anastasia and Chloe had visited with her before. The girls looked up at their father with bright, lumpish faces, confident of his indulgence.

Chauncey spoke. "No." The single word.

Nor did he seem out of temper. His face, shadowed only by the dim room. Drawn down, perhaps, a bit by recent misfortunes. Blurred by drink. All this was as nothing, a trifle, to Anastasia and Chloe.

The younger girl spoke, as her sister had failed. "Father," she begged, "might we then at least go outside the fortress walls for a while? To ride our palfreys in the fields a while, perhaps?" And in the pause that followed, Halimeda's screaming came ringing through the walls.

Both girls felt sure their second petition would be granted, since the first one had been denied. But Lord Chauncey said once again, "No."

"With a guard?" Anastasia tried.

Lord Chauncey set down his golden cup, and the girls ducked their heads. They expected to hear their father roar. But not so: his voice, when he spoke, was calm, with a dryness in it and a bitter edge they had never heard before in him. "I have not failed to note," Lord Chauncey said, "that I have but two children remaining to me, and you are they. Nor have I failed to remark the workings of some strange sort of doom. You are to remain within walls, as your mother told you long since. You are to avoid even the gardens, or anywhere there might be trees."

Lord Chauncey's daughters left their father's audience chamber in petulance and bewilderment, their mother's shrieking loud in their ears.

Within a few days Anastasia and Chloe took to sleeping in the same chamber, in a great four-posted bed made of strong old oak, clinging together against the sound of the screams. It was Xanthea's bed, Xanthea's chamber, farther than their own from their mad mother's screaming—though not far enough. When Anastasia and Chloe could not sleep, they whispered with each other, often resentfully, keeping their voices low so that the servants would not hear. The two girls held Xanthea to blame for their annoying situation. If Xanthea had not gone off with the stranger, Anastasia and Chloe declared, then her younger sisters would not be confined within walls.

"She's well out of this," Anastasia whispered sourly to Chloe, "if she's not dead."

"And if she's yet alive," Chloe whispered back, "I'll warrant you she's enjoying—enjoying—" The younger girl faltered, for she was not yet certain what it was that women enjoyed with their lovers. But Anastasia replied easily enough.

"If the stranger's face is anywhere near as fair as the rest of him, assuredly," she agreed with zest. "And to think he chose that ugly, hatchet-faced Xanthea! But perhaps she's dead. Perhaps, when he unmasked her, he killed her. Folk say he is some sort of demon."

The girls cowered. Their mother's screams surged, seeming to rock the room. They did not notice that the bed was moving.

"You really think he's a demon?" Chloe gasped.

"I'll warrant he killed her. And if she's not dead," whispered Anastasia vehemently, "I swear I'll kill her myself. I hate her."

The bed closed over them. Bedposts of hard old oak clutched their bodies, oak cut in Wirral years before, the strongest wood of that mighty forest. With the power of a hundred warriors' striving muscles the oak pillars pulled the girls up against the great slab that was the headboard and gripped them there as if pressing them to its bosom, and pressed, and crushed, and their cries went unheard amidst the screams of their mother. Then, though Halimeda continued to scream, her daughters cried out no longer, and the oaken grip gave their limp bodies back to the fortress.

In the air there drifted the smell of violets.

The world spun on about its business. Knaves trysted with maids. True spring had come. Somewhere in woodland the violets were blooming.

The lady had passed days in her chamber, some-

times shrieking Iantha's name for hours on end, sometimes weeping and sobbing out, "Iantha," sometimes
pacing and prowling the room and whispering the
name with each step, but never ceasing to keep that
name on her lips, even when she slept, for she
would murmur Iantha's name in her sleep. She ate
very little, and grew flower-thin, flower-frail.

But on the day when the scent of violets drifted in
the air, the lady of the fortress arose silent and calm.
In her dreams she had sensed an ineffable fragrance,
and the same fragrance still lay on her thoughts. She
stood at her high, small chamber window, feeling the
springtime air on her face. The day was fair, warmed
with sunlight, fresh with breeze, and on the breeze
she seemed to scent the whispering perfume of woodland violets. She knew it was impossible. Not even
in the farthest distance could she see the shadow that
was Wirral. But she felt Wirral reaching into her
dreams, her thoughts. And far away, on the wood-
cutter's road, she saw a stranger coming.

Halimeda went and sat down and had her maids
tend to her face and hair. "I will go out today," she
told the servants, and she ordered them to bring her
a dress of spring-green. They obeyed her uneasily,
not daring to tell her that her chamber door stood
locked by Lord Chauncey's command, and only by
his command could they unlock it again.

But Halimeda did not attempt to go out the door.
Once she had been arrayed to her satisfaction, she
ate, then sat serenely waiting, and the servants bus-
ied themselves about the tidying of the room, casting
sidelong glances at her and at each other, puzzled.

And before the morning was old, the door opened—
though no one afterward could say how it was
opened—and a stranger stood there, bearing a bou-
quet of violets in his hand.

The maids admitted later that they stood stupidly gawking at him, for his extreme beauty stunned them. And the wild, glowing gaze of his eyes seemed to stop their hearts. But the lady Halimeda rose graciously to meet him.

"Wirral sends greetings," he told her, offering the violets, and she took them in one hand and linked the other through his arm. Together, like old friends, they went out, as if going a-Maying, and none of the servants dared to stop them for the sake of the fierce sheen of the strange man's eyes.

When the lady and the stranger came to the courtyard, as the servants watched, and the grooms at the stable door stood watching, the stranger stopped where he stood and loosened the lacings of his tunic, and two squirrels leaped out onto the ground, one gray and one fox-red. And they turned into a bright chestnut horse and one of dapple gray, each with curving neck and coddled mane and each bridled and saddled and ready to ride; the sidesaddle, for the lady, being on the gray. And her horse went gloriously arrayed in trappings of spring-green and violet. Lightly she mounted it, and took the reins in one hand while she carried her flowers in the other, and with the stranger at her side on the red horse she rode out the fortress gates and away, the way no one but woodcutters went, toward the forest named Wirral.

Half the day later, Lord Chauncey missed the sound of his wife's screaming and noticed that most of the servants had fled, for none of them came to bring him wine. And he went in search, and found Halimeda's chamber empty, but a faint scent lingering therein. He could not at first name it, until he saw lying on the floor a single wilted violet.

In a far turret of the fortress stood a chest wherein

lay some things Lord Chauncey had long since wanted to throw away, but which Halimeda had kept. For she was one who dreamed and remembered. So her lord had permitted her to keep the things, so long as she did not speak of them in his hearing and so long as she hid them from his sight. And she had obeyed: but even so, he knew where she had secreted them.

He stared at the violet lying, shriveled and dying, on her chamber floor, for a considerable time, and all the wine he had drunk left his head and blood, and he felt himself stark sober and face to face with fate.

Then he turned and left the chamber, and the few servants who remained in the fortress fled away from before him as he strode along the passageways and climbed the stone spiral steps to the turret, to the hot, dusty garret room under its pointed roof.

He did not take time to bring the chest down, but opened it then and there. And there in that low-raftered room he stood and ungirded his lordly sword and let it clank to the floor. He took off his tooled boots of soft russet-dyed leather, took off his fine clothes through which ran thread of real gold and tossed them aside, letting them fall where they would. He put off linen smallclothes. To the skin he stripped, and then he pulled from the chest crude leather trousers, stiff with age, and the leather vest and thorn-torn shirt and heavy shoes of a woodsman. He put the things on. He put on the unadorned leather belt that held leather sheath and long steel hunting knife. And from the bottom of the chest he took a cudgel, a weapon such as commoners carry, and he hefted it. His hands still knew the feel of it, and the leather clothing still remembered the shape of his body, though it chafed his softened skin.

He left a lord's finery strewn on the garret floor and went to say farewell to his remaining children.

Though likely they would scarcely recognize him. In a sense, he was not their lordly father any longer. He was a common, churlish fellow, a bastard named Chance.

Anastasia and Chloe were lazing late in their beds, it seemed. They often did that since they had been confined to the keep. There was little else for them to do. He would commend them to the care of his chamberlain and command them to stay within walls; they would be safe thus, or as safe as walls and his will could make them.

But he did not find the girls in their chambers. The rooms stood empty. Nor could he find a servant to tell him where they were. From room to room he walked, and still the smell of violets hung in the air, filling him with an unreasoning dread. He searched until he came to the door of Xanthea's chamber, and pushed it open, and saw the crushed and crumpled bodies on the floor. Then he stood and stared.

Then, turning away, he descended the stairs, crossed the courtyard and walked out the gate, leaving his dead and his fortress behind him.

Xanthea's lover came back to her canopied bed under the light of a waxing moon, and she embraced him gladly, even more so than ever, for he had been gone from her a night and a day and half a night.

"Come with me," he told her when their more urgent needs were satisfied, "and I will show you what I have brought back with me."

So Xanthea put on her silk robe with the collar furred in miniver, and in bare feet she padded the palace ways to the room where Wirral led her. And there, under the soft glow of moonlight and fine wax candles, on a couch of green velvet, she saw her mother lying, so thin and pale that at first she thought

Halimeda was dead, until she saw the rise and fall of her steady breathing.

Xanthea gasped and reached toward her mother as if to touch or wake her, but Wirral stopped her with a gentle hand.

"Let her sleep until something wakens her," he said. "She is much in need of slumber."

"Why have you brought her here?" Xanthea whispered, glad enough to let Halimeda lie, for in truth there was not much of which she wished to speak with her mother.

"Because of the one who will follow her." Wirral took Xanthea's hand. "Come, you are restless? Let us go out. The forest is beautiful at night."

They went out, and walked hand in hand under the huge butts of trees older than the fortress of Wirralmark, beneath the waxing moon, until they saw before them the stirring of small folk on the ground. Then they stopped, and Xanthea's lips parted in astonishment. For seldom were Denizens to be seen so openly except at their revels, and never had she seen any stand as grave as did these. Among all of them she saw not a smile or a sparkling eye.

They were the young prince and his mate, the fair-skinned beauty Xanthea had noticed at the revels. And a few others, and in their midst the elder who led them all, his skin like the gray bark of a beech, his beard like moss. He stood very straight, very still, on the loamy earth between fern frond and the heart-shaped leaves of celandine, and when he saw Xanthea he bespoke her, but his voice came out of him low and halting, as if with effort.

"The moon waxes," he said. "The violets bloom, and I have grown old and slow. It is the time for planting."

Then the young prince embraced him, though the

elder Denizen did not move to return the embrace. He closed his eyes. And in a moment Xanthea exclaimed aloud, utterly startled, and felt Wirral's hand tighten on hers to support or silence her, for she saw the graybark—taking root. His limbs cleaved together and became part of his trunk. His face smoothed into gnarls, and branches sprang from his head, and he was growing, growing, and she stepped back, for already he loomed over her head—and within a few more heartbeats there stood a mighty beech where none had been moments before, its smooth bark silver-gray in the moonlight, and the Denizens stood small and grave at its base.

"You are now our king and leader," said one of them at last to the young prince who stood with his lifelove by his side.

He did not answer, but stood looking at pearl-gray bark, and in a moment he whirled and cried at Xanthea, passionately, as if it were somehow her fault, "Every year, less of us! Less of us to dance at the revels, less to make merry, less to make love for the forest's sake. Yet, though we take root like trees we need not die and rot—but that your father sends men to hew at us! Our curse on Chance. Our curse on him and all his kindred!"

Xanthea's mouth had gone dry. When she spoke, her voice came out as a harsh whisper. "Yet meseems I am blessed among my kindred, not accursed."

Her hand held tightly in Wirral's hand, she said that. But the Denizen smiled darkly and quipped, "Herseems, she deems! The lady sleeps and quaintly dreams." Like a squirrel he whisked away up the tree that stood where no tree had been before; his companions did likewise, and within the moment all had disappeared into the branches that spread above Xanthea like mighty, thick-muscled arms. The sound of trilling laughter floated down to her. "Farewell, Lady Fate!" a voice sang, and then the night stood silent.

Halimeda and her escort had left a plain trail, and Chance followed it, afoot, to Wirral. On the way he stopped at the lodge and took from the Wirral warden food for a few days, cheese and cold meat and rounds of hard bread, and a leather pouch to carry it in. For Chance had been warden himself, and survived Wirral for many years, and though Lord Chauncey had been half mad, as befits a lord of Wirralmark, Chance was canny.

He followed the moon-shaped marks of Halimeda's horse into Wirral, and all his fear and hatred of the place seemed laid aside with his finery. He felt, instead, only the thoughtful wariness of one who knows well the dangers he faces. Darkness came while he had not yet ventured far into Wirral, and he lay down where he was and slept.

The next day, and the next, he followed the trail into the penetralia of Wirral, places where even in his time as warden he had never ventured. Past the dense copse where outlaws denned in their caves. Past the fen where the corpse-white, single-eyed monster nodded. Past the deep, snake-infested dingle that might have been the navel of the forest. Past the chasms that steamed. The trail grew old, but horses' hooves make a plain mark; he followed. Then within a stride the trail disappeared, as if the horses had turned to air.

Chance looked around him. Many trees stood nearby, but among them he singled out a huge old oak, full of holes and hollows, the very likely abode of Denizens. He had seen none of the small folk on his way there, and only occasionally heard them snickering, a sound like that of nesting birds. But when he saw the oak he sat down facing it, laid his cudgel across his knees and watched.

He sat thus all night and into the next day. At dawn of that day he heard the stirrings of the Denizens in the branches of the oak.

Squirrels, he would once have told himself. Squirrels scampering. And perhaps indeed there were squirrels. But he heard a birdlike warble of laughter, and watched and listened more intently, though he did not move, and in a moment he saw the small face peeping at him.

It was the face of his son.

Chance shot to his feet, though he did not cry out, and the Denizens shook the small twigs of the oak with the force of their laughter. Justin laughed as well, and vanished.

"It's Chance again!" a piping voice sang out.

"Once more a man!" cried another.

"Back again where he began!"

Chance paid no attention to the mockery. He scarcely heard it. "My son," he breathed.

Justin did not know him, he could tell. If the lad had recognized him, the look in those merry eyes would have been one of fear. The thought wrenched at Chance's heart.

"What savage fate have you doomed on me?" he demanded of the Denizens.

They laughed, and as was their wont they did not answer directly. Instead, they sang,

> "Gift of manhead, gift of Xanthea,
> Gift of Wirral, gift of doom.
> Wirral lay with Xanthea
> In her mother's womb."

Chance scarcely heard what they were chanting, for he saw a movement in the black shadow of the

largest fissure of the oak, the movement of something more than a Denizen. And in a moment he
could discern the figure of a man. And in a moment
more the stranger who had carried off his daughter
from the Masque of Misrule stepped forth.

He knew it was the same one, for no two men
could have bodies so beautiful. And the face, as
beautiful as the body, so comely that for a moment it
stopped the shout surging to Chance's mouth. Skin
fair and fresh as the new leaves of spring, eyes feral
as a wolf's farseeking eyes, yet soft as dew on wild-
flowers. Browed like a hawk, yet with a mouth fit to
make a maiden weep with desire. No maiden had
ever wept thus for Chance. The shout hardened in
him again, but he knew not what name to call the
stranger.

"You!" he roared.

It was not necessary. Wirral had seen him and
faced him from the moment of coming forth. He had
come forth solely for this, to front Chance.

"You have stolen my daughter!" Chance thundered
at him. "Where is your weapon?"

But before the other could reply, Chance turned
startled eyes. Halimeda stepped forth from the oak.

When had her long, dark hair started to silver? He
had not noted it before, but now he saw the bright
hairs lying among the others like threads of moonlight. Her face, nearly as pale as moonlight, but
placid, smooth, every jot as beautiful as the face of
the girl he had once so hopelessly loved. And the
look in her eyes when she saw him, that sunrise
shine, warmed his heart.

"Chance!" she cried, and she hurried toward him,
hands outstretched. He laid down his cudgel, scorn-
ing the enemy before him, took her hands in both
his own and kissed them.

"Hali," he greeted her, "well met."

He tried to say a thousand things in those simple words. He tried to say them, also, with his brown eyes that met hers of dreaming sea-green. Perhaps she saw. Perhaps there was no need, already she knew, for she let the moment last only a heartbeat. Hastily, earnestly she spoke on.

"Chance, our daughter is within, well and whole and happy."

Wirral spoke for the first time. "The challenge is given," he averred. The low burr deep in his voice growled darkly, like a wolf hunting, hungry, in the night.

Chance straightened where he stood, his eyes keen. Halimeda saw, and clutched at his withdrawing hands with her own.

"What need is there to fight him?" she protested. "You are no longer a lord, with a lord's overweening honor."

"I am yet a man," said Chance.

"I need no weapon, commoner," declared Wirral.

Chance stepped away from Halimeda, caught up his cudgel and leveled a blow at the insolent fellow's head. Wirral eluded it easily. Combat was joined.

Halimeda retreated to the oak and stood by it, watching, her clenched hands held to her mouth. She had not said to Chance, though she had seen it to be true, that Wirral was Xanthea's lover. It had not occurred to her to do so, or to say that Xanthea's heart would be broken if Wirral were harmed, for all her fear was for Chance. Wirral looked far younger, stronger, more lithe, more fearsome in every way; how could he fail to defeat the older man? And the one who came out of the oak and stood by Halimeda's side, serenely watching, seemed to deem likewise.

And after only a few moments, Chance began to think the same.

The uncanny stranger came at Chance with his bare hands, and they were as hard as oak, his grip strong as a hawk's. After tearing loose from the first grasp of those hands—the fingers left deep, bloody gouges on his shoulders—Chance knew that his only hope was to evade that deadly touch. But blows of the cudgel seemed to stagger the other only for a moment, not to stop him. Many heavy blows Chance landed on him, to no effect.

Truly, no effect. Chance saw with a shock and a sickness of dread that he had not raised a bruise on that fair face, or drawn so much as a single drop of blood. Sweating, he found himself scrambling backwards, floundering against trees and around them, striking out—but no blows could hold off those terrible strong hands for long. Running backward, Chance knew that if he stumbled over a root and fell, he would be finished.

"Who are you," he yelled out in a sort of furious despair, "that you do not bleed?"

Without missing stride or breath the other said, "I am Wirral."

Then Chance felt the chill of foreboding, but also a hot, unreasoning rage. It was his old enemy. "By God, we hew at you!" he shouted, and he stood his ground beneath the oak, dropped his cudgel and snatched out his knife, slashing. The blade gashed Wirral's forearm and bounded off it like an axe striking strong, green wood. The wound did not bleed. Before Chance could strike again, the feral-eyed man caught his wrist with a grip fit to break bone, but Chance would not drop the knife.

"You killed my daughters!" Chance screamed, laying

Chloe and Anastasia to Wirral's account, which might not have been untrue. "You took my son!"

"Blame yourself for Justin," Wirral said. "You sent him hither."

One of his powerful hands held off Chance's hand that wielded the knife. The other sought Chance's throat, and with all the force of his arm Chance could not prevent it. Nor would he writhe away; he had done with running. In a moment he would be finished—

A heavy, dead bough fell from the oak directly onto Wirral's head.

It jarred the strong youth only for an eyeblink. But that moment was all Chance needed. The hawklike grip on his wrist faltered; he tore loose, leaving shreds of his skin behind; and his knife hand shot with redoubled force toward his enemy's chest. Before the oak bough had glanced off Wirral's shoulders and fallen to the ground, Chance's blade had sheathed itself in his heart.

Though, seeing what he had seen, Chance felt no certainty that it would kill him.

Wirral fell to the forest floor along with the bough that had been his undoing. Blood, bright red blood, spurted from his mortal wound. Somewhere close at hand a woman screamed; the soft, fierce eyes sought hers. But the beautiful face showed no pain. Nor did it speak. Instead, it simply disappeared.

There, on the loamy ground, lay a scrap of fox pelt, an outlaw's skull, and the bones of a deer, long since weathered white. And strong boughs of green oak, and leaves, and blue windflowers, strewn and wilted and bright with blood. And a few gray hairs from a wolf. Nothing more.

From overhead, from the place whence the oak

bough had fallen, came the shrill sound of Denizen laughter.

"We made him, Xanthea!" a birdlike voice cried. Chance looked up and saw the young prince he well remembered. The fellow seemed scarcely to have changed at all. Chance stood panting with his knife in his hand, its point sending slow red drops onto the Wirral loam.

"We made him just for you, Xanthea!" the Denizen cried. "For you, golden lady, we made him fair!"

"Full oft you have with Wirral lain!" called another.

"And you and Wirral have been one!"

"And one you twain shall remain!"

"And now by Chance he's slain!"

The voices shrilled dark and gleeful.

Slowly Chance turned and looked at his daughter. Xanthea, his firstborn child, and the only one who remained to him. He turned with a sure sense of doom, for it was for this, he knew, that the Denizens had sent the oak limb down on Wirral. To spare him for this. His own daughter.

There beneath the oak she stood, Xanthea, yet not the Xanthea he remembered. Her body, so tall, tall with pride and a vibrant energy. Her face—for the first time Chance saw truly her startling, great-eyed face, its uncanny beauty. Grotesque beauty, quite unlike her mother's smooth-faced loveliness. Xanthea's was a mad, verdant, shadowed beauty, as wild as the Wirral. Xanthea's ways, he deemed, as dark as midnight in Wirral. Xanthea, in Wirral conceived, of Wirral magic conceived and born, by Wirral bred— one with Wirral, as the Denizens had said. Xanthea was Wirral.

With a strange, slow, hating smile she regarded him. Then, like a doomster, she lifted steady hands and put on her mask. Her golden mask. In it, she seemed to loom, tall, tree-tall, still and fearsome.

Halimeda came and stood by her husband's side, slipped her hand into his.

"Wirral will take back its own." Standing like the goddess of the forest, Xanthea decreed it.

Chance found his voice. "It is the Denizens who have done this to you," he protested. "They have made you their tool. And you have let them."

Vehemently Xanthea told him, "Lay the blame to your own account. None of this could have happened had you loved me." Her glance through her golden mask raked them both, her mother and father standing before her. "Had you loved me at all, it would have held me, I could never have left the fortress walls. For all I have ever wanted is love."

Her weird lover had given her love enough to make her anew, give her selfhood she had never known. Now he lay, bone of deer and outlaw's skull, fur of fox and oak limbs.

"But failing that," Xanthea said, "I shall have vengeance."

And though he yet held the knife in his hand, Chance could not move as she walked up to him, tall, taller than he, and took it away.

Then she turned to the forest that waited, listening, all around. And she spread wide her long, strong arms and cried out a summons.

"My cousins!" she called, and they came to do her bidding.

Lord Robley, the smiling neighbor with the lovely wife, had not failed to make note of the strange goings-on at Wirralmark Manor by means of his spies. And no sooner had Chance gone away into the wilderness of Wirral than Lord Robley arrived at the head of several troops of men to take fortress and lands for himself. He met little resistance, even from the chamberlain and the household guards, for Lord Chauncey's followers were disheartened. There had been too many horrors of late, the finding of bodies in a certain bedroom being only the most recent.

Within a few days of his coming, Lord Robley had settled himself in power, sent for his wife and retinue, given commands. And the folk of Wirralmark accepted his commands almost gratefully. He was a hard lord, Robley, but they were accustomed to harshness in a lord. It was eeriness that unsettled them. The shadow of Wirral. And they hoped Lord Chauncey was dead and would not come back to make trouble for them all.

Even in their wildest whisperings, even in the ghastliest of the tales told in low voices before a dying fire in deep of winter, they had never foreseen how long the shadow of Wirral would grow.

Nor was it Lord Chauncey who came back to haunt them. It was his daughter. Chance's daughter.

On a moon-gray horse Xanthea came, the morning of Robley's fourth day in power, boldly and openly, riding aside with her oak-green gown flowing down around her feet. From her saddle hung a mask of gold, with the peacock feathers trailing down, and close beside it the carved wolf-mask. On her body Xanthea wore a girdle of emeralds and gold, a torsade of gold; no armor, no weapon of any kind. But at her back rose the dust of a great army.

A peasant boy first saw and brought the news to the fortress, running without ceremony in to Lord Robley's presence, gasping so that he could scarcely speak, his face so mottled and twisted that at first those who saw him thought he had gone mad. When Lord Robley heard his words, he felt sure of it. But then the watchman on the platform shouted down the same report, in a voice hoarse with fear.

Then Lord Robley himself looked, and then with small thought for anyone else he mounted the first horse he could come to, sent it out the postern gate and galloped away, though he was no coward. And all his troops who could manage it did likewise. For approaching they had seen warriors a hundred feet tall, wooden warriors with leafy helms. Trees.

Striding along on great, trampling roots they came, oak and ash and beech and elm, and their passing made a sound like stormwind in the branches of Wirral and left the land fallow. And few were those who would stand before them, for even the least of them, linden and rowan and cherry, a mere thirty feet tall, even these were more than a match for any man. They could be hewed, but they did not bleed. Some few brave tenants took axes and stood at the edges of their fields, attempting to turn the trees aside. Within a few moments they had been trodden into the ground, part of the earth they had tilled, and in years to come oak and ash, linden and cherry would grow out of their bones.

Wirral had reached out to take back its own.

Folk, even the soldiers of the fortress, screamed and ran before that army. It leveled cottages as it came. A trampling of roots, the thwacking of a few swinging limbs, and that which had taken men many years to build lay in splinters, ready to rot back into loam.

Xanthea rode her moon-gray horse through gates swinging open and unattended, into an emptied fortress. Trees followed her. Not trees, truly, but truly Wirral, spirit of Wirral. These were Denizens, generations of the Wirralfolk, the elders who had gone before. Voiceless though they had become in form of

trees, their great rage had moved them to follow
Xanthea's call. Xanthea dismounted, and took the
masks in her hands, and her horse turned to a squirrel, scurried to the top of an oak. Some of the trees
began to tear down the stones of the fortress walls,
prying them apart with a grip fit, like the grip of
roots, to crack boulders, then hurling them away as
children hurl pebbles.

"Leave the keep a moment longer," Xanthea told
them.

She walked through the empty, echoing passages,
and the stench of corpses from her former chamber
did not trouble her. She climbed the stone stairs to
the roof and watched the trees. All around the keep
they swarmed, for miles all around, trampling away
everything that bore the smell of man, just as they
had trampled Chance and his lady into Wirral loam,
the day before. And though they seemed as many as
the midges that swarmed over the fen where the
corpse-white monster nodded, Wirral had scarcely
thinned by dint of this slight stretching. Some few
saplings would gain more light, was all. Wirral stood
as it ever had, thick and verdant and perilous.

"Yours the final victory, Wirral," Xanthea whispered.

*I will never take another lover. I will never have
any lover but this.*

She went down, and stood aside, and the trees
tore the keep to bits, and Xanthea laid her masks on
the pile of rubble that was left.

At last, satisfied, the trees ceased their tramplings.
More slowly circling, they sought new places for
themselves, then stood still. They put their roots
into the cleansed ground. The day faded into a golden-
glowing dusk, and for miles around there was no
sound but the clear call of a bird. Xanthea ventured,

and wherever she wandered she found nothing of human making to disturb her eye. Nothing but Wirral. This portion grew thin, it was true. But the revels would go on. Before many years had passed, it would grow thick as grass. It would be well and whole again.

"Wirral, my love," she spoke aloud, "I will wait."

When full dark came, and in it the full moon, Xanthea strode away from the ruined fortress, back toward the place where she had left fur of fox and outlaw's skull, bones of deer and withered leaves and the soul of a wandering wolf.

Somewhere close at hand, though she saw no one, she heard the twittering chuckle of a Denizen.

"For Wirral is soft and Wirral is stark,
A blossom blue and an outlaw's bone,
The tooth of the wolf and the song of the lark,
And Wirral will take back its own!" it sang.
"Wirral will take back its own."

THE WOLF GIRL SPEAKS

When the men came
My pack mates ran
All but my mother
At the mouth of the den
Trembling—shot down.
The men reached in—
I cringed with the others
My brothers and sisters
Their puppy fur pressed
To my furless skin—
The men clubbed them dead
And pulled me outside
Though I bit and clawed
To the horrible harsh daylight
And tried to make me stand
On my long hind legs
I had not yet learned to weep
So I bared my teeth instead
And damn them they smiled.
We have saved the child they said
The poor wild thing
A good day's work
We have rescued her they said.

THE BOY
WHO PLAITED MANES

The boy who plaited the manes of horses arrived, fittingly enough, on the day of the Midsummer Hunt: when he was needed worst, though Wald the head groom did not yet know it. The stable seethed in a muted frenzy of work, as it had done since long before dawn, every groom and apprentice vehemently polishing. The lord's behest was that all the horses in his stable should be brushed for two hours every morning to keep the fine shine and bloom on their flanks, and this morning could be no different. Then there was also all the gear to be tended to. Though old Lord Robley of Auberon was a petty manor lord, with only some hundred of horses and less than half the number of grooms to show for a lifetime's striving, his lowly status made him all the more keen to present himself and his retinue grandly before the more powerful lords who would assemble for the Hunt. Himself and his retinue and his lovely young wife.

Therefore it was an eerie thing when the boy

walked up the long stable aisle past men possessed with work, men so frantic they did not glance at the stranger, up the aisle brick-paved in chevron style until he came to the stall where the lady's milk-white palfrey stood covered withers to croup with a fitted sheet tied on to keep the beast clean, and the boy swung open the heavy stall door and walked in without fear, as if he belonged there, and went up to the palfrey to plait its mane.

He was an eerie boy, so thin that he seemed deformed, and of an age difficult to guess because of his thinness. He might have been ten, or he might have been seventeen with something wrong about him that made him beardless and narrow-shouldered and thin. His eyes seemed too gathered for a ten-year-old, gray-green and calm yet feral, like woodland. His hair, dark and shaggy, seemed to bulk large above his thin, thin face.

The palfrey's hair was far better cared for than his. Its silky mane, coddled for length, hung down below its curved neck, and its tail was bundled into a wrapping, to be let down at the last moment before the lady rode, when it would trail on the ground and float like a white bridal train. The boy did not yet touch the tail, but his thin fingers flew to work on the palfrey's mane.

Wald the head groom, passing nearly at a run to see to the saddling of the lord's hotblooded hunter, stopped in his tracks and stared. And to be sure it was not that he had never seen plaiting before. He himself had probably braided a thousand horses' manes, and he knew what a time it took to put even a row of small looped braids along a horse's crest, and how hard it was to get them even, and how horsehair seems like a demon with a mind of its own. He frankly gawked, and other grooms stood beside him and did likewise, until more onlookers stood gathered outside the palfrey's stall than could rightly see, and those in the back demanded to know what was happening, and those in the front seemed not to hear them, but stood as if in a trance, watching the boy's thin, swift hands.

For the boy's fingers moved more quickly and deftly than seemed human, than seemed possible, each hand by itself combing and plaiting a long, slender braid in one smooth movement, as if he no more than stroked the braid out of the mane. That itself would have been wonder enough, as when a groom is so apt that he can curry with one hand and follow after with the brush in the other, and have a horse done in half the time. A shining braid forming out of each hand every minute, wonder enough—but that was the least of it. The boy interwove them as he worked, so that they flowed into each other in a network, making of the mane a delicate shawl, a veil, that draped the palfrey's fine neck. The ends of the braids formed a silky hem curving down to a point at the shoulder, and at the point the boy spiraled the remaining mane into an uncanny horsehair flower. And all the time, though it was not tied and was by no means a cold-blooded beast, the palfrey had not moved, standing still as a stone.

Then Wald the head groom felt fear prickling at the back of his astonishment. The boy had carried each plait down to the last three hairs. Yet he had fastened nothing with thread or ribbon, but merely pressed the ends between two fingers, and the braids stayed as he had placed them. Nor did the braids ever seem to fall loose as he was working, or hairs fly out at random, but all lay smooth as white silk, shimmering. The boy, or whatever he was, stood still with his hands at his sides, admiring his work.

Uncanny. Still, the lord and lady would be well pleased. . . . Wald jerked himself out of amazement and moved quickly. "Get back to your work, you fellows!" he roared at the grooms, and then he strode into the stall.

"Who are you?" he demanded. "What do you mean coming in here like this?" It was best, in a lord's household, never to let anyone know you were obliged to them.

The boy looked at him silently, turning his head in the alert yet indifferent way of a cat.

"I have asked you a question! What is your name?"

The boy did not speak, or even move his lips. Then or thereafter, as long as he worked in that stable, he never made any sound.

His stolid manner annoyed Wald. But though the master groom could not yet know that the boy was a mute, he saw something odd in his face. A halfwit, perhaps. He wanted to strike the boy, but even worse he wanted the praise of the lord and lady, so he turned abruptly and snatched the wrapping off the palfrey's tail, letting the cloud of white hair float down to the clean straw of the stall. "Do something with that," he snapped.

A sweet, intense glow came into the boy's eyes as he regarded his task. With his fingers he combed the hair smooth, and then he started a row of small braids above the bone.

Most of the tail he left loose and flowing, with just a cluster of braids at the top, a few of them swinging halfway to the ground. And young Lady Aelynn gasped with pleasure when she saw them, and with wonder at the mane, even though she was a lord's daughter born and not unaccustomed to finery.

It did not matter, that day, that Lord Robley's saddle had not been polished to a sufficient shine.

He was well pleased with his grooms. Nor did it matter that his hawks flew poorly, his hounds were unruly and his clumsy hunter stumbled and cut its knees. Lords and ladies looked again and again at his young wife on her white palfrey, its tail trailing and shimmering like her blue silk gown, the delicate openwork of its mane as dainty as the lace kerchief tucked between her breasts or her slender gloved hand which held the caparisoned reins. Every hair of her mount was as artfully placed as her own honey-gold hair looped in gold-beaded curls atop her fair young head. Lord Robley knew himself to be the envy of everyone who saw him for the sake of his lovely wife and the showing she made on her white mount with the plaited mane.

And when the boy who plaited manes took his place among the lord's other servants in the kitchen line for the evening meal, no one gainsaid him.

Lord Robley was a hard old man, his old body hard and hale, his spirit hard. It took him less than a day to pass from being well pleased to being greedy for more: no longer was it enough that the lady's palfrey should go forth in unadorned braids. He sent a servant to Wald with silk ribbons in the Auberon colors, dark blue and crimson, and commanded that they should be plaited into the palfrey's mane and tail. This the stranger boy did with ease when Wald gave him the order, and he used the ribbon ends to tie tiny bows and love knots and leave a few shimmering tendrils bobbing in the forelock. Lady Aelynn was enchanted.

Within a few days Lord Robley had sent to the stable thread of silver and of gold, strings of small pearls, tassels, pendant jewels, and fresh-cut flowers of every sort. All of these things the boy who plaited manes used with ease to dress the lady's palfrey when he was bid. Lady Aelynn went forth to the next hunt with tiny bells of silver and gold chiming at the tip of each of her mount's dainty ribbon-decked braids, and eyes turned her way wherever she rode. Nor did the boy ever seem to arrange the mane and tail and forelock twice in the same way, but whatever way he chose to plait and weave and dress it seemed the most perfect and poignant and heartachingly beautiful way a horse had ever been arrayed. Once he did the palfrey's entire mane in one great, thick braid along the crest, gathering in the hairs as he went, so that the neck seemed to arch as mightily as a destrier's, and he made the braid drip thick with flowers, roses and great lilies and spires of larkspur trailing down, so that the horse seemed to go with a mane of flowers. But another time he would leave the mane loose and floating, with just a few braids shimmering down behind the ears or in the forelock, perhaps, and this also seemed perfect and poignant and the only way a horse should be adorned.

Nor was it sufficient, any longer, that merely the lady's milk-white palfrey should go forth in braids. Lord Robley commanded that his hotblooded hunter also should have his mane done up in stubby rib-boned braids and rosettes in the Auberon colors, and the horses of his retinue likewise, though with lesser rosettes. And should his wife choose to go out riding with her noble guests, all their mounts were to be prepared like hers, though in lesser degree.

All these orders Wald passed on to the boy who plaited manes, and the youngster readily did as he was bid, working sometimes from before dawn until long after dark, and never seeming to want more than what food he could eat while standing in the kitchen. He slept in the hay and straw of the loft and did not use even a horseblanket for covering until

one of the grooms threw one on him. Nor did he ask
for clothing, but Wald, ashamed of the boy's shabbiness, provided him with the clothing due to a servant. The master groom said nothing to him of a
servant's pay. The boy seemed content without it.
Probably he would have been content without the
clothing as well. Though in fact it was hard to tell
what he was thinking or feeling, for he never spoke
and his thin face seldom moved.

No one knew his name, the boy who plaited manes.
Though many of the grooms were curious and made
inquiries, no one could tell who he was or where he
had come from. Or even what he was, Wald thought
sourly. No way to tell if the young snip was a halfwit
or a bastard or what, if he would not talk. No way to
tell what sort of a young warlock he might be, that
the horses never moved under his hands, even the
hotblooded hunter standing like a stump for him.
Scrawny brat. He could hear well enough; why would
he not talk?

It did not make Wald like the strange boy, that he
did at once whatever he was told and worked so hard
and so silently. In particular he did not like the boy
for doing the work for which Wald reaped the lord's
praise; Wald disliked anyone to whom he was obliged.
Nor did he like the way the boy had arrived, as if
blown in on a gust of wind, and so thin that it nearly
seemed possible. Nor did he like the thought that
any day the boy might leave in like wise. And even
disliking that thought, Wald could not bring himself
to give the boy the few coppers a week which were
his due, for he disliked the boy more. Wald believed
there was something wrongheaded, nearly evil, about
the boy. His face seemed wrong, so very thin, with
the set mouth and the eyes both wild and quiet,
burning like a steady candle flame.

Summer turned into autumn, and many gusts of
wind blew, but the boy who plaited manes seemed
content to stay, and if he knew of Wald's dislike he
did not show it. In fact he showed nothing. He
braided the palfrey's mane with autumn starflowers
and smiled ever so slightly as he worked. Autumn
turned to the first dripping and dismal, chill days of
winter. The boy used bunches of bright feathers
instead of flowers when he dressed the palfrey's mane,
and he did not ask for a winter jerkin, so Wald did
not give him any. It was seldom enough, anyway,
that the horses were used for pleasure at this season.
The thin boy could spend his days huddled under a
horseblanket in the loft.

Hard winter came, and the smallpox season.

Lady Aelynn was bored in the wintertime, even
more so than during the rest of the year. At least in
the fine weather there were walks outside, there
were riding and hunting and people to impress. It
would not be reasonable for a lord's wife, nobly born
(though a younger child, and female), to wish for
more than that. Lady Aelynn knew full well that her
brief days of friendships and courtships were over.
She had wed tolerably well, and Lord Robley counted
her among his possessions, a beautiful thing to be
prized like his gold and his best horses. He was a
manor lord, and she was his belonging, his lady, and
not for others to touch even with their regard. She
was entirely his. So there were walks for her in
walled gardens, and pleasure riding and hunting by
her lord's side, and people to impress.

But in the wintertime there were not even the
walks. There was nothing for the Lady Aelynn to do
but tend to her needlework and her own beauty,
endlessly concerned with her clothes, her hair, her
skin, even though she was so young, no more than

seventeen—for she knew in her heart that it was for her beauty that Lord Robley smiled on her, and for no other reason. And though she did not think of it, she knew that her life lay in his grasping hands.

Therefore she was ardently uneasy, and distressed only for herself, when the woman who arranged her hair each morning was laid abed with smallpox. Though as befits a lady of rank, Aelynn hid her dismay in vexation. And it did not take her long to discover that none of her other tiring-women could serve her nearly as well.

"Mother of God!" she raged, surveying her hair in the mirror for perhaps the tenth time. "The groom who plaits the horses' manes in the stable could do better!" Then the truth of her own words struck her, and desperation made her willing to be daring. She smiled. "Bring him hither!"

Her women stammered and curtseyed and fled to consult among themselves and exclaim with the help in the kitchen. After some few minutes of this, a bold kitchen maid was dispatched to the stable and returned with a shivering waif: the boy who plaited manes.

It was not to be considered that such a beggar should go in to the lady. Her tiring-women squeaked in horror and made him bathe first, in a washbasin before the kitchen hearth, for there was a strong smell of horse and stable about him. They ordered him to scrub his own hair with strong soap and scent himself with lavender, and while some of them giggled and fled, others giggled and stayed, to pour water for him and see that he made a proper job of his ablutions. All that was demanded of him the boy who plaited manes did without any change in his thin face, any movement of his closed mouth, any flash of his feral eyes. At last they brought him clean clothing, jerkin and woolen hose only a little too

135

large, and pulled the things as straight as they could on him, and took him to the tower where the lady waited.

He did not bow to the Lady Aelynn or look into her eyes for his instructions, but his still mouth softened a little and his glance, calm and alert, like that of a woodland thing, darted to her hair. And at once, as if he could scarcely wait, he took his place behind her and lifted her tresses in his hands. Such a soft, fine, honey-colored mane of hair as he had never seen, and combs of gold and ivory lying at hand on a rosewood table, and ribbons of silk and gold, everything he could have wanted, his for the sake of his skill.

He started at the forehead, and the lady sat as if in a trance beneath the deft touch of his hands.

Gentle, he was so gentle, she had never felt such a soft and gentle touch from any man, least of all from her lord. When Lord Robley wanted to use one of his possessions he seized it. But this boy touched her as gently as a woman, no, a mother, for no tiring-woman or maid had ever gentled her so. . . . Yet unmistakably his was the touch of a man, though she could scarcely have told how she knew. Part of it was power, she could feel the gentle power in his touch, she could feel—uncanny, altogether eerie and un-canny, what she was feeling. It was as if his quick fingers called to her hair in soft command and her hair obeyed just for the sake of the one quick touch, all the while longing to embrace. . . . She stayed breathlessly still for him, like the horses.

He plaited her hair in braids thin as bluebell stems, only a wisp of hairs to each braid, one after another with both his deft hands as if each was as easy as a caress, making them stay with merely a touch of two fingers at the end, until all her hair lay in a silky cascade of them, catching the light and glimmering and swaying like a rich drapery when he made her move her head. Some of them he gathered and looped and tied up with the ribbons which matched her dress, blue edged with gold. But most of them he left hanging to her bare back and shoulders. He surveyed his work with just a whisper of a smile when he was done, then turned and left without waiting for the lady's nod, and she sat as if under a spell and watched his thin back as he walked away. Then she tossed her head at his lack of deference. But the swinging of her hair pleased her.

She had him back to dress her hair the next day, and the next, and many days thereafter. And so that they would not have to be always bathing him, her tiring-women found him a room within the manorhouse doors, and a pallet and clean blankets, and a change of clothing, plain coarse clothing, such as servants wore. They trimmed the heavy hair that shadowed his eyes, also, but he looked no less the oddling with his thin, thin face and his calm, burning glance and his mouth that seemed scarcely ever to move. He did as he was bid, whether by Wald or the lady or some kitchen maid, and every day he plaited Lady Aelynn's hair differently. One day he shaped it all into a bright crown of braids atop her head. On other days he would plait it close to her head so that the tendrils caressed her neck, or in a haughty crest studded with jewels, or in a single soft feathered braid at one side. He always left her tower chamber at once, never looking at the lady to see if he had pleased her, as if he knew that she would always be pleased.

Always, she was.

Things happened. The tiring-woman who had taken smallpox died of it, and Lady Aelynn did not care, not for the sake of her cherished hair and most certainly not for the sake of the woman herself. Lord Robley went away on a journey to discipline a debtor vassal, and Lady Aelynn did not care except to be glad, for there was a sure sense growing in her of what she would do.

When even her very tresses were enthralled by the touch of this oddling boy, longing to embrace him, could she be otherwise?

When next he had plaited her mane of honey-colored hair and turned to leave her without a glance, she caught him by one thin arm. His eyes met hers with a steady, gathered look. She stood—she was taller than he, and larger, though she was as slender as any maiden. It did not matter. She took him by one thin hand and led him to her bed, and there he did as he was bid.

Nor did he disappoint her. His touch—she had never been touched so softly, so gently, so deftly, with such power. Nor was he lacking in manhood, for all that he was as thin and hairless as a boy. And his lips, after all, knew how to move, and his tongue. But it was the touch of his thin hands that she hungered for, the gentle, tender, potent touch that thrilled her almost as if—she were loved. . . .

He smiled at her afterward, slightly, softly, a whisper of a smile in the muted half-light of her curtained bed, and his lips moved.

"You are swine," he said, "all of you nobles."

And he got up, put on his plain, coarse clothing and left her without a backward glance.

It terrified Lady Aelynn, that he was not truly a mute. Terrified her even more than what he had said, though she burned with mortified wrath whenever she thought of the latter. He, of all people, a mute, to speak such words to her and leave her helpless to avenge herself. . . . Perhaps for that reason he would not betray her. She had thought it would be safe to take a mute as her lover. . . . Perhaps he would not betray her.

In fact, it was not he who betrayed her to her lord, but Wald.

Her tiring-women suspected, perhaps because she had sent them on such a long errand. She had not thought they would suspect, for who would think that such a wisp of a beardless boy could be a bedfellow? But perhaps they also had seen the wild glow deep in his gray-green eyes. They whispered among themselves and with the kitchen maids, and the bold kitchen maid giggled with the grooms, and Wald heard.

Even though the boy who plaited manes did all the work, Wald considered the constant plaiting and adorning of manes and tails a great bother. The whole fussy business offended him, he had decided, and he had long since forgotten the few words of praise it had garnered from the lord at first. Moreover, he disliked the boy so vehemently that he was not thinking clearly. It seemed to him that he could be rid of the boy and the wretched onus of braids and rosettes all in one stroke. The day the lord returned from his journey, Wald hurried to him, begged private audience, bowed low and made his humble report.

Lord Robley heard him in icy silence, for he knew pettiness when he saw it; it had served him often in the past, and he would punish it if it misled him. He summoned his wife to question her. But the Lady Aelynn's hair hung lank, and her guilt and shame could be seen plainly in her face from the moment she came before him.

Lord Robley's roar could be heard even to the stables.

He strode over to her where she lay crumpled and weeping on his chamber floor, lifted her head by its honey-gold hair and slashed her across the face with his sword. Then he left her screaming and stinging her wound with fresh tears, and he strode to the stable with his bloody sword still drawn, Wald fleeing before him all the way; when the lord burst in all the grooms were scattering but one. The boy Wald had accused stood plaiting the white palfrey's mane.

Lord Robley hacked the palfrey's head from its braid-bedecked neck with his sword, and the boy who plaited manes stood by with something smoldering deep in his unblinking gray-green eyes, stood calmly waiting. If he had screamed and turned to flee, Lord Robley would with great satisfaction have given him a coward's death from the back. But it unnerved the lord that the boy awaited his pleasure with such mute—what? Defiance? There was no servant's bow in this one, no falling to the soiled straw, no groveling. If he had groveled he could have been kicked, stabbed, killed out of hand. . . . But this silent, watchful waiting, like the alertness of a wild thing—on the hunt or being hunted? It gave Lord Robley pause, like the pause of the wolf before the standing stag or the pause of the huntsman before the thicketed boar. He held the boy at the point of his sword—though no such holding was necessary, for the prisoner had not moved even to tremble—and roared for his men-at-arms to come take the boy to the dungeon.

There the nameless stranger stayed without water or food, and aside from starving him Lord Robley could not decide what to do with him.

At first the boy who plaited manes paced in his

prison restlessly—he had that freedom, for he was so thin and small that the shackles were too large to hold him. Later he lay in a scant bed of short straw and stared narrow-eyed at the darkness. And yet later, seeing the thin cascades of moonlight flow down through the high, iron-barred window and puddle in moon-glades on the stone floor, he got up and began to plait the moonbeams.

They were far finer than any horsehair, moonbeams, finer even than the lady's honey-colored locks, and his eyes grew wide with wonder and pleasure as he felt them. He made them into braids as fine as silk threads, flowing together into a lacework as close as woven cloth, and when he had reached as high as he could, plaiting, he stroked as if combing a long mane with his fingers and pulled more moonlight down out of the sky—for this stuff was not like any other stuff he had ever worked with, it slipped and slid worse than any hair, there seemed to be no beginning or end to it except the barriers that men put in its way. He stood plaiting the fine, thin plaits until he had raised a shimmering heap on the floor, and then he stepped back and allowed the moon to move on. His handiwork he laid carefully aside in a corner.

The boy who plaited moonbeams did not sleep, but sat waiting for the dawn, his eyes glowing greenly in the darkened cell. He saw the sky lighten beyond the high window and waited stolidly, as the wolf waits for the gathering of the pack, as a wildcat waits for the game to pass along the trail below the rock where it lies. Not until the day had neared its mid did the sun's rays, thrust through the narrow spaces between the high bars, wheel their shafts down to where he could reach them. Then he got up and began to plait the sunlight.

Guards were about, or more alert, in the daytime,

and they gathered at the heavy door of his prison, peering in between the iron bars of its small window, gawking and quarreling with each other for turns. They watched his unwavering eyes, saw the slight smile come on his face as he worked, though his thin hands glowed red as if seen through fire. They saw the shining mound he raised on the floor, and whispered among themselves and did not know what to do, for none of them dared to touch it or him. One of them requested a captain to come look. And the captain summoned the steward, and the steward went to report to the lord. And from outside, cries began to sound that the sun was standing still.

After the boy had finished, he stood back and let the sun move on, then tended to his handiwork, then sat resting on his filthy straw. Within minutes the dungeon door burst open and Lord Robley himself strode in.

Lord Robley had grown weary of mutilating his wife, and he had not yet decided what to do with his other prisoner. Annoyed by the reports from the prison, he expected that an idea would come to him when he saw the boy. He entered with drawn sword, But all thoughts of the thin young body before him were sent whirling away from his mind by what he saw laid out on the stone floor at his feet.

A mantle, a kingly cloak—but no king had ever owned such a cloak. All shining, the outside of it silver and the inside gold—but no, to call it silver and gold was to insult it. More like water and fire, flow and flame, shimmering as if it moved, as if it were alive, and yet it had been made by hands, he could see the workmanship, so fine that every thread was worth a gasp of pleasure, the outside of it somehow braided and plaited to the lining, and all around the edge a fringe of threads like bright fur so fine that it wavered in the air like flame. Lord Robley had no thought but to settle the fiery gleaming thing on his shoulders, to wear that glory and be finer than any king. He seized it and flung it on—

And screamed as he had not yet made his wife scream, with the shriek of mortal agony. His whole hard body glowed as if placed in a furnace. His face contorted, and he fell dead.

The boy who plaited sunbeams got up in a quiet, alert way and walked forward, as noiseless on his feet as a lynx. He reached down and took the cloak off the body of the lord, twirled it and placed it on his own shoulders, and it did not harm him. But in that cloak he seemed insubstantial, like something moving in moonlight and shadow, something nameless roaming in the night. He walked out of the open dungeon door, between the guards clustered there, past the lord's retinue and the steward, and they all shrank back from him, flattened themselves against the stone walls of the corridor so as not to come near him. No one dared take hold of him or try to stop him. He walked out through the courtyard, past the stable, and out the manor gates with the settled air of one whose business is done. The men-at-arms gathered atop the wall and watched him go.

Wald the master groom lived to old age sweating every night with terror, and died of a weakened heart in the midst of a nightmare. Nothing else but his own fear harmed him. The boy who plaited—mane of sun, mane of moon—was never seen again in that place, except that children sometimes told the tale of having glimpsed him in the wild heart of a storm, plaiting the long lashes of wind and rain.

THE BARD

How did it happen that I am here, in this strange garb of female flesh and in this most strange place and time? I will tell you how it chanced:

"Think of a horse," I said.

The evenings were long, around the autumn camp-fires. There were no bards in the company, and not talk enough to beguile the hours. I had small knack for singing myself, though I loved it. So I said, "Think of a horse."

And then I said, "All right, Bellory, what is yours?"

"A black," he replied promptly. "A stallion, over sixteen hands high, with darting hooves and eyes like flame. Would that I had him when we meet with Merric!" For it was to war that our King had us marching.

"That was soldierly spoken, Bellory," the next man laughed. For Bellory wore gold armbands and tended to strut. But he took no offense with his comrade this night, not with Merric's holding little more than a day away. We all huddled for warmth of more than the fire. "What is yours, Breca?" Bellory asked.

"Bay gelding with black points," the older man growled. "Not flashy, but a stayer."

"Loren?" I asked.

"A sorrel mare," he replied quietly, for he was a gentle lad. "Sunny flanks and a mane like cream." Some men smiled, thinking of his fair-haired bride, but no one saw fit to jest. Others joined in unbidden. A gray, one said, with a fine dark eye. A piebald, said another grimacing, for that we must play the fool. An old roan, tired from the plow, said one who was tired from the march.

"And you, Gage?" Loren asked me suddenly. "What is yours?"

What was I to say, I who had started the diversion indeed? I had no answer ready, but all unawares one sprang from me. "A white," I said.

Silence worse than screaming burst from the group; I could have strangled in that silence. "It is an ill time for omens of death," Breca said at last.

"The sacred steed of the Goddess?" I chided with dry mouth. "Of the one who mothers us all upon the bosom of this land?"

"Blood serves to quicken that bosom," Breca answered stonily. Bellory's face was as pale as if he were already a corpse. Loren lay back stunned.

"Think on it no more," I told them grimly. "The omen is mine, and to myself I keep it." I rose and departed from the light of the fire, and no one followed me. Aimlessly I wandered through the camp, keeping to the shadows, beckoned by no one. The night was cold, but I felt doubly chilled by the strange and sudden turning of my fate. I tried to argue it away; 'twas but mischance—white was the only color that the others had not named. And indeed it was dreaming of a white horse that was the surest omen of death. . . . Therefore I would not sleep, lest I dream.

Other men wrapped themselves in their cloaks and lay down restlessly, spears at the ready. The fires retreated into ashes and the shadows spread. Bitterly I thought then of home and my saucy sweetheart Mindy. I had been loath to leave her, but when the King called. . . . All depended on his courage and honor, our King. Seasons and rainfall and crops and all wellbeing of folk and realm rode on him, and he bore it splendidly. I loved to watch him ride at our fore, golden on a golden steed, crowned and braceleted and with his long braids free to the wind—he scorned a helm, he! I feared death in his service, but I had been named as one who keeps his pledge, and above all I would keep my faith with the sacred King.

So I did not intend to leave the camp. Certainly I did not mean to run away. But I scarcely knew any more where my weary feet were carrying me. Without trying to, I made my way between the dozing guards and trudged across the grassy countryside.

For a long space of blackness I wandered along, not caring when I fell over stones or ragged turf so long as I did not sleep. Ever so slowly at last the blackness turned to gray and I began to wonder where I was. The land had turned steep; trees clung to the sides of slopes that stooped to deep rocky clefts. The camp was nowhere in sight. I must have left it miles behind. Fool, fool, a triple fool I berated myself, for I was more likely now to be slain as a deserter than killed in battle—thus had I given myself over to the Goddess! But I spied a glint of water amidst the rocks of the nearest gorge. Groggily I reached the stream and was kneeling to souse my head when I saw a woman further up the bank. She was shadowed by the looming land, but already in this twilight before the dawn she was at her washing. There is one who labors late and long, I thought.

I went to ask her where I was, for I yet hoped to slip back to my camp. I came up behind her, and she did not hearken to the sound of my footsteps. Then I caught my breath and stood still as the stones; I could not have moved if the King himself had plucked my sleeve. For it was Bellory and Breca and Loren that she washed. Their faces were pale and peaceful, but red tinged the stream.

The woman turned to face me. There was nothing fearsome in her aspect; indeed she seemed mild as the lover who lays her love to rest, and very fair. Yet I trembled at the sight of her eyes. Green they were, as green as grass.

"You are welcome, Gage," she greeted me, "for you spoke me well last night."

"These—my friends," I whispered. "How can they be already gone?"

"Nay," she laughed, with a laugh that gave no comfort, "the battle is not yet. These are but semblances, these and many others, to set the reckoning straight. You see I care for them well—I will do yours now, if you like."

My blood ran cold. Desperately I turned the talk away from her latest words. "And you—are you also a semblance, and no Goddess?"

She laughed again, but more gently. She was amused at my challenge, I think. "My form is true," she told me, "as are all the forms I take. I am mother and maiden and ancient hag, ancient as these stones. I am hill and stream and the bride of the sacred King. I am swan-white steed and blood-red stag, and today I shall be the black battle-raven. Which do you prefer?"

"I like well the stag and the steed," I answered wistfully. "But I like best your present form, Blessed Maiden. You are as fair as high grassland in the sunlight. . . . Grant me a boon, Goddess, since I seem doomed to die. Lie with me, fearsome lady. . . ." I stood quaking at my own boldness, yet I had made the venture with all my heart, for I had not lied when I named her fair.

She regarded me gravely, but she did not seem affronted. "Gage, they call you," she remarked. "One who will keep a pledge. Make me a pledge, then."

"Name it." I was reckless with a strange recklessness made of lust and despair.

"That when you have done, you will abide by my judgment."

"Indeed, lady, all my life has been under your judgment."

She came to me then, straight and sober, like a warrior queen. With silent grace she lent herself to my pleasure. She was a virgin, but she made no moan. She had been a virgin, I thought, many and many a time, for many a King. . . . I grew weak and tearful with the marvel of her, for she was indeed fair beyond perfection. I rolled away from her and lay still, and she said not word.

"The judgment," I spoke at last, oddly without fear. I lay at ease in the soft green grass.

"It is what it has always been," she said quietly, "that you are finally at one with me, I who am earth. I mother you forth, and at last to me you have returned."

"Yet Kings can bed you and live," I argued, almost lazily.

"Ay. Only the sacred King can rightly wed me, for

in me he weds the land which is his domain. . . .
You are no King, Gage. Yet this will I say for your
bedding: it has won your King the victory this day.
Of all his force only those three yonder will die."

Bellory and Breca and Loren. They would owe
me small thanks for my friendship, I who liked to
think of horses.

The Goddess bent her gaze on me with a tiny
smile.

"Pleasant has been your returning, I trust?" she
chided gently. "But there is further judgment. Since
you have known no pain of returning, you who have
united with me in death, neither can you know for-
getfulness. My birds will not sing for you, Gage."

I sighed away my mortality then. Home and
homefolk and my sharp-tongued sweetheart Mindy
. . . not until then had I quite given up hope of
seeing them again. Yet I was not overly sad. The
spell of the Goddess lay strong on me, though I did
not understand all that she was saying.

"A strange fate is yours, Gage," she mused. "Ask
of me a gift to lighten it, if you will."

I had no time to think. I opened my mouth, and
the words came forth.

"Music," I said. "He who makes songs and poetry
cannot ever be entirely sad, I think. Or if he is, then
the sadness is sweet. So let me be a singer of sweet
songs."

"You have chosen wisely," she assented, and rising, she left me. Like morning mist she was gone,
and gone in like wise were the corpses in the stream.
As I blinked and looked, a black raven flapped away.

The sun had long since found its way into the cleft.
I did not feel its warmth, but nevertheless I made
my way up the slope and took shelter under a tree.
There I might see all that came to pass.

In a little while the men of Merric arrived to set an ambush. I did not move for them—could I lose my life more than once?—but they took no notice of me, walking past me as if I were not there. They settled themselves among the trees and were silent. By noontime I could see the heat shimmering off the rocks below. Then, in the distance, I saw the dust of a marching army. Closer they came, and closer, with our golden King at their fore. I could see the faces of my comrades, streaked with sweat. I started down the slope to warn them and to join them; how could I do otherwise? But not a man of them glanced at me. Already some laid spear and shield aside and knelt by the stream, dipping water with their helms. Then the ambush struck. I have never been loath to fight, but being helpless was more than I could bear. I turned away to my tree, lay beneath it and closed my senses to the tumult below.

When next I looked all lay dark and silent in the dark of the moon. Only stars shed faint light. I picked my way down the slope once more. Bodies lay strewn like the rocks, but I could not distinguish among them. I could not find my friends, to care for them. So I wandered away, restless and stumbling, wondering whether I might ever be at peace. But I had not gone far when a shape of whiteness approached me in the dark, chill night, a shimmering shape of wonder: the white horse.

Tall, high-crested, small-muzzled and sleek of flank it stood. The twin orbs of its eyes glowed like the absent moon. It came to me with silent, powerful steps and bowed with courtly grace for my mounting. I got on it gladly enough, and we were off with a flash of silver hooves—whether on land, sea or air even from the first I could not tell.

There is little to say of that journey. I was lost

from the start of it, and whether it was time we
traversed or eternity, a thin stream or a broad pool,
I could not say. I remember only darkness with
flecks of gold and the swimming of the steed, that
liquid flight. . . . At last we came to a place of
somethingness, and there we stopped.

It was a silvery, misty, twilight land, yet not dim.
Rather, it shone with its own muted splendor. Tall
trees spread dusky silver leaves that rustled like silk.
Between the trees meandered dark streams with
scarcely a ripple; the water shimmered almost black.
Half-moon bridges arched over the streams, and
beyond, soft lawns rose to a castle and many dwellings, hazy even at that slight distance. Gray stone
buildings they seemed to be, but changeless as
mountains.

As I gazed, still sitting on the moon-white steed,
an eerie music sounded from behind me, like tones
of living flutes. I turned and saw the shore of the
dark, glowing pool from which, I guessed, I had
come, for it spread to no other side. A high-prowed,
beech-gray boat sailed there, bearing many men. Beside it in stately procession swam many fair white
swans. It was they who sang. They glided up the
streams toward the distant castle, still singing. Their
song was subtle and drifting, but in no wise sad; all
hard and delicate truth was in it.

Then the folk disembarked from the boat, quietly,
with faces both intent and serene. In their midst I
saw Bellory and Breca and Loren. I sprang down
from the steed and hurried toward them.

"Friends," I told them mournfully, "I am sorry."

"Sorry?" Bellory turned on me wondering eyes.
"For what? This is a fair place."

"Ay, that it is. But earth was as fair, and I have
caused you the pain of parting from it."

"Earth? Parting?" Breca and Loren too were puzzled. "Of what is this you speak, friend? Have we lived and met before?"

I stared at them and spoke no more. "It is as I said, Gage," a quiet voice told me. "My birds will not sing for you." I turned to the swan-white steed and knew it for a form of the Goddess; even as I looked it melted away and a woman stood there. But she was not the maiden I had known.

"Hail, All-Mother," said Bellory and Breca and Loren in soft unison.

"My greeting to you," she answered courteously, and they passed on. But I stayed, gazing, for even in the vastness of her age she was lovely—lovely and chaste.

"You must make your own music of comfort," she told me. "Be my bard, Gage." She handed me a silver harp wrought in shapes of all the marvels of that silver land. I took it and touched it with clumsy fingers, and music rang forth—music of all mortal joy and longing, music in harmony of imperfection such as the swans did not possess. And somehow words came to me, and I sang for her.

Thus I stayed and sat in her great hall and performed from the place of honor after many a feast. The guests listened with a bittersweet pleasure they scarcely understood, for my songs were of remembrance rather than of forgetting. After a turning of time that could have been a day or an eon, Bellory and Breca and Loren were returned to the world of memory; and after a while I, like them, reluctantly had to go.

But the fair Maiden's gift has not failed me. And so it is that I am here, in this strange garb of female flesh and this thrice strange land and time, to tell you the tale: still singing of my brown-haired Mindy and my bold companions and the horses running upon the soft, far reaches of the grassland beyond the golden halls of the sacred King. For I was ever one who liked to think of horses.

> *O alien age, where are the very steeds,*
> *The jewel-bright, the lovely ones,*
> *The swift, impassioned carriers of the Kings?*
> *The honey wealds are gone, the feral land,*
> *And gone with it the windborn ones,*
> *The sky-bred steeds that still the wanderer sings.*

BRIGHT-EYED
BLACK PONY

Wystan saw them coming from afar.

Coming through the forest, the tall black horse running between the twisted trees, so black in the somber shadows, the rider like a burr entangled in its mane, clinging, curled small against the assaults of twigs and boughs. Presently, as they came to a clearing, the rider straightened. He was but a slim youngster straddling the great war-horse, a lad with golden hair that flowed down around his shoulders and a long red cloak that reached nearly to his booted feet. Wearily he braced himself by his hands against the arch of the steed's neck as the horse plunged to a shying halt. Before him lay nothing but water, the wizard's lake, a seemingly endless expanse dimming into dusk and nothingness within a few furlongs.

"Forward," the youngster ordered.

The horse danced backward, threatening to rear. Swaying behind the steed's withers, the rider kicked and shouted, raising a willow whip. Mastered, the black leaped forward, splashed through shallows and swam with rolling eyes and vast nostrils toward an unnatural gloom. Dark mist or midday dusk—once in it, the horse could see nothing; rider, nothing. Nothing.

The steed's breath comes roaring in its chest; how long can it last? Why do I care, I, the recluse?

Blaze of bright sunshine and wooded shore. The horse scrambled out of the water and stood, trembling and breathing in great heaves, on the island.

A different sort of place, this of my making, I am a fool to let him set foot on it. But he would have drowned. . . . Such a slip of a lad to come here so boldly on the great horse.

The youngster was staring as the horse caught its breath. Blue trees, slender, graceful as dancers, upreaching, with smooth skin of pearl blue and leaves blue as lapis. Presently he sent his winded steed through them at the slow walk, gazing as if half-frightened. Fear that no longer pursued him, sending him fleeing, but confronted him, slowing his headlong course . . . Forest ended at a sunny tilled clearing.

"Ho," the lad murmured, and the horse stopped willingly.

Amber meadowland, chickens, sheep. A wisp of a rill leading up to a spring. A crazy sod cottage all in turrets and oriels, shapes no sod should take. An ordinary garden: rye, beans, cabbages. . . . A man, his strong, bare back turned to the sun, working the earth amidst the plants.

Swallowing, licking his dry lips, the youngster sent the horse forward, and the man straightened and watched intently as the rider approached. Meadow, rill, edge of the garden. The boy slipped down off his big black and covered it with his cloak before he spoke.

"I have come to see the sorcerer," he said, his voice tight, but level.

"And who might you be who come to see Wystan?" the laborer asked.

"I'll tell that to Wystan alone," the lad replied, tone hardening into sharp edge. He glanced angrily at his questioner, but the glance stayed and became a stare. The man stood lean, sturdily muscled, his mouth a flat line across the dun mask of his face. And his eyes, beneath brows as flat as his mouth, eyes like polished stone, unreadable.

"I see," the youngster said, his voice still tight and steady. "You are Wystan himself. I beg pardon, but I did not expect to find you planting spinach."

"Parsley," the sorcerer corrected him, unsmiling. He held up a pinch of the fine seed. "And there is more magic in this than in all my spells."

The boy stood at a loss for a reply. "As for my name," he said after a pause, reverting to the former matter, "it is Merric, son of Emaris, prince in Yondria. My father was the ruler until lately. My uncle killed him and killed my older brothers, and now he sits on my father's throne and keeps my mother his prisoner." The lad spoke collectedly, almost coldly.

"Assuming that this is true," said the sorcerer harshly, "what do you want of me? I take no part in the quarrels of princes." Wystan gave the youngster a piercing glance. Merric met his sharp stare unmoved.

Some sort of bitter strength in him. Not grief, perhaps, but certainly desperation.

"I want refuge, nothing more." Merric's shoulders straightened beneath his fine tunic of silk. "No one comes here. They are afraid."

"And you are not afraid?" Wystan asked with a hint of threat.

"Yes. Somewhat." Merric looked straight into the stonelike eyes.

There it is, that odd strength still! Yet the lad is lying; I feel sure of it.

"But I deemed a man of wisdom would feel no need to harm a child."

Wystan's face moved; his mouth twisted ironically. "A child, is it, now, when it suits you? You who make shift to ride the steed of a man, a warrior? Go away."

Merric stood where he was. "This is the horse my father has given me," he said hotly, "and not of my asking."

"So you are a child, then. Am I your nursemaid? I welcome no strangers here." *I dare not.* "Folk do well to fear me. Go."

"You cannot send me away!" the boy blazed. "You are—you are curious about me."

Now how in all the seven kingdoms did he know that? Is the youngster wizard get?

Man and Merric stood glaring at each other. Insects ticked away the moments amidst the grass.

"Very well," said Wystan at last. "Stay, then. But that great horse must go. This is only an island; there is not sufficient pasturage for him here."

Merric stiffened, turning his head to look at the black steed which stood sweating and puffing with its head drooping to its knees.

I could provide such pasturage, but I will not. This is a small test for you, my bold one.

"The beast is far too big for you, anyway," the sorcerer added scornfully. "It is as ridiculous to see a child on such a destrier as it is to see a big man on a pony."

"True enough. I had to climb the stall side-bars to

get onto him." Merric looked stricken. "But he carried me here bravely."

"Take him down to the shore," said Wystan indif-
ferently, "and let him swim back."

"But no, I cannot do that! He is stable bred; he
would come to harm on his own. I will . . ." Merric
swallowed, and his thin shoulders sagged. "I will
take him back."

*True for you, lad. Though now I am certain you
lie. Back to what?*

Defeated, the boy turned numbly, feet scraping,
gathering up the reins.

"Gently, Prince, gently." Wystan took a step closer
to Merric and the tall steed. "If it is verily the horse
you feel for, and not your own pride in his size and
beauty . . ."

"I am no longer a prince," said Merric, "and there
is some pride in me, yes, but more chiefly a wish to
do no harm."

That is interesting. Harm whom?

The lad was watching the wizard.

"Then see here," Wystan said, and fixing his
inscrutable eyes on something in the distance, he
laid a hand on the horse's lowered forehead. As
Merric watched, the great black steed shuddered,
shrank, and changed somewhat in shape, until all in
the moment it was a bright-eyed, shaggy black pony.
It lifted its head and glanced about curiously. The
red cloak dragged by small ebony hooves.

"Bigness is a great burden," said Wystan, "for man
and beast alike." His voice was gentler than before,
and something had changed in his face, his eyes.

"Many thanks." Merric's voice shook, he was surprised by childish tears. Blinking to hide them, he
turned away, patted the pony, bent to retrieve his

cloak. But Wystan frowned, for the boy had staggered as he moved.

"When have you last eaten, Merric?" he inquired sharply.

"Some few days ago. I was in haste."

"And would it have been above you to beg a bite from some peasant, or from me? Come on!" Wystan took the boy by his arm.

"I—must see to the black—"

"The beast is fine; look!" The sorcerer was shouting in exasperation. "His weariness is gone with his bulk. Come on!" He tugged the lad into his cottage, plainly furious.

Hours later Merric was fed, more or less washed, and bedded down in a pile of straw. Wystan sat close to the hearth fire, reading by its ruddy light, and Merric watched him sleepily.

"Your face is completely changed," he said when the sorcerer had closed the book.

For a moment Wystan went rigid; then he sighed, softened, and nodded. His eyes were glimmering, deep as the lake on which his island floated, and his lips moved in curves as subtle as its shores.

"I wore a mask earlier, as we all do from time to time." Wystan glanced at the boy. "As you still do. Have you not wept for your father and your brothers?"

"There was no time!" Merric snapped, all his sleepiness gone. "I had to ride or die!"

"But now there is time."

Merric did not answer. He stirred uneasily.

"I cannot see them in your eyes, your father and your brothers, your mother and uncle," the sorcerer said. "Tell me about them. Their names?"

"Some other time," Merric muttered. He turned his face away, pretending to sleep, and Wystan smiled.

He will stay here until he has ceased to hide.

The next day Merric rested, for the most part. The cottage seemed larger than it looked, all in towers and alcoves; he explored it. But a day later he went to look for his host. He took the black pony and hauled water from the spring to the garden, for the season was dry. Wystan had set up a big loom in the sunshine and was weaving a blanket out of wool. Though the cloth was coarse, it was long, tedious work. The sorcerer sat patiently on a tall stool, sending the shuttle back and forth.

"That is woman's work," Merric told him peevishly.

"Very well," Wystan remarked and instantly changed into a muttering crone who puttered about with the warp and weft. Merric stepped back, startled and frightened.

"Which one is you?" he cried.

"Which one is you?" the crone cackled back. "Which is you, the prince or the water-bearer?" Merric fled, and she laughed heartily as he trudged up the dusty hill to the spring.

Time after time, that day and the next, he led the pony down with clay pitchers full of water and poured them in futile-looking patches on the arid earth. The third day he did the same. But when the sun was high, Wystan spoke to him, and he changed his pitchers for baskets and led the pony toward the forest to gather fuel. His legs ached with walking; the way seemed long. The pony plodded and nipped at weeds, as a pony will.

"Come on, damn you!" Merric shouted, for perhaps the dozenth time that day, tugging hard at the strap. This time, being out of sight of the cottage, he lashed the little beast on the belly with the whiplike leather end. The pony gave a frightened leap, show-

161

ing the whites of its eyes, and Merric turned away
from it to lash fervidly at the trees. In a moment his
shoulders slumped, his hands went slack. Frightened
yet further by this odd and perverse flogging, the
pony lunged away from him, snatching the lead from
his loosened hands, and it galloped back toward the
cottage, its hooves making a sound as of stamping
rabbits.

There was still the wood to be gotten in. Hardening his face, Merric followed the black pony.

It had taken refuge with Wystan and was grazing
placidly beside his loom when Merric plodded into
view. He went to the pony softly and picked up the
trailing lead strap. Wystan seemed to take no notice.
Merric turned—

"Do not go," said Wystan tonelessly from behind
the loom, "if you are going to beat the little black. I
can fetch wood myself."

"I do not mean to," Merric said in a muffled voice,
but even as he spoke his arms stiffened, his hands
clenched into fists. He flung away the lead line, let
himself drop to the hard, dry earth, pummeled it.

"Damn the beast," he cried, "it was the power and
beauty of it that I loved, to my shame. Now that it is
a drudge, like me . . ." His tears sprinkled the sere
earth.

"Now I know for certain," said Wystan coldly,
"that you are, as you said, a child."

"Damn you too!" Merric shouted at him.

*So who is the child here? For all his spleen, I think
he is not one to hide himself for long on a mystic isle.*

Merric was struggling up, tears spent, turning away,
bound away somewhere, anywhere. Wystan got up
from his loom and went to stand beside him, stop-
ping him with a touch.

"We are all children," he said far more softly. "And the most part of grief is rage. So weep for your dead."

Merric faced him, unable to hide from his eyes, unable to do otherwise than face the one he had just cursed. "I lied," he told him, hot fury shaking the words. "My father and brothers are not dead. I wish they were! I hate them!"

Wystan nodded, odd glinting lights swimming into his gaze. "Yes . . . and the most part of your rage is grief."

"I hate them, I could kill them, I fled from my own hatred!" Merric shouted, tears starting again. "By my soul, Wizard, what manner of monster am I?"

Wystan snorted. "You'll have to study long to be a monster."

"But . . ."

" 'Twas not I who stayed your hand from flogging yon pony. I or anyone else. You did it yourself."

"But . . ."

"But nothing!" Wystan roared. *Furious. Furious at him for making me feel.* "It is past noon; would you fetch the wood? There is no fuel for a cooking fire, and I am hungry."

"I—am sorry—"

"Stop whimpering." Wystan glowered darkly. "You are worthy of whatever friendship you can wring from me, and not because you are a prince, either. Because you are here; no better reason. Go fetch wood."

Merric went, afoot and with the baskets over his arms, leaving the pony to graze.

The cottage stood silent that evening, and Merric went early to his bed. Much later, after Wystan was asleep, the prince got up and quietly went out. Wystan was awake instantly upon the soft closing of the door, following Merric anxiously with his mind's eye.

I—had not thought he was of the sort to run away. Not more than once—

Then the sorcerer sighed and smiled, a genuine, warm smile with no one to see it. The prince had gone to the moonlit meadow, searching for a certain dark and shaggy form, and when he had found it, an ungainly, soot-colored lump dozing on the ground, he had curled up beside the warm, furry flank of the black pony. Wystan watched him for a long time as he slept with his face half-buried in the coarse mane.

Merric came in groggily for breakfast the next morning. "You smell of horse," Wystan told him.

Merric said nothing, only made a small face at him over the food.

"I can see them in your eyes now," Wystan remarked after the eggs were gone. "Your father, your brothers. I do not think they intended to be cruel to you."

"Perhaps not." Merric sighed, pushing his plate away. "Perhaps it is just that—they are interested only in power and the usages of power, indifferent to everything else."

"And they assume that your interests are the same."

"I must wear a royal cloak, ride a tall horse—" Merric stopped himself, recalling how he had missed that horse. "I am not so much unlike them," he admitted. "But—they are indifferent to the other things in me, things they do not care to see—"

"Poetry," said Wystan.

And magic too, I think. Though I will not say so at this time.

"I suppose," said Merric in some small surprise.

164

He gave the sorcerer a searching glance. "How did you know?"

"I merely surmised," Wystan hedged, and the boy did not persist, for another thought shadowed his face.

"I daresay I should go back." Reluctance dragged at the words. "They will be looking for me, and they will be angry."

"I think not angry," said the sorcerer, for he knew family. But he had been doing some questing, three days past, and he had seen no sign of searchers in the forest beyond the lake or the meadows beyond the forest, the villages, the strongholds, no one looking for the golden-haired prince. Odd. Sufficiently odd to make him uneasy.

"Stay a few days yet," he told Merric. "If anger there is, it will have passed into fear by then, and they will welcome you home the more ardently."

"I am willing enough to stay," said Merric.

Rain had come to water the garden. They spent the day in the cottage, animals and all. Merric brushed the cockleburrs from the black pony's mane, then turned to Wystan for amusement. Presently the sorcerer found himself showing the boy his books, talking of his craft, telling tales, describing wonders, talking as he had not talked to another mortal in perhaps a decade. They did some small magics at the table, laughing, making a marvelous game of it. Supper was late. Rain darkened into dusk and wind and thunder, fearsome, but the cottage felt snug. Merric slept peacefully on his bed of straw, and that night Wystan slumbered soundly.

Thus it was that he did not sense the stranger's coming.

The man pounded at the door in the darkest of the

dark hours before dawn, and Wystan stood rigid, shocked stark awake in consternation. No one had ever come upon him so unawares, not since he had withdrawn to his magical island. No one.

I have let down my defenses, somehow—

Merric merely stirred drowsily on his pallet of straw.

"For the love of mercy!" the man cried in the night, and Wystan stirred up the fire for light, then moved stiffly to the door, his face a mask. The stranger stumbled in, soaking, out of the downpour.

"Sorcerer," he appealed, "I am the most miserable of mortals."

A stocky man, one who was losing the battle with age. Face pulled downward now in long, haggard collops of flesh that looked gray even in the firelight. Wystan let his mask slip for a moment in his astonishment, for this was the man he had seen in Merric—though the fellow's look then had been one of authority.

"I am King Emaris of Yondria." Just a hint, a flash, of the authoritarian in those words, at once gone. "Or, until four days past I was. . . . My sons have turned against me. My sons, my very own blood and get, have turned on me to strike me down." The king spoke in a torrent, tempestuously, glaring all the while intensely at the sorcerer, scarcely noticing the youthful servant or apprentice who stood in the shadows beyond the hearth. "My eldest, Morveran, and the next younger, Emerchion, they who were supposed to be the comfort of my old age, though as of yet scarcely past their passage—they have plotted together and seized my crown and throne. Only by grace of my wits have I escaped with my life. And the youngest, Merric, has gone into hiding some-

where, in league with them to get himself out of the
way of their scheme—"

"I have not!"

Merric strode forward to confront his father.

No loving reunion, this.

The prince was full of shock and wrath. "I would
never—I have been here all along. I abhor—if you
knew how I despise all such schemes of power—"

But Emaris did not answer the anger, for all his
passions were lost in astonishment. "Merric!" he whispered. "But—when did you come here? And *how*
did you come here?"

"Five days ago. Or six . . ." The youngster stood
more quietly before his father. "The black swam me
across."

"But—that crossing—" The king shook his head
dazedly. "It is fearsome. The haze, the gloom, unnatural. Only my desperation gave me courage to try
it. And my despair gave me no choice. . . . And my
dapple-gray carried me through the darkened day
and into the tempest of the night, until finally it
foundered and sank, and I swam on alone. And only
at the limit beyond limits of my strength did I make
the shore. So how could you, a youngling . . . ?"

"I am no stranger to despair," said Merric very
quietly. But he had never known such despair in his
father. King and youngest son stood gazing at each
other as if they had never seen each other before,
and watching, Wystan forgot to harden his face.

*I—have let myself be drawn nearer to that peo-
pled shore. My island floats closer to it, even as I
sleep. Else he would never have attained it . . .*

"My mother?" Merric asked at last.

"She is in safety on your uncle's estate. In hiding.
There is a small cottage in the wood. . . ." Emaris

167

let his words trail away, thinking. But it was the boy who voiced his thought.

"My brothers are not evil youths. They would not have harmed you or my mother, I think. They let you escape."

"Yes. However roughly."

"They are impatient. They think too much of power."

"I have taught them all too much of the usages of power," said Emaris, and for the first time he looked kingly, speaking his regret. He straightened himself, and the haggard look left his face. Wystan stirred uneasily.

"King," he addressed him, not calling him liege, for he gave allegiance to no monarch, "King, what is it that you want of me?"

"Hope."

Food and a warm fire, dry clothing and sleep half answered that, and the wizard bestowed them. Emaris slept past noon of the next day. But Merric was wakeful and troubled, and wandered the woods with the black pony as Wystan sat at his loom.

"What ails you?" the sorcerer asked him curtly as he sat by his father at the evening meal of bread and cold mutton.

Merric did not hesitate, though he had to swallow twice before he spoke. "I feel that what has happened is somehow my fault," he said softly, and Wystan snorted.

"How so?" he demanded. Emaris listened intently.

"My—spleen, my hatred—"

"That is a child's talk. Feelings don't count. Deeds do."

Child's talk, is it? Feelings have made me flinty. Feeling breached, invaded. How long has it been—?

"But," Merric said, words rising on a wind of

168

desperation, "I—thought of something like this, or imagined it, blood shed for the sake of power and the throne. I—and I did not face it, it frightened me. I fled from it."

"So that is what sent you here," said Emaris, wonder in the words.

"I—should have stayed. Perhaps—they would have been ashamed, in front of me."

"It was a cruel time, lad," said his father with fervor. "Far too fearsome for a youngster. You were well out of it."

"And speak no more of fault," Wystan told Merric sternly. "Of foresight, perhaps, but not of fault. The Sight, misunderstood."

Emaris turned to him. "You mean—the boy has—"

"The Sight, and perhaps some powers. Yes. I think so."

"Well." The former king stared at his son. "He was always—different. And I, like a fool, I combatted it."

"If his powers can now be nurtured, he might yet mean your hope."

"We can go to the cottage, join your mother, bide our time." Emaris leaned toward his son. "And when you are ready—the throne. Perhaps not for me. Perhaps for you."

Merric stood up, shaking, his face taut with anger no longer hidden. "I detest such schemes of power," he said in a voice potent with fury. "I will have no part of plots of power, now or ever, power of magic, power of the sword; I do not want them. Nor do I want the throne."

"You've small choice, my son." Emaris stood up as well, but not to intimidate, nor to plead, only, for once, to speak truth. "Your brothers will quarrel—

see if your Sight does not tell you the same. There will be turmoil, black times for courtiers and common folk alike. The throne wll tremble. Invaders will come, they who always lie in wait. Yondria will fall—unless the rightful king can save her."

Merric turned and ran outside, into the gathering dusk, fleeing over the meadow to take refuge with the black pony.

"Where has he gone?" Emaris exclaimed.

"Never mind." Wystan stood, keen-eyed, nodding to himself. "He will be back soon enough. He is not one to hide for long."

Unlike one whom I know. It was not the father so much, the mother—though they did not understand me, they tried to love me, but I would not let them, and I scarcely understand myself, I, the great sorcerer. And it was not the comrades who had their own concerns, or the sweethearts, the ones who spurned my timid courtship, or even that one special beloved, she who loved another. So I swore never to let myself be hurt again. But it was all these things—and no one of them nearly as bad as what has happened to this man, this boy. And they will soon find their way back to the fray.

In the morning the boy was at the door with the pony. The little black had been brushed until its shaggy fur shone; its full mane had been brushed and combed into a silken fall, its ebony hooves polished with oil.

"Is that—your charger?" Emaris let his jaw drop in astonishment.

"I like him like this." Merric hugged the black pony around the neck; its head stood no higher than his. "But if he is to carry my father and me homeward," the boy added with a reluctant glance at Wystan, "I suppose he will need to be tall again."

"Stand back," said Wystan. He came forward, caressed the pony under its chin, and it shot up again into a war-horse of eighteen hands' height, powerful and graceful.

"Well." Emaris swallowed. "We must both thank you, Sir Sorcerer."

Wystan said nothing, only brought a packet of food and a blanket, new woven. He glanced at Merric, gave a small, wry smile. There was that between the two of them that went deeper than words, than thanks. The wizard stood by silently as the boy bridled the giant black.

There were no surprises for me, anymore, until these two came.

"You take the reins," Emaris told his son. "He is accustomed to you." The man mounted, helped the boy up before him.

"Come back, someday, and be my apprentice," Wystan said to Merric. "I will send the island to meet you sooner next time."

"You . . ." Merric gaped at him. "You did that?"

"Even as I send it closer to the shore now, for your sake."

"Come with us, rather," Emaris offered, "and be his tutor." But Wystan shook his head.

To leave my longtime refuge? Unthinkable . . .

It was an awkward parting. Father and son rode away, hands half-raised, hesitant, in farewell, and the wizard stood darkly, wrapped in himself. His hands did not move out of the folds of his tunic. Before the black horse had traversed the meadow, the boy chirruped, and it broke into a canter, then passed out of Wystan's eyesight, into the lapis forest.

Nor did he watch it any longer with his inner eye.

Mount, man, and boy found the island shore. Beyond the quiet water of the lake, the mainland showed plainly in the distance, unobscured by any hint of mist or haze. Sunlight rested on the green hilltops.

"Forward," Merric ordered.

The black steed leaped into the water, swam strongly. The mainland soon grew nearer, but the shore just departed seemed to fall no farther behind. Merric glanced back at it, puzzled, and then Emaris. It took the two of them several moments to comprehend.

"By my body," the former king exclaimed at last, "it's following us!"

Black hooves caught on gravel bottom. The horse carried them onto the shore of their homeland. Once on grass, Merric pulled his destrier to a halt, turned. Father and son watched as if spellbound while the island glided up to the main as gracefully as a tall-masted sailing ship coming to port. It joined almost seamlessly to the shore.

Wordlessly they got down off their horse and waited. In a few moments Wystan appeared from between the blue trees, walking fast, with a neatly wrapped bundle on his back and a staff in his hand. He stepped to the mainland. But the feel of that unmagical earth seemed to stagger him for a moment, and Merric and Emaris went quickly to his side. Wystan let his hand rest on the shoulder of the boy.

And as they watched, the island sailed away, into the distances of the nameless lake, into a bright sunlit haze, into oblivion.

I—swam out there, years ago, thinking to drown. The island formed itself out of my dreams as I went under. . . . I climbed back to life by clinging to the roots of it. Now it is gone.

Not even the great black steed could carry three.

"Well," said Emaris gruffly, "let us all walk together, then, and the horse can bear the packs."

"A pack animal," Wystan stated, "ought to be of a more manageable size. Do you not think so?"

Emaris merely smiled, but Merric nodded eagerly, his eyes shining.

Then Wystan turned to the mighty war-horse. It put its head down to greet him, and he laid one hand on the glossy mane between the ears. The steed whinnied gladly, gathering, shifting shape beneath his touch. When he took his hand away, standing on the shore was a small, bright-eyed black pony.

COME IN

Come in, Reality, come in.
Bloodied body on my doorstep,
Crawl across my good clean floor,
Clutch at my ankles,
     Pull me down,
     You corpse,
Long-nosed, barbaric, fetid
—Don't care what you did—
Come in. The fire is in my groin,
     My gut.
I'll put you in my pot
And melt you into wine and tears
     And incense.

THE PRINCE
OUT OF THE PAST

Kam Horseleech awoke with a start, not knowing for a moment where he was. That always happened to him at Ithkar Fair, starry sky overhead instead of the familiar thatch, no warm form of wife. Usually the drunken cries of ill-assorted fairgoers served to alert him, but there was no noise, it must have been that most hushed time of night a few hours before dawn. What had roused him?

Still groggy, he sat up and glanced around. Moonbeams, shadow and soft light, tents and wagons. Smells and sounds—quiet stirrings of all sorts of animals, someone's nag stamping, lop-eared rabbits rustling in their cage and a cheetah in one farther away—nothing untoward. Kam yawned, his mind moving hazily. Sleep after a trying day, that nomad's mare foaling breech and the cut on that supercilious noble's prize ambler, the man peering over his shoulder as he worked. No matter. Go back to sleep.

Yet he had felt a summons, firm as the grip of a hand on his upper arm. But no one stood near.

Well, it would do no harm just to have a look about. . . .

Kam got up, stumbling slightly over his own sizable feet. Automatically he ran a hand over his shock of hair and through his rough beard, picking out bits of straw. A big hand, not at all clever by the looks of it, but good with horses. . . . He stumped off at random, trying to be wary. It went against his nature to be suspicious, but this was the most disreputable sector of the fair, as he had been warned many times by both friends and experience. All those who stank, whether animal or human, were pushed outward from the sweet-smelling temple center of the fair to lodge here at the fringes. So if he did not want to be knocked on the head by bravos or to step on a snake-charmer, he had to be careful. What lay in shadow of tents and trees . . . and that moon-glade, now, just ahead. It would not do to step out in it without having a bit of a look around. . . .

He stepped out in it nevertheless, for he was one who liked the light, and a most unaccountable feeling took hold of him.

Now what was that grip, gentle, invisible hands of—moonlight?—on his bony wrists, tugging at him, on his shoulders that were round and stooped from toil, guiding him? Not even crying out—but with bushy eyebrows arched high in astonishment—Kam found himself threading his way quite surely through a haphazard maze of sleeping bodies, past the offal of distant food booths to a region that smelled strongly of manure—

Until he came to a stop, and all the stench and squalor around him seemed distant and unreal, for he saw only those who stood in the moonlight before him.

Being what he was, he noticed the horse first. It

stood very still, white flanks mottled gray by leaf-shadow in moonlight, shimmering, almost spiritous, but so big, a destrier without peer, massive neck highly arched and the small ears almost hidden in mane, noble nostrils, dark eyes, ripple of muscles in great shoulder—and standing with one hand resting lightly on the great shining curve of barrel, the master—

Kam turned his eyes slightly to see who it was who owned such a steed. Another mincing noble, he judged it would be. But no—this man looked to be neither perfumed noble nor worldly priest nor commoner nor nomad nor soldier nor merchant nor any other sort of man that Kam could put a name to, nor even one of those nameless overseas barbarians. He was—what was he, in the moonlight? He met Kam's stare quite equably.

"Goodman horseleech," he said, "thank you for coming."

Young, he was very young, and handsome—and yet the curls of his fair young head shone pure white. And something in his voice was not young at all—there were ages of quiet in that level voice. A glint of sheen about him—crown, or helm, or sparkle of armband, or brooch at the cloaked shoulder? Kam was never to remember clearly, for he was caught in a trance of strangeness and shifting moonlight. And that face dimly lit and the eyes deep pools of shadow—he was perhaps not of unusual height, perhaps of a height with Kam if Kam had straightened fully, but he seemed tall, even when he bent to run his hand down the horse's sleek side.

"It is the hock, here," he said.

Kam noted the swelling, moved closer numbly to explore it with large, deft and gentle fingers, noting in the same trancelike fashion that the steed bore not a thread of harness. "Spavin," Kam said, his voice coming out curiously rusty.

"I know. That last battle, too much, the terrible weight—he has been lame for a long time, and has worn the hoof all uneven with it. What can you do for him, goodman Kam?"

He hated to answer truly. He swallowed first. "Very little," he said finally. "If I could have treated it sooner, just after it happened—"

"I know. I lay abed, a spear-tip buried in my thigh, and by the time I— Well . . ." The stranger paused, glancing, if Kam could judge, obliquely upward, toward where the moon hovered, gathering thoughts. "The talk of Ithkar Fair is that you are the best healer of horses south of the mountains," he went on at last. "Surely there is something you can do."

There were remedies. Kam had tried them at various times, reluctantly. "Some men burn the spavin with white-hot iron to draw the devil out," he said, his voice as quiet and even as that of the one he faced. "Others pierce it with tapestry needles or slender knives."

"And you say?"

Kam tried not to scowl. "I say let ill enough alone. Pain and disfigurement—"

"And small enough result. Yes." The stranger turned slightly, his hand still on the great steed's back. "Have you no magic, goodman Kam?"

A chill that was not the night breeze touched Kam—fear, but not of the stranger. It was the well-inbred fear of one well mannered who has always obeyed the law. "You know the priests guard magic quite jealously," he said too hastily, too anxious to tell the other that which should not need saying.

"Magic is forbidden in Ithkar except when judged harmless or a minor part of a man's stock in trade."

"Well, then say that I forced you to do my will." There was not the slightest hint of threat in the youth's voice—only eagerness. "With this," he added, and from a scabbard under his cloak he drew forth a long, slender sword that shone like new silver in the moonlight.

A sword!

Kam gaped, knowing now quite certainly what he had managed not to know before: that this man, this horse, were not of earthly sort. The fair-wards let no weapons into Ithkar Fair, whether lance or dirk, whether on noble, cleric, or commoner. None. Years had taught him that the rule was as dependable as the sunrise. And here stood one with a shining sword in hand—he could not, then, be one who had entered this place by any earthly gate.

"Who are you?" Kam whispered.

The other seemed suddenly abashed and sheathed his sword. "Does it matter?" he asked.

"To be sure, it does!" Kam exclaimed, though he could not have told why. "Who—*what* are you?"

"The prince out of the past."

Names of dead heroes, champions of the Three Lordly Ones in the noble times long past, filled Kam's mind in disorder, like half-remembered music. "Who—which one?"

"All."

Kam stared, beyond his depth, uncertain whether to kneel, pledge fealty, kiss the moonlike glint of a ring. But he was a plain man, he could do none of those things. Only one thing could he do for this prince, and silently he turned to the horse to attempt it.

"Even the spirits are drawn to Ithkar Fair," the

champion said, all in a soft rush, as if he had at last
found someone he could talk to. "This fair draws all
to it, best and worst. . . . We walked here side by
side all the long way, the steed and I. He is limping
worse than ever now. I wish I could have carried
him, for he carried me many a sore time."

Kam had placed one hand on the horse's flank and
the other on the hot and tender hock, and he stood
puzzled and distraught. "Lord," he said, "I cannot
feel him."

The youth smiled quizzically. "He's solid enough."

"Yes, but I mean—I cannot feel his being, his
. . . ." Kam did not know the word for "essence," but
he knew horses, their shying, their slobber, their
passions—for grass and home and each other, their
oblique thoughts, their fears—his body bore the half-
circle moonlike marks of their hooves. And he knew
that what stood so tamely under his hand was not
horse as he understood it.

"What is he?" Kam asked.

"All." Now it was the prince who fumbled with
words. "The . . . greatness, the majesty of . . . all
such horses, as I am . . . of men."

Kam closed his eyes, tried to remember the tales
he had heard as a boy, tales of a golden time of high
court and high courage, long ago when the Three
ruled. . . . None of them came clear, but a sort of
vision drifted to mind of the steed that bore the
champion joyously across the countryside, that lent
its weight to the blow of his lance, that took him
curvetting out of the hands of the enemy—under his
touch the great kingly destrier stirred, lifted his lovely
head, and softly whinnied.

"Yes!" It was the prince, an excited whisper.

Kam placed both hands on the hock, embracing
the injured part with their warmth, and let the magic

come. "Lordly Ones," he whispered, "Lordly Ones on your seven pillars of cloud white as pearl, white as moonlight, white as white gold, help me. . . ."

It shot through him with javelin force. He heard and felt that the charger reared up with a great neigh, and he felt the prince catch him as he fell backward, strong arms and warm, but he could see nothing, and in a moment he knew nothing more.

He awoke some hours later to bright sunlight and the unwelcome sight of a fair-ward standing over him, scowling under the shadow of his brass helmet.

"Up, horseleech, and come with me," the fair-ward ordered.

Kam did not get up. He felt far too weak. Instead, he looked around him. He lay on a pile of straw in an unfamiliar place—where were his blankets? A half-grown urchin stood nearby, and a nice-looking shaggy gray pony with thick mane on a well-arched neck. Dapple gray—or was the gray mostly dirt?

"Caught red-handed," the fair-ward grumbled, prodding him with his bronze-shod quarterstaff.

Kam struggled to a sitting position. "What is the charge?" he asked.

"Magic! When I came by here yesterday that pony was spavined so bad ye could see it with no eyes. Today it's sound. Get up."

The news rather than the order brought Kam scrambling to his feet. The urchin faced him at the pony's side, unsmiling. A curly-headed, freckle-faced lad, his hair sun-bleached nearly as white as tow, he stood no higher than Kam's chest. But his eyes, startlingly dark, looked merry and wise and very old. Stuck in his belt he wore a long stick.

"Come along," the fair-ward said, and Kam went without a word.

The priest who heard the case was young, golden-robed, newly shaven of head, and newly cynical since having become privy to the inner workings of the temple. He regarded Kam impatiently.

"Have you any defense?"

Penalties for the use of magic were severe. Kam could be declared outlaw, lose his home and possessions and his rights as a freeman. Most practitioners resolved this matter with a simple bribe, for the priests were mercenary. Kam had no bribe and no defense except the truth.

"The champion. . . ." No, it would not be truth to say that the prince had made him do it. The healing had been Kam's gift of the heart. "The Lordly Ones empowered me to help the horse."

"Pony," the fair-ward corrected.

The priest sighed hugely. Ai, the credulousness of these peasants! Would they never learn anything other than their literal-minded, superstitious beliefs? Still, the man was evidently not a shyster or a sneaking wizard. Even the fair-ward admitted that Kam had a reputation for honesty.

"If I let off everyone who spoke of the Three," the priest said rather sharply, "the fair would be topheavy with trickery, shoddy wares sold under a veil of glamour."

Kam glanced up from where he had been studying his large toes. "Well, if it is trickery to heal a suffering beast," he said just as sharply, "then I stand guilty."

"There is a need for codification of these matters of healing," the priest grumbled, more to himself than to Kam. The problem was irksome, and he had not had his morning pastry. He decided to delay judgment.

"We'll see if you have anything more to say after a night down below," he told Kam, and waved a slender hand in dismissal."

"Down below" turned out to be a cell with chains and shackles and nothing to eat. Kam sat there disconsolately through the day and into the night. But when moonlight began to make its way through the single high window, Kam felt misery leave him, to be replaced by a quite unreasonable hope. He watched as, the moon traveling toward its setting, pale shafts of light inched nearer and nearer to him. At last, just as he had known they must, they touched the shackles on his wrists—

And the chains fell apart with a faint silvery clink, and invisible hands helped Kam to his feet. Utterly astonished in spite of his hope—for it is one thing to expect the impossible, and another thing to see it happen—Kam let himself be led through a moonstruck and unlocked door and a maze of temple catacombs to a seldom used entry, which opened dustily before him. Moonlight fell on cobbles outside, and the prince out of the past and the steed of all steeds awaited him as before.

"Why do you not ride?" Kam asked anxiously. "Is the horse not well?"

"Well and whole. You ride. You must be weak. Have they beaten you?"

"No." Kam was touched but not surprised by the concern in the champion's voice. "Thank you, my lord, but I need not ride. I cannot, anyway. I—I have never sat a horse."

"Never, and you all your life a horseleech?" The marvel of that smile in the moonlight. "Well, I am blithe indeed that you are not outlawed or hurt. Let us walk together, if you will not ride."

They set off companionably toward the outer sector of the fair enclave, where drunkards brawled and peacocks shrieked and jugglers and horses were lodged, horses for sale, trained performing horses, pack horses and saddle horses, Kam's love and livelihood. As they walked the most wondrous horse he had ever seen walked freely beside him, its hooves chiming against the cobbles, with not a trace of a limp.

But the prince limped. Of course, the wound in the thigh. "Are there no leeches for you at Ithkar Fair?" Kam asked.

"Not such a healer as you, goodman." The prince smiled again. "Never mind. The steed will carry me."

He made ready to ride when they reached Kam's small campsite. He needed the height of a wagon-bed to help him vault to the horse's back. Before he climbed up, Kam took courage to ask him something ignoble.

"Lord—will there be a fair-ward awaiting me with the dawn?"

The prince genuinely laughed, a ringing, lovely sound. "Nay, I think not," he declared when he was done. "The priest has had a difficult night, and some of his notions have been shaken. He is not a bad sort, you know, really."

"Or he would not have given me a second thought."

"Yes. I think you will find he will be glad enough to let you be."

Once again it was the quietest hour of night. The moon was nearly down. The youth sprang to his steed.

"Farewell, goodman Kam," he said, and with a touch he started to turn the marvelous mount away. Then he turned back and stretched out a silver-ringed hand. "I have no payment to offer you, and I have not even told you—many thanks."

Those eyes, deep pools of shadow . . . Half in fear

and half in longing, Kam ardently wished that he could see those eyes more clearly.

"You have made me rich," he replied. "My lord. . . ."

"What is it?"

"Who—what lad are you by day? In the light of the sun?"

"Helpless yet, but all hope, unwounded. The prince that will be."

"Ah." It was a sigh of fulfillment. "Call on me, champion," Kam said.

"I will. Kam . . . farewell."

They touched hands, and then he was gone, the sound of his charger's hooves ringing away rapidly in the night. He would make good speed before sunrise.

When even the sound had left him, Kam turned and looked skyward. At the horizon the jewel of white fire that was the moon dipped and sank. Kam felt oddly alone, he who always came alone to Ithkar Fair.

"Prince that will be," he murmured. "And may that day come soon."

AMENDS

A Tale of the Sun Kings

The procession wound through streets lined with cheering people. Hal and Alan, the Sun Kings, had returned to their court city of Laueroc after a month's journey. The news had flown; everyone had turned out to greet them.

They rode at the head of their retainers. They made no showy cavalcade; the Kings shunned ostentation at any time, and that day their plain clothing was travel-stained. But their horses were beautiful, they themselves beautiful and well loved, the circlets, silver and gold, riding high on their youthful heads. The crowd cheered them wildly. Alan grinned and hailed people he knew. Hal, more restrained as always, glanced about him. Petitioners waited at the castle gates, shouting like the rest— One face among the many caught his searching eye, the one that did not cry out a greeting, that looked back at him white and still. Hal pulled his steed to a halt as memory

189

took hold of him. Vision, rather, seen through eyes not his own. . . .

Ward shivered in a winterbound cottage darkened by early dusk, snow blowing in through the cracks death-white and a fiercer storm coming on. They were all sick, lying abed, mother and the boys and the small sister, everyone except himself and the useless old man his father. Not much to eat, nothing to burn except the innards of the cottage itself. They would destroy their home from within, feed it to the fire as the fever fed at their vitals; they would die. The youth rose, gave to the small blaze the three-legged stool he had been sitting on—and then came the knock at the door.

"Open it, Ward," said his father numbly from his place by the hearth.

"Who could it be except lordsmen?" the young man flared in reply. "Let them knock."

The father rose stiffly and went to the door himself, undid the string latch. The door swung open with a bang, blown aside by the wind. No lordsmen stood there. Instead, there in the white whirl of snow stood two youths, hoods back in defiance of the cold, their cloaks whipping about them. Ward stared. They looked no older than himself, and yet far older. Behind them loomed dark, leggy shapes—their horses. Horses! He resented them already.

"Your hospitality, Goodman, or we are likely to perish in this smother." It was the grave-faced one who spoke, as much in command as in request. Ward noticed his gray eyes, curiously intense. Noticed them from all the way across the room.

"To be sure, you are welcome," replied his father courteously, "though we've little enough to offer you."

Hot anger flamed up in Ward, warming him as the

fire could not. What would these strangers care if they ate everything and left his family destitute? He stepped forward, fists clenched, but no one looked at him.

"Did I see a cowshed yonder?" the second youth asked. He was blond and held his mouth in a faintly humorous half smile.

"Ay. Naught in it."

"I'll put the horses there, then." The two of them swung into motion in the manner of men who have long been accustomed to each other's ways of doing things, wordlessly. In a moment a knobby pile of bundles and gear had grown on the doorstep, the blond youth had led the horses into the gathering darkness and the other had stepped inside, swinging his pack.

"I am Hal," he said quietly, "and my brother's name is Alan."

"Worth, they call me," the goodman introduced himself, "and yon is my eldest, Ward, and the wife Embla, and the younger ones. . . ." His tired voice faltered away.

"And all sick with fever," Hal muttered. He dropped his pack and strode straight across the room, kneeling and feeling at the woman's forehead with a delicate fingertip touch.

"Let her alone!" Ward shouted, startled. Most folk would have shied away.

Hal did not move. "Put on some water to boil," he said absently. "We'll make her a broth, some tea—"

"There's nothing except potatoes and old turnips!"

"Ward!" his father reproved him.

Hal got up and crossed to his pack, loosened the fastening. He drew out a sack of oats and one of maslin flour and a chunk of meat wrapped in the raw deerhide. Alan blundered in at the door, shouldering

191

an enormous bundle of firewood. He grinned at the goodman, who was staring at him openmouthed.

"We try not to come visiting emptyhanded," he said, easing his load to the earthen floor. Hal had shoved the foodstuffs aside and was rooting impatiently in the recesses of his pack.

"Alan, see if you can't get some water started. I can't find my agrimony—oh, there it is."

Alan stood still. "Sickness," he murmured, looking across the room to where a sufferer stirred and trembled.

"Ay. Where's a pot? By the mothers, must I do everything myself?"

"I will take care of it," Worth said unexpectedly. He dipped the water from a covered bucket. A half-fearful hope enlivened his face, made it look years younger. Ward stirred from his stance in the middle of the floor and sullenly sat on it, idle. He felt hateful, and guilty at his own anger. These two had brought help, but he could not like them any the better for it, not when they made him feel foolish. He almost wished they had been brigands after all.

His ill humor kept him from enjoying the food much, though it was the best he had eaten in months. Real meat, venison! Hal made a rich, good soup with a sort of bread in it for strength. He spooned off the broth and fed it to the invalids. He and Alan did not eat much. By the time everyone was done it was late, very dark, and the fire was dying to a flicker. Alan rose, yawning, and set about fastening a blanket over the worst portion of the wall. It blew and billowed as if there were no wall at all.

"What a wind," he grumbled. "Listen to it, would you!"

Moans and howls sounded overhead. Something

sobbed just above the rafters. Worth gasped and dropped with a clatter the pan he was washing.

"That's no wind," he stammered. "Black Nick is on the wild hunt tonight, him and his red-eared hounds, come to take souls as lords take deer, the mothers help us!" The words caught in his throat.

"He shall not have them," Hal said flatly. He took a seat by the little girl who lay and whimpered on her cot by the wall. "Get that fire going."

Worth numbly obeyed, his face twitching. Ward could not move; he felt frozen. Something was mewling and wailing around the eaves. "It sounds like babies," he whispered.

"The souls that run before," Hal said sternly. "Pay no attention. I tell you, he shall not have these."

"How do you propose to prevent him?" Alan asked, almost as if it were possible.

"It is fear that draws him here like a scent, the fear and despair—feel them in the room, here, almost as solid as the night? I have felt them since I entered. Fire and warm food weren't enough."

A high-pitched distant yelping sound, overhead, where it had no right to be—wild geese, Ward thought. But it was not the season for wild geese.

"We have no elfin balm," said Alan.

"I know. You think I haven't longed—well. Let me try it with the plinset."

Alan handed over the instrument in its leather case. Hal took it out carefully, warm gleaming of well-loved wood. . . . Music was a rare occurrence. A chant or a few sung words flung to the wind might be all a person heard from one year to the next. When Hal struck a soft chord, it was as much a sound of wonder and delight as the hunt was a sound of terror.

"Lint in the bell," Hal murmured. He sang the

song of the blue flax flowers and the summer sun. Alan joined in on the choruses, tuning his voice a triad away, lending resonance. The sound of music shut out for the listeners the weird noises without; the room filled with the glow of imagined sunlight. Hal went on at once to another song, this one about heartsease and the flower of that name.

He defied the powers of winter and death—but only as an embrace defies hatred. Some of his songs were full of valor and glorious folly, some witty, some of them sad, but all were very much alive, all warm. The bedridden folk stopped their shivering and moaning. Even the fire seemed to glow more steadily and brightly.

The children settled one by one into peaceful slumber, and then the mother, and then Ward, leaning his head against the wall where he sat by himself in the farthest corner. He was aware for a while of Hal's playing, and then he swam like a trout to a deeper place, so he thought. . . . Then he had a strange and vivid dream.

It seemed to him that the door burst open with a freezing blast of air. And there in the black entry of night stood a specter, eight feet tall, a skull for head and branching from the skull two great forked horns. Hal rose to face it, his plinset in his hands.

"You shall not have them, Arawn," he said.

Arawn was the black rider's name in the western tongue. His shadow loomed huge upon the wall. At his shoulder nodded the gaunt head of his pale, luminous horse, and around his heels crowded the red-eared hounds, uneasily whining.

"How can you defy me?" Though the giant spoke hollowly through his naked, clacking teeth, he seemed amused.

"I defy you with mortal defiance," said Hal. "The spirit that has always defied you. Take your leave."

"Why, you poor fool," Black Nick boomed, "don't you know it is no use? Poor silly hero—give way, now, before I take you as well. I suppose next you will be offering yourself in their stead."

"Nay. You are to have none of us this night." Hal stood taut but firm.

"And who are you, that you think you can deny me my rightful game?" All amusement had vanished from the spectral hunter's voice.

"I am Hal, son of Gwynllian, heir to Torre and Taran and the Blessed Kings of Welas, Star Son, Son of the Mothers, Very King."

"No court has hailed you," Black Nick mocked.

"The time is not yet. The gypsies hail me, and the elves, and the spirits of the dead."

"Yours is a mighty magic," the prince of darkness said, "but not mighty enough to halt me. Give way." Towering, he took a step forward. Hal trembled, struggling within himself, forcing himself to say yet one more thing.

"I am Mireldeyn," he whispered, "and I bid you begone."

Black Nick stopped where he stood.

"Well," he said, in a voice impersonal and oddly gentle. "Well. You know then that there is a price to pay."

"I pay with every breath."

The specter gave a nod, perhaps a sort of bow, his spreading antlers scraping against the rafters. Then he turned and vanished in a single stride. The door banged behind him, and it seemed to Ward that Hal went limp and nearly fell, that Alan appeared from somewhere, caught hold of him to support him. What happened after that he could not tell, for he was asleep. Was he not asleep?

When he got up in the morning Hal was lying near the fire in a sleep that was almost a swoon. Alan was quietly cooking oatmeal, and Ward's mother was sitting up in her bed, staring at the strangers. The children lay sleeping peacefully, and so did Worth. Ward stumbled over to his mother's bedside.

"Are—are you all right?" he stammered, unbelieving.

"I seem to be much better." Embla turned her puzzled eyes on her son. "What has happened, Ward? I remember music, the sweetest of music—"

"Nothing. Nothing has happened." Ward shook his head vehemently, shaking off memory, shaking off shreds of dream.

Snow still fell heavily, but the wind calmed. The snow ceased to seem an enemy, became an insulating downy comforter that sealed them, cocoonlike, from all harm. Alan trudged outside and returned with firewood and more meat from the haunch he had hung behind the cowshed. The snow was his veil; no lordsmen would threaten. Alan made stew, and the children sat up and ate it, all three of them, while Worth moved from one to the other to his wife in restless joy. Hal still lay in a stupor. Alan hauled and heaved him into a bed and he hardly stirred.

"Will he be all right?" Worth asked anxiously.

"Ay, he is just—tired. He was up all night—nursing them," Alan said awkwardly. "Herbs—"

"And something more," Worth stated with a keen glance.

Ward thought of his father as a coward because he quietly met the demands of the lordsmen who kept him constantly poor. Surely the old man did not mean—no. It was too frightening. It was just a dream.

Even though Alan seemed more strained and anxious than he had any reason to be.

In midafternoon Alan made an abrupt gesture and went over to wake Hal, took him in his arms, pulled him up against his powerful chest. "Hal!" he called him, but Hal's head hung limp; there was no response. Alan spoke very softly in his ear: "Mireldeyn." Ward stood near enough to hear the word. Hal's eyes fluttered open and he made a dry sobbing sound.

"All right," Alan murmured. "It's all right. Wake up. Please." He helped Hal to sit up on his own. And to Ward's astonishment and chagrin, his father went and knelt by the bed.

"Lord," said Worth huskily, "they are better, they will be well. A thousand thanks—" Hal gave him the ghost of a smile.

"Never mind that," he said. "You have turnips. Would you get me one? I ought to eat."

"A turnip!" Worth protested. "Lord, there is meat."

"I get meat all the time. You take the meat. I'll take a turnip."

They spent the evening gathered around the hearth, all of them, even the little ones, talking and talking in a sort of celebration. It was family talk, tales of good times or funny times, touching only lightly on the hardships, the grinding difficulty of life under greedy lord and evil king. Ward sat scowling in their midst, full of rebellion. How could they prattle so? Saved, for what? Brutish slavery, he thought. Hal did not sing. He sat quietly, looking pale, and when the rest of them went to sleep he paced about, the hollows of his cheeks and eyes looking huge in the dim light. Ward, half-wakeful, was aware of his pacing, aware that Alan kept him company and whispered with him from time to time. He chose not to be aware that they spoke of the specter, and Mireldeyn, and the price that must be paid, the loneliness.

The next day Embla was up and about for a while. The snow stopped. Toward evening Hal and Alan packed their things, planning to be off in the morning. They sat by the fire for an hour and went early to bed. That night everyone slept.

Everyone except Ward. When the fire had died down from embers to ashes he slipped from his bed and crept softly to the piles of gear near the door, opened a pack. In the shaft of moonlight that wavered through the single window he examined the contents—

"Ward!" It was his father, whispering. "What are you doing?"

"Digging carrots!" he whispered back hotly. He rummaged in the pack, muttering to himself. "Here we are to sit, starving, and likely they have gold, booty, who knows what."

"Are you mad?" his father gasped. "Are you my son? You would thieve from those who befriended us?"

Ward made no reply. He drew from the pack a burnished helm and stared at it in the moonlight. There were old songs about a sunset king who would rid Isle of the oppressors; Ward discounted them. But he admired the helm. It shone with the subtle glow of rare silver.

"There," he breathed.

"Put it back!" hissed Worth.

"Nay, indeed. I plan to feed my brothers and sister if you will not." Ward reached for Hal's sword. Worth restrained him.

"You will get yourself killed!" he cried, forgetting silence. "If I did not submit to the lord's demands we would all be dead!" His wife stirred, and he lowered his voice again. "Put that helm back. What, boy, do you think they will tamely let you have it?"

Ward shook off his father's grip. "They are outlaws," he said impatiently. "They have no recourse."

"No recourse!" Worth choked, then laughed heartily and silently, a rare event for him and one his son could least stand, to be laughed at. "Do you mean to tell me you have not noticed Hal's power?" he gasped. "You cannot face him and prevail."

Anger and frustration rushed through Ward—the interfering old man! He struck out at his father with the hand that clutched the silver helm, knocking Worth sideways with a metallic thud. The next instant he was himself flung backwards, landing hard on the dirt floor. Hal's hands pinned him there, and he lay frozen, unable to move, stunned by the blazing wrath in those moonlit eyes; he had never seen such flashing fury. Hal panted with rage, and yet when he spoke he spoke evenly. "Now listen," he said. The phrase was a command. "I will lie and watch you filch from my pack, and if there were any coin in there I'd let you have it. I would have given it to you before now. And I will lie and watch you finger my helm. But I will not lie and watch you strike your father. That you do at your peril."

Worth was standing behind Hal, pale. "Don't hurt him, Lord," he begged, and Ward realized with a sudden pang that Worth's fear was all for his worthless son.

Hal got up and in the same effortless motion he lifted Ward upright, grasping him by the shoulders, shaking him. "If I had a father like yours," he said intensely, "if I had ever had a loving father, even for a day—"

"Hush, Hal." Alan stood beside him. "You'll wake the little one."

He released Ward and turned away from him. "Let's go."

"In the middle of the night?" Alan asked mildly.

"Ay, so much the better. The wind is up again; it will cover our traces before dawn. Let's go." He turned to the goodman. "The deer is hanging in the brush behind the cowshed, frozen. Eat it or trade the meat for what you need."

"What can I give you for thanks?" asked Worth. "I owe you so much. . . ."

"Your loyalty. You will know what to do when the time comes."

Now Hal was King, Sunset King. Worth had helped make him so. And now he had encountered Ward again. The youth stared back at him, white-faced, and he had seen himself through those frightened eyes.

Hal vaulted down off his elfin steed, waved his retainers onward and strode to where Ward stood, took his limp hand in welcome. The youth trembled under that touch.

"Ward! I can't believe it!" Alan stood by Hal's side, warmth and concern in this voice. "What brings you to Laueroc? Nothing wrong, I hope?"

The youth lifted his lowered eyes, incredulous. They were greeting him as old friends! His lips moved, but he could not produce an answer.

"Is your father all right?" Alan asked worriedly.

"Fine!" Ward stammered. "He lost an arm in the fighting—" He looked down again. His so-called coward of a father had led the assault on the lord's stronghold while he, Ward, had trembled in line, missed his aim—

"But he is all right without it?" Hal asked.

Ward nodded.

"Of course, he would be," said Hal. "He has that quiet courage. How are your mother and the little ones?"

"Fine." Ward managed the one word and no more. He faced his King whom he had wronged, his King who had swept away the lordsmen like dirt off the land. His head swam and he could not meet those gray eyes. "Lord," he whispered, "please kill me and have it done with."

"Mothers, what am I to do with him?" Hal appealed. "Ward, can't you tell I mean you no harm?"

"Bring him in," Alan said. "This is going to take a while." At a soft glance from Hal he smiled and went in himself, to his castle chamber, his lady and his supper. Hal led Ward and the horses to the stable. He rubbed his steed dry with a cloth while Ward watched in wonder. How one so kingly could care for his own—

"Surely you don't really want me to kill you, Ward," Hal remarked. "What is the matter? Why have you come to see me?"

"I—Lord, I am so ashamed. I must make amends somehow."

"Why? That row we had?" Hal paused as he pulled down fodder, looked at the youth. "It was nothing. We can forget it, we have both grown since then. Alan tells me that everyone hates his father one time or another, that it is part of the love."

Ward winced. He had lately left his father with a harvest to get in, all for no better reason than his own uneasy ache. "I feel as if I've done nothing right in all my life," he said.

Hal snorted, blanketing a horse. "Let go of shame for a while, Ward, and think! Turn and face the thing that is chasing you."

The youth stood stiff with fear again. "But that's just it," he whispered. "The shame."

"Not a certain dream in the night?"

Ward shook and sweated as if the fever had hold of him at last. "I knew it was real," he said hoarsely.

"I gave you strong herbs," Hal said. "You should have been fast asleep. You should never have seen."

"I was a coward, I would not move to help you—"

"Help me!" Hal exclaimed. "Even Alan could not help me much that night. I could scarcely help myself. I could scarcely stand."

"I am a coward!" Words burst out of Ward. "I saw your power, you defeated Death himself, you are— you are a wizard, or a god, I don't know what you are, you saved us all and I hated you for it, I am such a wretch! I am terrified of you, I wish you would strike me so I could hate you—" Ward covered his quivering face with his hands. "Liege, help me," he choked.

Incredibly, he felt arms around him. "It is all right, truly it is," said Hal softly. "Those were dark days, dark years. You were filled with bitterness, and I—after that night with Arawn I was so tired I had no patience, no strength to befriend you. I must always struggle to befriend. Your fear is the price Arawn mentioned, the price I pay."

Ward stopped trembling and glanced up, startled. Hal nodded at him, his face bleak, his gray eyes unnaturally bright.

"It is not just you. . . . Ward, whatever gave you the notion that you are a coward, that you do nothing right? You are here, are you not? Here, inches from me? Why?"

"Amends. . . ."

"Then you are honorable as well as brave." With a

small smile Hal released him. "There is no need for amends. Just seeing you here is enough."

"It is not enough," said Ward with a daring that surprised him. "Lord, there must be something I can do."

"A penance?" Hal grumbled. "No need." But Ward did not hear; a thought had taken hold of him.

"You say my fear—people's fear—is the price you pay for—being what you are?"

Hal only nodded, watching him.

The youth felt as if he was risking his life. All wary instincts made him feel that way. Nevertheless, he squared his shoulders, straightened himself with a long indrawn breath and met the bright gray eyes. It had to be done, even if he should die for his temerity—

"Why, then, Liege, if it pleases you, I for one will no longer be afraid," he said, unwavering. And he saw with delight that for once in his life he had done something exactly, ineffably right. Joy touched those shining eyes.

"Amends are made," Hal said.

THE DOG-KING
OF VAIRE

I am Fabron, speaking to you from the reaches of the wind. I was king of the canton of Vaire in Vale when I was alive. I came to my throne by virtue of threats and greed, but I tried to be a good king. I wanted to be well remembered. I rode the rounds of my canton yearly, hearing my people's concerns, and every horse and retainer of my entourage wore ornaments of my own making, most of them gold. I had been a smith, and smiths were honored people; we worked magic with metal, and metal conferred its own ancient magic on us: we were healers, smiths and the sons of smiths. At least, some of us were. . . . For myself, I wore a breastplate all in chain links, and a chain belt to my sword, and the staghound—the emblem of Vaire—leaping on my helm. I dressed in sober velvets to set off my artistry. Jewels and brooches show better thus.

But it was not in such array that Frain first saw me—Frain, my son, who did not know me. Spring had come and was turning into summer, but I was not holding court or preparing to ride through my domain. Mela, my wife of many years, lay ill with a wasting fever, and I stayed constantly in her chamber, seeing no one. She did not ask for me. Indeed, she had turned dead to me many years before, after we had sold Frain. Not that she was cold or disobedient—she was ever an obedient wife—but something had died within her. I did not understand; I thought we would have many babies, and what matter was one the less? High King Abas had had need of a child to prove his continuing fertility and to keep his vassals content. He had paid me dearly for it, first in gold, and later in power when I threatened to expose him. But I had paid dearly, too, over the years. Frain was our first child and our last. I had not reckoned, perhaps, on the anger of the goddess who abides in all women. So Mela lay moaning and did not speak to me or cry out my name, and I could not help her. I felt somehow to blame—I always felt to blame for any ill in her life since I took Frain from her.

The door opened. I looked up wearily, expecting another officious servant, but it was Wayte, my captain of guards, with an iron dagger at his throat. Other guards were milling about outside the door like beleaguered sheep. They were armed, of course, and so was Wayte, but they risked his life if they drew a weapon.

It was Frain who held the dagger on Wayte. I knew him at once, for I had made shift to see him a few times during the years, standing behind a buttress and watching him in the courtyard at Melior when he was too young and careless to notice. He was a sturdy youth now, with auburn hair and high, freckled cheekbones, and an earnest, open look about him. He seemed hardly more dangerous than the toothless baby I had given for gold. Yet there he was

with his arms locked around Wayte's shoulders and
the dagger at his throat. The captain stood almost a
head above him.

"I beg pardon, my lord," he said to me. "They told
me I could not see you, but my business could not wait."

His voice was clean and courteous, like his looks,
but there was nothing crawling about it, no anxious
entreaty. He is a prince, I thought, and I longed to
go to him and embrace him. Instead, I kept my place
and spoke gruffly through my beard. "Let that so-
called captain of mine go," I said.

He did not move. "Your word, my lord, that I will
not be harmed."

I nodded, waving the other guards away. Frain
loosened his grip, and Wayte bowed and left without
a word, his face angry and white. The fellow was
expecting my wrath; he did not know the joy he had
brought me.

"Prince Frain," I asked as collectedly as I could,
"what brings you here?"

He whistled softly. "I had not expected, my lord,
that you would recognize me! Have you heard of the
events in Melior, then?"

"No, I have had no news from Melior. I know your
face, that is all. What has happened to bring you
here with your fine linen half torn from your back?"

He glanced down at himself ruefully. "Your guards
would never have admitted such a vagabond. Have I
your lordship's leave to seat myself?"

"Of course, of course!" I exclaimed hastily, suddenly
aware of the poor account I was giving of myself. I
was in a lethargy of despair from Mela's illness,
roughly dressed, scarcely washed or combed, and
now scant in courtesy. I bustled to clear a space on
my cluttered couch. "I beg your pardon. Please sit
and tell me what news you will."

Such a tale he told me. His so-called brother Tirell had rebelled against his mad father at last, it seemed. Abas had done murder, and Tirell had led Frain on a wild ride into Acheron itself—Acheron, where no sane man will set foot. And then fighting, and a strange, ominous black beast—I gaped in amazement, but Frain's voice was so careful and modest that I believed every word he told me. Finally, in canny desperation, Tirell had sent Frain to me.

"Tirell hopes—no, expects—that you will help us overthrow Melior," Frain explained.

"He is mad, you have said," I remarked dryly.

"Aye, so he is. Though perhaps"—Frain cocked a clear eye at me—"not in that regard."

"How is he mad, then?"

Frain sighed, thinking, and for the first time I saw real pain in his fine brown eyes; he had kept away from emotion before. "He has taken his love and grief," Frain said slowly, "and turned it all to hard hate and vengeance with a cutting edge. He hardly moves or speaks except for vengeance. There is no human warmth in him these days, not toward any being of human kind."

"But he fends for himself well enough day to day?" I asked.

"All too well," he wryly agreed.

"And you, Prince Frain—" How I yearned to call him Frain, my son. But I would not do that. Long silence is not lightly to be broken.

"You need not call me prince," he put in. "I have never been 'princed' much. Tirell is the prince in Melior."

"And you, Frain," I said softly, "do you accord with Prince Tirell in this bid for the throne?"

"I have followed him since I was old enough to walk."

"And now that you are old enough to think," I returned sharply, "will you follow a madman?"

"Thinking is the least of it," Frain replied slowly. "To be sure, he is brave, and comely, and honorable in his way, and there is vision in him, perhaps even some wisdom. But I believe I would follow him even if he were a wretch. Because of something in me; I don't know what."

I could not say a word.

There was no replying, in any event, for a long, anguished moan filled the room. Mela had awakened from one of her brief sleeps. I hastily crossed the room to be at her side, taking her dry hand in my own. But she looked through me and past me, as always, seeing nothing to help her. Frain stood beside me, and I caught my breath; her vague gray eyes flickered onto his face. But then she turned away her thin face and tossed her head to and fro in a sort of weak, distracted protest against her own misery. Her red hair lay snarled on the pillow, angry and unkempt. I placed a hand on her brow to still her.

"I could try to heal her," Frain whispered. The words seemed dragged from him. "Tirell says there is healing in me."

"Prince Tirell may speak truth," I said roughly, trying to hide my sudden hope. "Though I know more of healing than he is ever likely to learn."

"I know you were a smith." Frain turned to me with his steady, questioning gaze, and I could scarcely meet his eyes. "Can no one, then, heal those who are dearest to them?"

"Perhaps not, Frain," I said quietly, for that was truth, "but I lost my gift for healing years ago, when I grew too fond of wealth—wealth and power."

"My baby!" Mela whispered, and her frail hands moved on the bedsheets.

"Try, Frain," I told him, "but do not take it too hard if you fail. She is far gone."

"But what should I do?" he asked.

"What do you think?" I asked in turn.

"There is something to do with metal," Frain said slowly, as if the fact puzzled him. Of course, he did not know who he was, what he had come from, that he should be a healer. "I used a knife last time. But I hate to touch her with such an ugly thing."

"A knife can cut away blight from the stem," I said. "Clean pain can heal. Use it."

He did not tell me that he had hardly eaten for days, nor that he had ridden far, in haste, and with little rest. I learned that later, much later, when we were at Melior. He stood by Mela's bed with his back straight and his head bowed, like a hostage for her, and laid a hand on her hot brow. She stirred beneath his touch and whispered again. He curled his fingers around the iron knife blade, sheathing it with his own skin, and moved it over her heart, over her hands and head. He trembled, and I knew what he was feeling, remembered it well. The power moves in you and through you from depths beyond knowing or from some place beyond being; I never understood which. It carries you out of self and you shrink in fear. But I don't think Frain was afraid. He stood with Mela in her own dark place, bent over her, embracing her, struggling to lift her, to free her. Her whole body trembled and strained with the effort, though he had not actually moved; every sinew of his spirit was taut. For the space of countless heartbeats he fought for her, with her, against her—

And for an instant I thought he had succeeded. Her bleary eyes met his and cleared. "My baby!" she breathed. Then an awful tumult of feeling surged into her eyes—love and rage—and the rage snapped her away from him. I saw it happen. Frain swayed as if he had been struck. His knife clattered to the floor, and he clutched at a bedpost for support. He clung to the heartless wooden thing and sobbed.

I went and put my arms around him. He let go of the bed and cried against my shoulder, cried like the child I had never known. "Easy, lad," I murmured, swallowing, patting him clumsily. "Stop your shaking, now."

He raised his wet face. "She is trapped in a tangle of rage and despair," he said wildly, "roots and strength-sucking vines, anger—I tugged and tugged—"

"I know," I told him.

"The knife would not cut her free. Knives are like water in that place. I—I was a drifting thing, I didn't know who I was, I couldn't remember my name." He gulped for breath. "I—there was something—if I had only known. . . ."

If you had known she is your mother, I thought with a pang, it would only have increased your heartache. He had given everything, down to the last dram of his strength; he could scarcely stand. I had never seen such courage. I know that such had not been my courage in my day.

Mela lay quite still. "Is she—dead?" whispered Frain.

I reached out and touched the pulse of her neck. "No, but she is beyond knowledge or pain, and I am glad of it. She will die soon." I guided Frain toward the door. "Come."

He was still trembling. "I am sorry . . ."

"I told you she was far gone," I said more gently than I had ever heard myself speak. "You did no harm, and more good than you know. Come." I took him down the corridor, half supporting him. The guards watched us pass in barely concealed astonishment. I led him into my own bedchamber and laid him down, took off his boots and covered him and pulled the curtains around him. "Sleep," I ordered, and left him there.

My wife died two nights later. I did not see Frain in the interim, though I often thought of him. I ordered the servants to extend to him the fullest hospitality: bath, clothing, food, whatever he needed. I knew he would feel weak and drowsy for a few days after what he had done for Mela, so I was not really expecting him as I sat with her. In fact, I suppose, he avoided the sickroom, for he was still very young. Death makes grim company. But it came easily enough for Mela. She slipped away without a movement or a word to me. I wept a bit, and then I slept for a good while.

By the sun, it was past noon of the next day when I awoke. I immediately went looking for Frain, and found him readily. He was in my chamber, dressed but resting. He winced when he saw me, so I knew he had heard the news.

"I am sorry about Queen Mela, my lord," he said.

"There are some who cling to their ills," I replied. I felt calm, almost dreamy, but he had started me crying again even so; I could feel the tears on my face. I let them run. Kept within, sorrow turns to poison.

He had started to rise when I entered, and I had waved him back. Now I sat beside him. "I have never seen courage to match yours in a healer," I said.

He shrugged. "Tenacity. Dogged pertinacity, if you will. In Melior, people call me Puppydog behind my back because I can't be put off." A note of bitterness crept into his voice, even though he tried to speak lightly, and my tears abruptly stopped. I sat straight up in indignation that anyone could speak of him so.

"Because you are faithful, you mean? But it seems hardly fair—"

"Faithfulness is not too highly regarded in Melior."

"Well, it is here," I said warmly. "And I wish people would remember that the dog is the emblem of honor and fidelity." I leaned forward, my elbows on my knees, gesticulating. "Have you heard the legend of the Dog King of Vaire?"

He shook his head, settling himself in willingness to hear. So I told the tale.

"On the night in which Nolan of Vaire was born, his sister, the magical she-dog Vlonda, birthed two pups, and they were called Kedal and Kedur. They lay with Nolan in his cradle. One was black and one was white, and the baby was red as fire. In seven short years he grew to be a tall man, and the pups grew to be giant hounds, each big enough to fell a stag by itself. They were all constant companions to each other, and the dogs served Nolan as well as if they had been men.

"Now in those beginning days, dogs were not yet heard of. That is why Aftalun had bedded and then transformed Vlonda, the warrior maiden: to give this gift to man. Wherever Nolan went with his hounds, people watched in envy and awe. The dogs fought beside him in battle, guarded his sleep, kept his possessions safe from thieves, provided meat for his table, and helped him, and in course of time his children, through danger of every kind. They fought with fierce animals, ran through fire, swam through floods, climbed towers, and jumped pits in his service, and neither of them ever mouthed a complaint. Nolan, their master, was the best king Vaire has ever known, and no one in the realm lacked anything during his reign.

"Nolan lived for two hundred years. Before he was an old man, every great lord had a dog; wars were fought for the stealing of dogs. But the most faithless followers were put to shame by the faithfulness of the dogs, for it is in the nature of a dog to be constant, and in the nature of a man to be willful. That is why each can help the other. But petty men came to envy the dogs, and hate their nobility, and kick them for spite, and use their name as a name of reproach.

"Nolan saw all this with sorrow. He feared that his loyal companions might be subjected to insult after he was gone—for Kedal and Kedur, being born of Aftalun, were immortal. So, in his old age, Nolan turned his canton over to his sons and set out for a final adventure in the mountains to the south. Kedal and Kedur bounded around him like young pups. When the three of them reached the slopes of Lord Tutosel, he breathed easier, for he judged that they would meet no people there. But at the top of the first pass their way was blocked by a hideous, misshapen old man. 'Filthy curs!' he shrieked. 'Go dig in garbage; go roll in manure!' Nolan tried to silence the old man, but it was too late; the mocker slipped away, and the dogs had turned to stone.

"Nolan spent the rest of his days in the mountains, living in the open, windy pass by the two stones that once were his faithful servants. Folk will point out to you the peak where Kedal and Kedur still watch over Vaire with tears rolling now and then from their blind, stony eyes. For what Nolan feared has come to pass: every shepherd boy now has a dog, and men have forgotten that dogs are the gift and get of the gods. But no one goes near those mountain ways, for Vlonda remembers. She roamed long in search of her brother and her sons, and folk say she still skulks, brooding, beneath the shadows of Kedal and Kedur."

*   *   *

"I have never had a dog," Frain remarked. "Abas hates them. He will not allow any in Melior's court."

I got up, and he got up as well, courteous youth that he was. I took off my fine cloak of royal blue, my golden stag-hound clasp. It was presumptuous of me to place the emblem of Vaire on Frain, but I refused to worry; in this way, at least, I would claim him as my son! I put the cloak around his sturdy shoulders, fastened it with the red-gold clasp.

"Wear this," I said, "and if anyone calls you pup, smile." I suppose I was weeping again. He put his arms out to me, hesitantly. I welcomed his embrace. I wept quietly for a while, to get it out of the way, but I was thinking far ahead. I knew that I would never willingly be far from him again, that I would ride with him even if it meant following his mad fool of a brother.

"Stay here a few days," I told Frain, "and stand by me at the burial. Then I will go with you to see Tirell."

"Thank you, my lord," he stammered. He was startled. "And thank you for the tale as well," he added. "I will remember it."

I did not know that I had named the place of my own death, telling him that tale. I, the ambitious smith, the extortionist and usurper, would die at the feet of the ancestral staghounds of Vaire. And not kingship or power or a healing touch or all of Frain's faithfulness would be able to save me.

WE BUILD A SHRINE

So we build a shrine to suffering,
Sprinkle ourselves with our own holy tears
And eat the bread of bitterness
And lift our voices to the god of suffering
Saying, for these my enumerated sorrows
    I deserve:
Your love, your kiss of favor, your praise,
Pity, respite, reward, bliss
      eternal, embrace, accolade—bah!

I wish I could leave my childhood
Behind me as my father left Ireland,
Step onto the boat to somewhere else.
He put an ocean between him and that
Petty, bitter, lush green land, every sod of it
    soaked with blood,
Land of sorrows—
But the Irish never really leave.
The brogue stays on their voices, on their
Tongues that sacramental blood-red wine,
That holy water in their eyes, on their lips
    that ancient cry—
And as I bewail my childhood,
They bewail the childhood of their race.
And so and still we build a shrine
    to suffering.

PRIMAL CRY

Coal town. Hoadley, PA. Big house on the hill, high Victorian, mansion almost. That would be the mine owner's place, formerly. Avenue of elms all stumps since Dutch elm disease. Some other houses just below, ornate, less big. Doctor, lawyer, mayor, maybe. Several houses, comfortable, along Main Street. Stores, school, Post Office. And taverns, numerous, one on every corner. And churches, nearly as numerous. Slovak, Irish, Polish, Italian, Greek, Lithuanian, Brethren, Lutheran. Railroad tracks right through the center of town, length of Main Street. Below that, houses again, row on row, two stories, peaked roofs, weathered siding or peeling fake brick made of asphalt. Nothing extra. Plain sparrow-brown boxes, enough of them to fill seventeen streets, numbered. Below again, the warehouses, the tarpaper shacks, the creek, orange from acid runoff. Only bony piles and scrub forest beyond.

Me, I'm an outsider. Only lived in Hoadley a few months. Like another world, Hoadley.

Nancy Springer

We moved to Hoadley when Brad took a job with one of the private-sector agencies in Steel City. Career-change counselor. The mills had closed, see. I was four months pregnant with our first child, so no use hunting a job. No jobs to be had, anyway.

Just waiting for baby, I was good and bored when I met Deb.

Brad found the apartment in Hoadley. One of the big old places on the hill, cut up—we had the whole first floor. Felt like mine barons. No ten-acre lawn, no wrought-iron fence, no avenue of elm trees, but yes bay windows, yes bevel glass framing the great door with the fanlight above, yes deep shady porch. Looked down over strata, social. Fine view of the slag heaps. Big brick house next door, similar.

Met Deb at the County Historical Society a few doors away. Place with real slate siding, old horse-drawn ambulance parked on the lawn. Christmas time, I wandered down there to take in the crafts display. Deb was there behind the counter, flanked by blue-haired wrinklies. Odd. She's about my age, late twenties, tall and slim, terrific clothes, got life enough for the whole place. Cute face, lots of glossy black permed hair, ditzy way about her. Overgrown kid.

She showed me the counted-cross-stitch ornaments and the candlewicked pillows. All the while she and the wrinklies were pumping it out of me that I was new in town, and where I lived.

"Gee, I'm your neighbor," Deb said. "I'm Debora Michaels."

The way she said it, every syllable stressed, Deb-ah-rah, sounded like royalty. Always called herself Debora. She never said so, but it didn't take me long to notice she hated hearing it shortened to Deb. I called her Deb every chance I got.

"Lin Burke," I said. That's me. Lin the loner.

"Come and meet my parents as soon as you're settled," Deb told me breathlessly. "Any time at all. My father's family is from Connecticut. His mother's people trace back to the Mayflower. My mother's ancestors on both sides are Germans from the Brandywine. They go back to Revolutionary times, and there's a Saltzgiver buried in the cemetery at the Old Swedish Lutheran church in West Chester."

Who the hell was she trying to impress?

Weird, that she was still living with her folks at her age, in the big brick place right next to ours, Roman blinds, corner turret. Couple days later, bored, I went over.

Mr. Michaels was home for lunch. Local bank president, courtly gentleman, none too talkative. Mrs. Michaels was a round-faced, fluffy woman. She talked enough for both. Did I like Hoadley? It wasn't what it used to be. Time was when the trains roared through day and night and the snow lay black with soot all winter. Been years since the mines and mills ran, sky glowed red toward the City. Mine owners long gone, like the elms. Took what the town had to give, raped it some say, went away. Left scars and bony piles behind.

"Good riddance," said Debora. "The place is a lot cleaner now."

"But the people have no work, dear," her mother told her. "A lot of them can't meet their mortgage payments. Your father has to find ways not to foreclose."

"I don't know why they don't move away. Move to Arizona or Nevada."

"But their families are here, their friends are here." Mrs. Michaels sounded shocked. Why, I didn't understand.

There were lots of things I didn't understand.

Pictures of Debora all over that house, photos, little girl in Polly Flinders dresses, expensively hand-smocked. Mary Janes, banana curls and white straw hats. Easter pictures, First Communion pictures in front of the Lutheran church. High school graduation draped shot. College, black mortar board and tassel. Banker's little girl on the front porch swing, looking down over Hoadley. Only child. I have vices, but nosiness is not one of them. Nothing struck me as odd.

Time went on. I did Christmas, started natural childbirth classes down in Steel City at the hospital, read the newspaper, learned to know Hoadley. Some place, Hoadley. Especially in deep January. Child abuse cases every second week in those houses down below Main Street, the gray-brown ones. Once in the grocery I saw a woman with a bruise on her cheek. She said she fell. Everyone laughed. Even she laughed. But I read in the paper about a woman, a big woman, nearly three hundred pounds, killed her husband. He came home drunk and ugly, and she sat on him. Sat on his chest until he was dead. Said she didn't mean to kill him. They didn't arrest her. There was another thing somebody told me about. Happened a few years before. Woman died, and when they went through her things they found babies in her attic. Five of them, all dried up, long time dead, stored in boxes.

Backward. That's what Hoadley was like, backward in time. Like the last fifty years forgot to happen. Like people were stuck in the past. People my age would tell me how Pa used to come home mean from the mines and whip them, whip all eight kids, or ten or whatever. People Pa's age would tell me how a man's pay was owed to the company store before he even got the scrip. People a generation older, still living, would tell me how they came over from the old country. Ireland, Poland, Italy, Rumania. Steerage, with their families. A younger brother died, or an older sister, or an aunt. Looking for the land of opportunity.

I would see the families on Sunday, the big families from down below Main Street, out driving in their old beat-up American-made cars, or walking to church in clothes from the Goodwill store, laughing and quarreling.

Deb came into my kitchen limping. "I about killed myself on the ice," she complained. "It's these boots."

Spike-heeled, periwinkle-blue Guccis, on the ice that coated the whole world at that time of year. "Don't you have something with some tread?" I grumped.

"Sensible shoes make me feel dowdy." She took off her fur jacket. I saw that she was wearing a silk shirt and her Jordache jeans, the ones that fit so tight she had to lie down on the bed to zip them up. And never would I admit to her how good they looked with the Gucci boots. Or how good she looked. Damn, she was beautiful. Could have been a model.

"So you'd rather be dead than dowdy," I said.

"God, Lin, you are such a party pooper."

I saw Deb from time to time. Didn't really like her. She got on my nerves. Backward, like the town. Airheaded. Went to the Spirit Church, for Christ's sake, the one some fly-by-night preacher had started up in an empty warehouse on the edge of town, and I could guess what her longtime Lutheran parents thought of that. Saved and devout, Deb was. Intelligent, but narrow—when she got a brainstorm, she would broadcast it again and again, to different people or even to the same one. Me, for instance. Drove me up the wall. But we were sort of thrown together, being neighbors. At least she was interesting to talk with. There weren't that many people in Hoadley I liked to talk with, not once I got tired of hearing about steerage and the company store.

"I just found out the most fascinating thing," she told me, breathless as always.

"What thing?"

"Burt Bacharach is my fourth cousin once removed on my mother's side!"

How she loved to drop names. Burt Bacharach, for God's sake. Only Deb would have cared.

She used to come over in the afternoons and drink coffee with me until Brad came home. "She's infantile," he said after he had met her a few times.

I grinned, agreeing. She was.

"A real rich brat. Running around in her designer clothes and her Corvette when there are people living on beans and day-old bread." He met those people in his work a lot, and it upset him. "I don't understand why you're buddying around with her."

"She's the only person I've met in this town who ever talks about anything except hard times and the high cost of ground beef," I said. "Anyway, she's funny." I liked to laugh at her. Helped my ego.

Deb was active in the local genealogical society. They met twice a month in the library, a makeshift storefront place. Afternoons, since everyone was unemployed. Deb didn't have any paying job either. She had majored in American History at U. of Pitt in Pittsburgh, and then she had come home to Hoadley. No problem—she wasn't complaining, so why should I. She was more serious about her research than most people are about their salaried careers. Than most Hoadley people were about the lottery, even.

"My great-great-great aunt on the Michaels side is a matrilinear descendant of the Stuarts—"

"Ed Stewart, the lumber man over in Hemlock Bend?" I said, pretending to misunderstand.

"The *Scottish* Stuarts," she corrected me sniffily. "As in, King James. As in, Mary Queen of Scots."

Sure.

She was sort of an evangelist for genealogy. Had it mixed up in her half-assed religion somehow. Kept inviting me to go along to her meetings. Nothing better to do, so I would go, sit back and smirk while she and her colleagues argued about sources. Contemplating my swelling abdomen and my own superiority took up most of my attention. But one gray afternoon in the library, I got jolted out of my stupor.

There was a round of relative-upsmanship going on. Deb had indicated that a solitary French Huguenot forebear on her mother's side might be a scion of some French royal bastard—I've forgotten the details. Royalty bores me. But a blue-haired bastion of the Historical Society was bent out of shape.

"By the way, dear," she said blandly, "I've heard news of your natural mother. Did you know that her husband has left her?"

Deb tilted her chin up an extra notch. "I read it in the newspaper," she shot back without an instant's hesitation. "So fair of them, how they print almost everything. That Phyllis Snyder who's been passing bad checks—isn't that your niece?"

Her adversary went white, fumbled for a rebuttal, then lapsed into silence. No pussycat, Deb. No ordinary genteel banker's daughter.

Ice cool, gorgeous and unperturbed, she continued outlining her plans for researches French. Her parents had offered to pay her way overseas. I looked at her until I realized I was staring. Then looked down at my pregnant belly, knowing what I should have suspected long since. The daughter with the glossy black hair, the dark eyes and the many passions was not born of quiet John Michaels and his round-faced German wife.

Deb told me about it later, in my kitchen, over coffee. She brought up the subject herself.

"It's no secret." She shrugged off the blue-haired wrinkly's snub. "The whole town knows I'm adopted."

"And you know who your birth mother is?"

"Sure. She's Italian. Catholic. She used to live down at the lower end of 11th Street, but she's moved out to Mine 27 now."

Another gridwork of gritty brown houses, at the edge of Hoadley. "Do you ever see her?"

"No!" With vehemence. "I stay away from her, and she stays away from me."

I sat back and waited for more fireworks.

"She didn't want me," said Deb intensely. "She gave me away."

The woman had paved her daughter's way to easy street. But if Deb wanted to feel sorry for herself, I wasn't arguing. "How come?"

"I was a scandal. Her husband was away, working at the Lackawana mill."

"Oh." Better and better. "Do you know who your father was?"

"No." Fiercely. "And I don't want to know. I don't care."

I sat back some more.

"DeArckangelo arranged the adoption," she said. DeArckangelo was Hoadley's most prominent lawyer. Lived in the thickly gingerbreaded house beyond Michaels's. "It was legal, and my parents told me all about it as soon as I was old enough to understand. And they never cared that my hair isn't ash blond like theirs. My mother used to fuss with it and put it up in barrettes and pincurls. She said I was pretty."

Pathos. Deb waited for me to tell her how pretty she was. I wouldn't give her the satisfaction.

"You have brothers and sisters?"

"Half brothers. And I am not interested in researching my natural family," she added, rather tangentially. I hadn't asked her.

"If you'll excuse a stupid question," I said, "why are you so interested in researching your adoptive family?"

"Interested" seemed hardly the word. "Obsessed," I should have said. She looked at me as if I had suddenly sprouted an extra head.

"Because I want to learn everything I possibly can about my ancestors. When I meet them, I want to be prepared."

She really believed—she really thought—even though she went to that cockamamy church, I had assumed a college graduate would have outgrown believing in the afterlife. Enough for one day. I was glad to see Brad when he came home and Deb went away.

"The woman is insane," I told him over supper.

He was in a sour mood. "That's no woman," he said. "That's an overgrown baby."

"Still wants her mama? But the Michaelses dote on her. Their world revolves around her."

"I wish yours didn't," he snapped. I goggled at him.

"I don't give a damn about her one way or another! I don't care if I never see her again."

But I let her in when she came over the next day with more revelations for me. And there she sat at my kitchen table, earnestly explaining to me her views of the hereafter.

"Well, if heaven is what you want," she said, "I mean, heaven is in your mind, and I started my research years ago, before roots were popular, and that's what I really want, to meet my ancestors and— and find out all the answers to all the questions I have to ask them." Interesting theology, if somewhat disjointed. "So that's what I believe. For me."

Silence.

"I think of it as a big family reunion," she added dreamily. "That's my idea of heaven. Picnic tables under the elms, and wine and real china plates, and all my ancestors there in their sunbonnets or their pinstripe suits. Great-great-grandfather Israel Wheeler from Connecticut. And great-great-great-GREAT-grandmother Felicity Saltzgiver from Chester County. She had seventeen children."

"Better her than me," I said.

Deb ignored my irreverence. "Her husband Noah Saltzgiver fought in the Civil War," she went on, still staring off in what was perhaps meant to be an inspirational manner. "He was decorated. I like to think sometimes that maybe someday—when I go to them, you know—maybe he will turn to Felicity, or maybe she will turn to him, and one of them will say, This is our great-great-great-great granddaughter whom we have never met. . . ."

All such notions aside, I hope that someday, under some circumstances, it will be remembered of me that I did not laugh at her.

"Except sometimes I worry," she added.

"Worry about what?"

"When the research isn't going well, I get the feeling that they're keeping the answers back from me. That they don't really want me at all. They don't want me in their lives."

Why would they? God, the woman was a lunatic.

"But then it goes better again, usually. So I guess they'll accept me after all." Deb slumped chummily in my old kitchen chair, rendered loquacious by warmth and coffee. "You know what?"

"What."

"I've had other genealogists ask me to marry them."

"Those guys at the meetings?" Kind of narrowed it down. Almost all those people who did roots in Hoadley were women.

"Right. Matt Kohut and Chris Burkheimer. They each asked me to marry them, years back, different times. But Matt is engaged to Carol Tonolini now."

What brought this on?

"I just didn't feel ready to marry anyone. I still don't. Not until I have my research all done."

Oh, Jesus.

Matt Kohut was a tan-faced, sandy-blond guy with a real Hoadley face: straight nose, flat mouth, prominent Slavic cheekbones. A hunk. Chris Burkheimer was another hunk, a former football hero and, I heard, a practical joker. They seemed out of place in the library. Deb had evangelized them into genealogy in the first place, and out of inertia they had stayed. But it was Chris and Matt and Carol Tonolini who first gave her the notion that she didn't have to wait until she died to meet her "ancestors."

Matt, Chris, Carol Tonolini and Chandra Drisana. False name, Chandra Drisana. Even I could tell that, and I'm no genealogist. She was a drifter, floated in sometime in late January, early February. When the whole world was the color of road slop. Hoadley was close enough to the turnpike that vagrants drifted through from time to time, hit up the churches for a few bucks, tried out the local taverns and went on— quickly. They sensed they were not welcome. Everyone else in Hoadley had lived there since great-

229

grandpa came over from Bavaria or wherever. Chandra Drisana stayed a little longer than most. She was a thin, ravaged-looking woman, older than me, or maybe she just looked older. Very long coarse straight hair, aggressively long, the color of the slag heaps streaked with ice. Plain face, wide mouth, and a sort of gypsy look about the way she dressed. She wore skirts and blouses and shawls even in the horrible Hoadley winter weather. The Salvation Army got her a room by the week in the old hotel, a few doors down from the library.

We met her in the library. She spent a lot of her time there, doing research in the occult, she said. I don't know what she expected to find in that repository of Zane Grey novels, that haven for Harlequin Romance addicts, but she was always there. The old watchdog of a librarian would not let her take books out, so whatever she found she read right in the library, hunched over a table. But I think she came mostly to soak up the heat. Cheap hotels are cold.

She gave me the creeps. The first time I saw her, I tried to ignore her. But she beckoned me over as soon as she saw my pregnant belly.

"Six months," she said.

I nodded, unimpressed. A horse doctor could probably have told as much by looking at me.

"I am a psychic healer," said Chandra in tones intended to thrill. "Let me lay my hand on your swelling, and I will tell you the sex of your unborn child."

"No, thank you." I didn't want her touching me. Started to walk away, but she grabbed my arm.

"Did you know that the baby whimpers in the womb? Each soul utters a primal cry, its very own, a cry that disturbs its dreams all its life. Love me, wails one. Let me be free, cries another. I will not submit, another will shout, and yet another, Embrace me, in wordless cry. The task of an entire lifetime is to soothe the primal cry."

At my elbow I saw Deb listening with a fascination that bordered on awe.

"A mother's task is to start her child on the innate path. Let me lay my ear against your side, and I will tell you your infant's primal cry."

I jerked my arm out of her grasp and stalked off to fume in the stacks. It was a small library, though, and I could still hear Chandra. And Deb. Eagerly discussing Chandra's skills as a psychic healer.

Matt and Chris had some ideas about that.

We had a week of warm weather in late February, a false spring before winter settled back in for another three months. Deb walked the block and a half to the Genealogical Society meeting, since it was so nice out, and I stayed home to fill out some catalog orders for the baby things I needed. That was a mistake, maybe. Though I doubt I could have done or said much if I had gone with her. Anyway, Matt and Chris walked Deb home in the springlike sunshine, past the elm tree stumps, and then she came to see me, all excited. Matt and Chris had told her that Chandra Drisana could help her make contact with her ancestors.

"A *seance*?" I protested. "Deb, that's a pile of crap."

"It's not a seance. It's a circle of psychic healing."

"Who needs healing? The dead woman with seventeen children?"

"It's not for healing," said Debora frostily. "It's for strength. The circle of us together, we can venture backward in time, beyond the womb. To the place where the families are. The dead and the unborn."

She wanted me to be in on it, of course. As always, my cynicism seemed only to encourage her. Nothing could make me take part, but I did finally say I'd come along and watch. I dreaded it. Boredom or my sense of superiority couldn't have dragged me to a seance. But—go ahead and laugh, I know this is me, Lin Burke the loner, talking—I had a feeling I ought to go and try to keep Deb out of trouble.

So there sat Lin Burke at the irrational affair taking place in Chandra's fleabag hotel room. At night, of course, amid flickering candles and incense. Five in the circle—Deb, Chandra, Chris, Matt and Carol. I said I'd watch, and Chandra just looked at me, then went ahead and set up. She laid out an old plastic shower curtain on the bare floor. A five-pointed star on it, drawn in magic marker—hell of a thing to call it, magic marker, at a seance or whatever. I said something about it, but nobody got the joke. Chandra set some mismatched dinette-set chairs on the points of the star, facing in. She was very careful how she placed them. Then the five venturers sat down. Deb was wearing a look as if she was taking first communion or losing her virginity in the back seat of a Mercedes. She had told me breathily that this was the most important day of her life. If I had vomited, I suppose she would have blamed it on my pregnancy.

The fearless five crossed their arms above their bellies and joined hands at close quarters. They sat with their eyes shut, breathing deeply, and Deb's heightened expression changed after a while to one calmer but even more rapt.

"We are children," Chandra intoned.

They sat being children. I yawned.

"We are very young."

Deb looked it, too. The soft, pouting way she held her mouth—I expected to see her insert her thumb and suck. Chandra had hold of her one hand and Matt the other, or maybe she would have.

"We are babies."

Deb's knees swiveled outward and her feet cocked so that the soles faced each other.

"We are babies unborn. We are in the warm, dark womb."

So help me, Deb drew her feet up so that she assumed, as nearly as she could, the fetal position. The others sat still.

"We are smaller, smaller. Back, back to the place of origins. We are each a single cell. We are nothing."

They sat very still, looking like elaborate dolls, scantily breathing.

"Yet we still are," Chandra whispered. "We exist. We are souls, the soul circle. We are seekers. We seek Debora's family."

Deb had relaxed from her fetal pose, but despite her closed eyes her face looked frightened, strained. The five "seekers" sat silently for a few minutes. Then I noticed faint movement. Chandra was stiffening, sitting up straighter in her chair. As if someone had stuffed her broomstick up her ass, I thought.

"Hostility," she said sharply.

I glanced at Deb. She looked terrified. Her face, screwed up as if she would cry with fear. More. Heartbreak. I sat with my cynicism suddenly gone, passionately hating what was happening.

"Something is wrong," Chandra shrilled. "I sense hostility."

"It's me," I said out loud, very coldly. I thought the sound of my voice would jolt them out of it. No such luck.

"It's them," declared Chandra, though not, seemingly, in answer to me. "The ones at the tables. Grandfather Michaels, great-grandfather Elijah Michaels. And their wives. And the Wheelers, the Stewarts. And Noah Saltzgiver in his broadcloth suit, and Felicity in her gray bonnet and wedding dress."

The soul-scared look on Deb's face—I could not keep from staring at her. But even so I clearly saw a slight movement beyond her. Chris Burkheimer blinked one eye open, caught Matt Kohut's eye and smirked. And I knew who had told Chandra what to say.

"They want us to go," Chandra declaimed in breathy tones. "There must be some mistake. They say Debora is seeking the wrong family. A family to which she does not belong."

I could have killed. No matter what sort of a snotty bitch Deb was, no matter what she had done—

"We're not welcome," declared Chandra. "We must go back."

Out of my chair at the same moment, I reached for Deb. "Come on. We're getting out of here." But she did not seem to hear me or feel my hand.

Chandra snapped her eyes open and looked straight at me. "No, wait," she ordered. "We must exit. We are something now, each a single cell in the warm dark womb, growing, dividing. . . ."

I stood still for this bullshit only because I was afraid Deb would crack up otherwise. I waited until they got past the child. All the while Deb did not make a sound. She had not made a sound even when they had stabbed her in her back and twisted the knife. But her face was shrieking a strangled cry.

"We are no longer children," Chandra finished. "But we are yet growing."

They all let go of each other's hands and opened their eyes. Before they could say anything I took Deb by the shoulders, urged her up off her chair, grabbed her coat and purse and steered her out the door. She still had that awful look on her face.

"Deb," I yelled at her, "it's all a bunch of crap!"

Before I could say more, Matt and Chris came running after us. "Deb," Matt said, "I'm really sorry."

"You should be!" I retorted.

"Now what's that supposed to mean?" It was Chris, the practical joker, all hot and bothered. Protesting too much.

"You know damn well what I mean," I told him. "Come on, Deb." I got the coat on her, took the keys from her pocket, got behind the wheel of her Corvette and drove her home.

"They told Chandra what to say," I explained to her. "All that stuff about picnic tables and Noah Saltzgiver, that's stuff you told them, maybe years ago when you were dating them."

She wasn't listening. "They hate me," she whispered, and looking at her I saw she didn't mean Matt and Chris, her rejected suitors.

"Come on, Deb," I pleaded. "That's a pile of shit. Anyway, you're you and it's now, 1983. You're here. Your parents love you. It doesn't matter where you came from."

That was about as heavy as I'd ever talked with anyone. But it made no impression on her at all. "I saw them," she said numbly. "Around the picnic tables. Under the elm trees. They looked at me and told me to go away. Go back to Eleventh Street. They don't want me."

"This is the goddamn twentieth century, for Christ's sake!"

I took her to my place and worked on her for two hours over coffee, trying to argue some sense into her, while Brad sulked and watched TV in the other room. I even thought of calling that so-called preacher of hers, and decided against it. He was crazier than she was. Finally, late, after the lights had gone out over at her place, I gave up on her and sent her home. At least the mindless crying look had faded somewhat from her face.

A trace of it stayed there, though, for months.

Chandra had left Hoadley by morning, on a Greyhound bound for Akron. No fool, that one. She knew the Michaelses would have crucified her if they'd heard. I wondered what Chris and Matt had given her besides bus fare, or if she just liked messing up people's lives. I wondered if Deb's parents would want to crucify me as well. In fact, I think no one ever told them what had happened. Deb least of all.

The winter crawled on into a slow spring. Tree buds swelled like something sore, turned red and stayed that way. Some of the ice became slush and mud. The Spirit Church preacher spearheaded a drive for a new building, then disappeared along with the funds, and Deb started going to the low-roofed, square-steepled Lutheran church with her parents again. Not much else happened.

I was fixing up the baby's room. Deb hung around. She would go shopping with me or come into the apartment and watch me hang curtains or whatever. She never offered to help, no matter how much my frontage got in my way. I think she felt out of her element but at the same time, for some reason, fascinated. And fear still hanging like tears at the corners of her eyes.

"You love the baby already," she said to me one day. "Don't you?"

I had bought some flowered paper and was lining drawers in a little dresser. When she said that I stopped with scissors in air. Very uncomfortable. Scared, even. I'm not used to thinking in those terms, as if love is something you can get hold of. Something solid, like money in the bank. Though I guess you take that on trust, too.

"I have no idea," I said.

She seemed shocked. "But you *want* the baby, don't you?"

"Of course." What sort of peabrain did she think I was? "I wouldn't be in this condition if I didn't."

"Well, then you must love it."

"Give us a chance to shake hands first, would you?" I went back to cutting my drawer linings.

"I sent for my birth certificate," said Deb suddenly.

"Huh?" I couldn't follow her leaps of logic, or illogic, sometimes. "Are you going to France after all?" Thinking maybe she needed it for the passport.

"No, not that birth certificate. The one my natural mother filed before she—gave me up. It just came in the mail today. You know what?"

"What." Morosely.

"She named me. Christabella."

"Good lord, what a name."

Deb ignored that. "Christabella," she repeated. "Christabella Infusino. She gave me a name."

I stared at her blankly.

"So she couldn't have hated me all that much!" Deb blurted at me. "She had a name picked out for me. She must have wanted me at least a little bit, maybe before I was born."

I excused myself, went into the bathroom and sat there until I felt calm again, cradling my pregnant belly in my hands.

Sometime within the next few days I noticed that Deb had started taking walks all the way down to 11th Street. Down to the tacky side of town, down the heaved-up sidewalks past the potholes. The first raw weeks of March she walked down there almost every day—walked, by damn, and this is the periwin-

kle boot girl, the white Corvette cat, walking down
11th Street in the rain with her slicker hood up and a
pair of squelching tennis shoes on her feet.

She didn't ask me, but I started to walk with her.
Sort of happened out when she went by. We didn't
talk much, thank God. I could stand her better when
she didn't talk. Actually I found that I no longer
entirely disliked her, those days. And I guess she
didn't mind having me along for the walk. She would
slow up and wait for me as I waddled along beside
her, seven months great with child.

"That's where I was born," she told me. "Right in
the house."

It was that particular house that she walked to, of
course. A rotting wooden hulk patched with tarpaper,
moss growing on the roof, porch falling off. No one
lived there any more—the place was condemned. A
couple of Italian guys, brothers-in-law, unemployed,
were going to tear it down for the lumber. Mid
March, they started.

The weather hadn't warmed up much. Just the
same, Deb and I would stand a few minutes and
watch them work. We got to know them a little,
enough to say hi, complain about the weather, joke
that their wives would be jealous if they saw us
hanging around. They were gutting the interior first,
sheltering from the cold wind. Day by day we watched
as they brought forth fixtures out of a dark, gaping
doorway.

"The warm, dark womb," Deb remarked once,
maybe the first time she had come close to mention-
ing the "circle of healers."

"A promiscuous womb," I quipped. I cannot seem
to help being flippant. "Wide open to all comers."

Deb actually smiled. "That explains the variety of
the offspring."

The men brought out wooden cupboards, metal sinks and a porcelain one, oak doors, hardware, a chamber pot and some lengths of lead pipe. They took the window sashes out. The house stared blindly. Chunks of plaster and bits of lath started to drop down. They were ripping out the walls to get at the studding.

"Jesus shit!"

White face at the ravaged window above us. Husky Italian staggered beyond words, gesturing for help. Somewhere inside, the more articulate brother-in-law kept up bursts of startled profanity.

"Screw me silly, what is it!"

Deb reached the stairs while I, very pregnant, was still lumbering through the door. The commotion came from the second floor—

When I saw what it was about, I stood as stunned as any of them.

No insulation in the walls of that old place. And in the space between plaster and lath and the outer sheathing lay something that just fit there, snugly, as if in a coffin.

A—homunculus, a human something, a tiny, shriveled brown mummy curled up there in the wall, its head the largest part of it, feet bent under and hands up against the twisted, brittle mouth, disintegrating hands—but the face, intact. Eyes shut, squeezed tight in pain or rage. Mouth wide open to wail. And the leather thong still furrowing the puny neck. Someone had strangled a baby.

A gasping breath, then the cry. For an awful instant I thought it was coming from the dead thing in the wall. It seemed to be everywhere. It seemed to fill the world.

It was Deb. Not a scream, what she was doing, not a shriek of fear that would pass or hatred that would vent. Not a weeping. But a cry, a terrible, dry-eyed, utterly abandoned infant's cry, the throat-tearing cry of total dependence. For a moment I stared at her, couldn't think or act, I was so shaken by that cry. Her face, contorted, teeth bared to the gums, eyes buried in pain, skin the color of a bruise, straps of muscle standing out on her neck—and her hands rose to meet her gaping mouth—

"Mother of God," one of the Italians moaned.

I jerked myself loose from that place, got hold of her by the wrists and took her out. Her noise eased up once we reached the street. I hustled her toward home, and the police cars went screaming down Eleventh Street beside us. That walk home seemed to take millennia. All through the streets of Hoadley, out of the walls of the sparrow-brown houses row on row I imagined I heard crying, primal cries. Want me. Mother me. Love me.

The local paper ran a photo of the mummified baby the next day. It could have been as much as a hundred years old, the coroner said. Probably had nothing to do with Debora's natural family at all. But Deb had that awful look on her face again.

I didn't see her much after that. For all I know she is still living at home. They might have hired a private nurse for her by this time. I don't know. I don't care. Within three days I had talked Brad into breaking the lease, and I had found us an apartment in Steel City. I did not want my baby to be born in Hoadley.

Here is an excerpt from Mary Brown's new novel
The Unlikely Ones, *coming in November 1987 from
Baen Books Fantasy—SIGN OF THE DRAGON:*

MARY BROWN

THE UNLIKELY ONES

After breakfast the next morning—a helping of
what looked like gruel but tasted of butter and nuts
and honey and raspberries and milk—the magician led us outside into a morning sparkling with
raindrops and clean as river-washed linen, but
strangely the grass was dry when we seated ourselves in a semicircle in front of his throne. Hoowi,
the owl, was again perched on his shoulder, eyes
shut, and he took up Pisky's bowl into his lap.
Although the birds sang, their songs were courtesy-
muted, for the Ancient's voice was softer this morning as though he were tired, and indeed his first
words confirmed this.

'I have been awake most of the night, my friends,
pondering your problems. That is why I have con-
vened this meeting. We agreed yesterday that you
had all been called together for a special mission,
a quest to find the dragon. You need him, but he
also needs you.' He paused, and glanced at each
one of us in turn. 'But perhaps last night you
thought this would be easy. Find the Black Mountains, seek out the dragon's lair, return the jewels,
ask for a drop of blood and a blast of fire and Hey
Presto! your problems are all solved.

'But it is not as easy at that, my friends. Of your
actual meeting with the dragon, if indeed you reach

him, I will say nothing, for that is still in the realms of conjecture. What I can say is this: in order to reach the dragon you have a long and terrible journey ahead of you, one that will tax you all to the utmost, and may even find one or other of you tempted to give up, to leave the others and return; if that happens then you are all doomed, for I must impress upon you that as the seven you are now you have a chance, but even were there one less your chances of survival would be halved. There is no easy way to your dragon, understand that before you start. I can give you a map, signs to follow, but these will only be indications, at best. What perils and dangers you may meet upon the way I cannot tell you: all I know is that the success of your venture depends upon you staying together, and that you must all agree to go, or none.

'I can see by your expressions that you have no real idea of what I mean when I say "perils and dangers": believe me, your imaginations cannot encompass the terrors you might have to face—'

'But if we do stay together?' I interrupted.

'Then you have a better chance: that is all I can say. It is up to you.' He was serious, and for the first time I felt a qualm, a hesitation, and glancing at my friends I saw mirrored the same doubts.

'And if we don't go at all—if we decide to go back to—to wherever we came from?' I persisted.

'Then you will be crippled, all of you, in one way or another, for the rest of your lives.'

'Then there is no choice,' said Conn. 'And so the sooner we all set off the better,' and he half-rose to his feet.

'Wait!' thundered the magician, and Conn subsided, flushing. 'That's better, I have not finished.'

'Sit down, shurrup, be a good boy and listen to granpa,' muttered Corby sarcastically, but The Ancient affected not to hear.

'There is another thing,' said he. 'If you succeed

in your quest and find the dragon, and if he takes back the jewels, and if he yields a drop of blood and a blast of fire, if, I say . . . then what happens afterwards?'

The question was rhetorical, but Moglet did not understand this.

'I can catch mice again,' she said brightly, happily.

But he was gentle with her. 'Yes, kitten, you will be able to catch mice, and grow up properly to have kittens of your own—but at what cost? You may not realize it but your life, and the life of the others, has been in suspension while you have worn the jewels, but once you lose your diamond then time will catch up with you. You will be subject to your other eight lives and no longer immune, as you others have been also, to the diseases of mortality.

'Also, don't forget, your lives have been so closely woven together that you talk a language of your own making, you work together, live, eat, sleep, think together. Once the spell is broken you, cat, will want to catch birds, eat fish and kill toads; you, crow, will kill toads too, and try for kittens and fish; toad here will be frightened of you all, save the fish; and the fish will have none but enemies among you.

'And do not think that you either, Thing-as-they-call-you, will be immune from this; you may not have their killer instinct but, like them, you will forget how to talk their language and will gradually grow away from them, until even you cross your fingers when a toad crosses your path, shoo away crows and net fish for supper—'

'You are wrong!' I said, almost crying. 'I shall always want them, and never hurt them! We shall always be together!'

'But will they want you,' asked The Ancient quietly, 'once they have their freedom and identity returned to them? If not, why is it that only dog, horse, cattle, goat and sheep have been domesticated and even these revert to the wild, given the chance? Do you not think that there must be some reason why humans and wild animals dwell apart? Is it perhaps that they value their freedom, their individuality, more than man's circumscribed domesticity? Is it not that they prefer the hazards of the wild, and only live with man when they are caught, then tamed and chained by food and warmth?'

'I shall never desert Thing!' declared Moglet stoutly. 'I shan't care whether she has food and fire or not, my place is with her!'

'Of course . . . Indubitably . . . What would I do without her . . .' came from the others, and I turned to the magician.

'You see? They don't believe we shall change!'

'Not now,' said The Ancient heavily. 'Not now. But there will come a time . . . So, you are all determined to go?'

'Just a moment,' said Conn. 'You have told Thingmajig and her friends just what might be in store for them if we find the dragon: what of me and Snowy here? What unexpected changes in personality have you in store for us?' He was angry, sarcastic.

'You,' said the Ancient, 'you and my friend here, the White One, might just do the impossible: impossible, that is, for such a dedicated knight as yourself. . .'

'And what's that?'

'You might change your minds . . .'

'About what, pray?' And I saw Snow shake his head.'

'What Life is all about . . .'

432 pp. • 65361-X • $3.95

To order any Baen Book by mail, send the cover price plus 75 cents for first-class postage and handling to: Baen Books, Dept. B, 260 Fifth Avenue, New York, N.Y. 10001

Here is an excerpt from Heroing *by Dafydd ab Hugh, coming in October 1987 as part of the new* SIGN OF THE DRAGON *fantasy line from Baen Books:*

Hesitantly, Jiana crawled into the crack.

"It's okay, guys," she called back, "but it's a bit cramped. Toldo next—wait! —Dida, then Toldo. I want . . . the priest in back." She felt a twinge of guilt. What she really wanted was the boy where she could reach out and touch his hand when needed.

Dida whimpered something. Jiana turned back in surprise.

"What's wrong?"

"Oh, love . . . are we really going—into *there?*"

"Dida, it's the only way. Are you a mouse? Come on, warrior!" He pressed his lips together and crawled toward her hand. When she touched him, she felt him trembling.

"Don't fear. I came through here, remember?"

The tunnel smelled as fresh as flowers after the stench of sewage. Jiana could breathe again without gagging.

The ceiling of the passage sank and sank, until she was almost afraid it would narrow to a wedge and block them off. But she remembered her harrowing crawl from the prison, her heart pounding with fear, feeling the hot, fetid breath of *something* on her neck, and she knew the passage was passable. At last, they were scraping along with their bellies on the floor and their backs against the splintery ceiling. Jiana wondered how Toldo Mondo was managing with his prodigious girth.

Suddenly, she knew something was wrong. She crawled on a few more yards, then stopped. Dida was no longer behind her. She heard a faint cry from behind her.

"Jiana, help me—please help me . . ."

"Lady Jiana," called out Toldo, "I think you had better come back here. The boy . . . seems to have a problem." Jiana felt a chill in her stomach; Toldo sounded much too professionally casual.

"What's wrong?" She turned slowly around on her stomach, and inched her way back to where the two had stopped. She stretched out her hand and took Dida's; it was clammy and shaking. With her fingers she felt his pulse, and it was pounding wildly.

"I can't do it," he whispered miserably. "I can't do it—I just can't do it—all that weight—I can't breathe! —I can't . . ."

"What? Oh, for Tooqa's sake! What next?"

As if in answer to her blasphemy, the ground began to shake and roll. Again she heard the scraping, grinding noise, only this time much closer. Dida continued to whimper.

"Oh gods, oh gods, oh please, let me out, oh please, take it away . . ."

"Too close," she whispered, trying to peer through the pitch blackness.

"Oh my lord," gasped Toldo Mondo, "don't you hear it?"

Again the ground shook, and this time the scraping was closer yet, and accompanied by a slimy sucking sound.

For a moment all were silent; even Dida stopped his whimpering. Then Jiana and Toldo began to babble simultaneously.

"I'm sorry," she cried, "I'm sorry, o Ineffable One, o Nameless Scaly One, o You Who Shall Not Be Named! I never meant—"

Toldo chanted something over and over in another language; it sounded like a penance. The fearful noise suddenly became much louder.

"Toldo! It's coming this way! Oh lordy, what'll we do? Crawl, damn you, crawl, crawl! And push the kid along—I'll grab his front and drag!"

"You fool! It's here! Don't you hear it? Am I the only one who hears it?!"

"Shut up and push, you fat tub of goat cheese!"

In a frenzy, they began to squirm away from the sound, dragging Dida, and Jiana discovered that the tiny crawlway was as wide as a king's hall, though the ceiling was but a foot and a half off the floor. Dida was no help. He was in shock, as if he'd been stabbed in a battle. He could only move his arms and legs in a feeble attempt at locomotion, praying to be "let out."

After a few moments, Jiana realized she was hopelessly lost. Had they kept going straight from the hole by the river, they would have found the next door. But they were moving to the right, and she did not know how far they had gone in the pitch black. In fact, she was not even sure which way they were currently pointing; the horrible noises had seemed to change direction, and they had concentrated on keeping them to their rear.

"Oh gods, I've done it now," she moaned; "we won't ever get out of here!" A sob from Dida caught at her heart, and she cursed herself for speaking aloud.

"We shall make it," retorted Toldo Mondo. "There must be *something* in this direction, if we go far enough!"

Soon, Jiana herself began to feel the oppression of millions of tons of rock pressing down on her. She had terrifying visions of being buried alive in the blackness by a sudden cave-in caused by the movements of whatever was behind them. With every beat of her heart it got closer, and the shaking grew worse. She could clearly hear a sound like a baby sucking on its fist.

"Jiana, go!" cried Toldo in a panic. "Crawl, go—faster, woman! It's here, it's—Jiana, I CAN SMELL IT!"

"How does it squeeze along, when even we barely fit?" she wondered aloud. *You're babbling, Ji . . . stop it!*

She surged and lunged forward, not letting go of Dida, though he was like a wet sack of cornmeal. And then, there was a rocky wall in front of her. There was nowhere left to crawl.

Coming in October 1987 * 65344-X * 352 pp. * $3.50

C'MON DOWN!!

Is the real world getting to be too much? Feel like you're on somebody's cosmic hit list? Well, how about a vacation in the hottest spot you'll ever visit ... HELL!

We call our "Heroes in Hell" shared-universe series the Damned Saga. In it the greatest names in history—Julius Caesar, Napoleon, Machiavelli, Gilgamesh and many more—meet the greatest names in science fiction: Gregory Benford, Martin Caidin, C.J. Cherryh, David Drake, Janet Morris, Robert Silverberg. They all turn up the heat—in the most original milieu since a Connecticut Yankee was tossed into King Arthur's Court. We've saved you a seat by the fire ...

TRAVIS SHELTON LIKES BAEN BOOKS BECAUSE THEY TASTE GOOD

Recently we received this letter from Travis Shelton of Dayton, Texas:

I have come to associate Baen Books with Del Monte. Now what is that supposed to mean? Well, if you're in a strange store with a lot of different labels, you pick Del Monte because the product will be consistent and will not disappoint.

Something I have noticed about Baen Books is that the stories are always fast-paced, exciting, action-filled and seem to be published because of content instead of who wrote the book. I now find myself glancing to see who published the book instead of reading the back or intro. If it's a Baen Book it's going to be good and exciting and will capture your spare reading moments.

Another discovery I have recently made is that I don't have any Baen Books in my unread stacks—and I read four to seven books a week, so that in itself is a meaningful statistic.

Why do you like Baen Books? Drop us a letter like Travis did. The person who best tells us what we're doing right—and where we could do better—will receive a Baen Books gift certificate worth $100. Entries must be received by December 31, 1987. Send to Baen Books, 260 Fifth Avenue, New York, N.Y. 10001. And ask for our free catalog!